PRAISE FOR
CHARLIE N. HOLMBERG

THE PAPER MAGICIAN

"Charlie is a vibrant writer with an excellent voice and great world building. I thoroughly enjoyed *The Paper Magician*."
    —Brandon Sanderson, author of *Mistborn* and *The Way of Kings*

"Harry Potter fans will likely enjoy this story for its glimpses of another structured magical world, and fans of Erin Morgenstern's *The Night Circus* will enjoy the whimsical romance element . . . So if you're looking for a story with some unique magic, romantic gestures, and the inherent darkness that accompanies power all steeped in a yet to be fully explored magical world, then this could be your next read."
    —Amanda Lowery, *Thinking Out Loud*

THE GLASS MAGICIAN

"I absolutely loved *The Glass Magician*. It exceeded my expectations, and I was very impressed with the level of conflict and complexity within each character. I will now sit twiddling my thumbs until the next one comes out."

    —*The Figmentist*

"*The Glass Magician* will charm readers young and old alike."
    —Radioactive Book Reviews

THE MASTER MAGICIAN

A Wall Street Journal *Bestseller*

"Utah author Charlie Holmberg delivers . . . thrilling action and delicious romance in *The Master Magician*."

—*Deseret News*

THE PLASTIC MAGICIAN

"The everyday setting with just a touch of magical steampunk technology proves to readers what an incredible job Holmberg does with her world building. Fans of previous Paper Magician books will love this addition to the world, and readers new to it will quickly fall in love with the magic-wielding characters."

—*Booklist*

THE FIFTH DOLL

MYTHS &
MORTALS

ALSO BY CHARLIE N. HOLMBERG

The Numina Series

Smoke and Summons

The Paper Magician Series

The Paper Magician

The Glass Magician

The Master Magician

The Plastic Magician

Other Novels

The Fifth Doll

Magic Bitter, Magic Sweet

Followed by Frost

Veins of Gold

MYTHS &
MORTALS

THE NUMINA SERIES

CHARLIE N. HOLMBERG

47NORTH

Text copyright © 2019 by Charlie N Holmberg LLC

Published by 47North, Seattle

www.apub.com

Amazon, the Amazon logo, and 47North are trademarks of Amazon.com, Inc., or its affiliates.

ISBN-13: 9781542041713 (hardcover)
ISBN-10: 1542041716 (hardcover)
ISBN-13: 9781542041720 (paperback)
ISBN-10: 1542041724 (paperback)

Cover design by Ellen Gould
Cover illustration by Marina Muun

Printed in the United States of America
First edition

To Mary Ann, the most Christlike person I know.
Even though she says she's not. Because she's silly.

Prologue

In a room clouded with cigar smoke, Sandis stood between two men who had betrayed her. In front of her, her great-uncle; behind her, Rone. If Rone was to be believed, her great-uncle had sold her to Kazen, her worst enemy. Then again, Rone had been the one to *deliver* her to the summoner.

Sandis had been looking for her great-uncle for weeks. Talbur Gwenwig, her grandfather's brother. The only living family member she had left, even if he was a stranger. She had envisioned their reunion countless times and in countless ways, but never quite like this. The dim office with its aged wooden walls had no windows, nothing to air out the stench of the burning roll held between the stocky man's fingers. The only light came from two lamps, one on his simple desk, the other in the far corner. The light was a dehydrated sort of yellow. She could barely breathe—but that might have been due to Rone's presence behind her.

Hugging herself, she took a step away from him, and closer to Talbur. She saw a few traces of her father in his face, something that let her relax a fraction. His hair was thinning and receding from his forehead. He had a large nose and wide-set eyes, the same shade of brown as hers. She guessed him to be in his sixties.

His words, *"I was so hoping I'd get a chance to meet you,"* rang in her ears, colliding harshly with what Rone had told her just an hour before.

If he'd truly sold her off, he wouldn't have expected to meet her. Right?

She shifted her weight from one foot to the other. Her clothes, despite the rough wash she'd given them in a horse trough, were growing stiff around her. The blood would never wash away completely. But she didn't want to save the clothing. This uniform marked her as a vessel. It would expose the golden Noscon brands cascading down her back the moment she removed Rone's jacket.

His jacket. She didn't want it. She didn't dare remove it.

"You knew I was coming?" she asked, taking another step toward him and away from Rone. Tension rolled off Rone like steam. Because of Talbur, or because he'd lost his priceless amarinth?

"Knew? No. Only hoped. Grafters are a tricky lot." Talbur dragged on the cigar and let a spicy cloud pass from his lips. "I wasn't sure where you'd end up, or even if dear Engel here would keep up his end of the bargain."

Sandis stiffened. Refused to look back at Rone, though she direly wanted to read his face. Was he angry that her great-uncle questioned his loyalty to the stack of cash likely still tucked away on his person? Was he hurt by the reminder of what he'd done?

Rone had come back for her. Helped free her. But he'd been the one to cage her in the first place. Sandis couldn't sort through it all, not now.

Celestial, she was so tired of crying.

"You sold me." It wasn't a question.

Talbur reached toward an ashtray and tapped his cigar against its side. "I am a broker, my dear girl. I merely made the arrangements. Your master came to me a while ago, believing you'd come looking for me. I didn't even know you existed! Apparently you're quite the magnificent woman. It is woman, yes? How old are you?"

Sandis swallowed. "Eighteen." The walls felt too close. Her hands sweated, and her nostrils burned from the cigar smoke. And yet, outside this room, she had nothing. *Nothing.* Nowhere to go, no one to trust.

Kazen had tried to sacrifice her to the demon Kolosos. She could still feel the heat in the back of her throat, the *other* sensations from her near brush with possession—or death. Although she'd acted as a vessel many times in the past, it had always been for Ireth, the fire horse. Ireth, who, against all odds, had managed to communicate with her. She and the numen had shared a special connection, one that had allowed her to summon him into *herself*, if only for a matter of seconds. But Kazen had ended all of that. Stripped Ireth's name from the base of her neck so she could serve a new monster.

But Ireth had never been a monster. Not to her. Not that it mattered, anymore.

The thought of him sent a hard pang of loss through her chest. Without Ireth, her only options occupied this room with her: two men who could not be trusted.

Still, Talbur was family. She had *family*, and it was sitting right in front of her, separated only by an old wooden desk. That meant something, didn't it?

Talbur nodded. "Yes. That grafter was very interested in having me return you, should you come knocking on my door. Paid a remarkable sum, with a bonus after I delivered you. Of course you never came. But Engel here did."

Behind her, Rone took a heavy step into the room. "Don't act innocent, you piece of sh—"

"My, my." Talbur took another drag on his cigar, this time letting the smoke blow out his nostrils. Sandis watched it dissipate, unsure where else to look. "Such language in front of a lady. I speak only the truth, Mr. Verlad. And might I offer you similar advice? Don't act innocent. See here." He gestured toward Sandis with the lit end of the cigar. "You're hurting her again."

Sandis stiffened and forced her face to slacken. What had her expression been? She blinked, ensuring her eyes stayed dry. She would not look at Rone. She *would not look at him.*

Her chest hurt, like her body was too weak to hold up the leaden ball of her heart.

"My dear woman." Talbur rotated his chair and focused solely on her, his cigar seemingly forgotten. "I looked into you. The daughter of my nephew, Hammett. I knew the lad when he was a boy more than as an adult. Never met the lass he married. Never met you.

"But how you do pique my curiosity." He smiled, and despite everything she knew about him, that single gesture puffed oxygen on the tiny ember of hope burning in her gut. The one that was nearly extinguished under a pile of dark ash. "Everyone wants you. And I must wonder, what if we had known each other earlier? What if I had met you as a great-uncle meets his great-niece, and not as a broker meets a pawn in someone else's game? I am terribly sorry. You've obviously been through quite the ordeal."

Sandis remembered the blood dried into her clothes. Acid climbed up her throat, and she pressed her tongue to the roof of her mouth to keep it at bay. This was Galt's blood. He had been an enemy, to be sure, but she would forever be haunted by the memory of Kazen slaughtering him in front of her. Of his blood seeping between her toes. Kazen had killed his own friend and follower in an effort to draw forth Kolosos. There was ox blood on the clothes, too. Maybe even Kazen's.

Talbur snuffed his cigar in the ashtray, despite it being barely spent, and gestured to the chair on the other side of the desk. "Sit, my dear. I'd like to get to know you. I'll send my secretary to get you something to eat and something to wear. And a pitcher. You're quite the mess."

Sandis swallowed before inching toward the chair.

Rone stormed forward until his darkness filled her periphery, forcing Sandis to turn away or break the promise she'd made herself. *You will not look at him.* "You bastard. If you think you can win her over with pretty words and ignore everything that—"

"Mr. Verlad." Talbur's voice was so strong, so low, so *final*. He looked Rone in the eyes. "I do not believe I invited you to stay."

Rone's fury flashed hot as a bellows. "You think you can make me leave?"

"Please, Rone." Sandis's harsh whisper sounded like fingernails sliding across splintered wood. She stared at the corner of Talbur's desk, unwilling to turn her head toward either of them. "Please, just go."

"Sandis." His voice was strained as he moved toward her. She retreated from him, and he stopped. "I had to. He gave me emigration papers. My mother is safe in Godobia now."

Sandis took a deep breath, though it shuddered through her throat. A cool flare of relief pulsed in her gut. At least he'd betrayed her for something important, something far more precious than the trivial sum Kazen had claimed he'd accepted. Documents like that were nearly impossible to come by—she remembered her father filing for them once. Two years of waiting, only to get a denial.

One set of emigration papers. One thousand kol. The price for her life. "I'm glad."

"Please." His shadow moved nearer. "I came back for you."

Sandis's nails dug into her palms as tears—*damn these tears*—blurred her vision. He'd come back eventually, yes, and before it was too late. He'd helped her escape the prison he'd willingly cast her into.

But he hadn't come back when she'd screamed his name in that alleyway. He hadn't come back when she'd begged him to change his mind. Hadn't rescued her as grafters and mobsmen alike descended upon her. As Kazen pushed his hand into her hair and took away every shred of freedom she'd fought so hard to gain.

Rone had sold her, and therefore had sold Ireth, too—her one and only reliable companion.

"Please go." She had to whisper so he wouldn't hear the tears in her voice. Tears that joined the countless number she'd already cried for him.

Rone didn't reply. Didn't move.

Talbur cleared his throat. "You heard her. I do have the means to forcibly remove you, my boy. But my dear niece has had a long day. It would be better if you didn't make her suffer more."

The floorboards creaked as Rone's weight shifted. Sandis could imagine him glaring at her great-uncle, fire in his eyes.

Then he strode out of the room, slamming the door behind him.

Chapter 1

Sandis stood in her bedroom, which was half the size of the entire flat she'd grown up in. The bed was too wide and too high, the walls too white, the curtains too gauzy. The carpeting, also pale, was thick and long and gave under her feet like newly fallen snow. Something about the colors reminded her of Kazen's lair, but she wouldn't let herself dwell on the similarities. If she started thinking of that other life, she'd think of the vessels she'd left behind. Of sweet Alys, bleeding on the floor from a gunshot wound to her arm . . . The others hadn't been wounded in her escape, but she worried about them, nonetheless. Kaili, quiet and nurturing. Rist, temperamental but caring. She even thought of Dar, though he'd always been so aloof and self possessed.

Even after a few weeks, Talbur's home in District Three felt foreign. Wrong. Like it shouldn't exist in the world Sandis knew. In this room, she was apart from time and place. She was someone else.

That someone else looked in the mirror above her vanity and picked up the polished wood comb, one that mimicked the design of the ancient Noscon people who'd once inhabited the land on which Dresberg now nested. It was a forgery, of course—such a thing couldn't have survived through so many years. She pulled it carefully through her hair, which the maid had trimmed for her the day after she met Talbur. It still hung above her shoulders, straight and clean cropped, but now it was just a little longer in the front than in the back. Apparently, it was more fashionable than the cut Kazen had given her. The cut made to expose the golden script burned down her spine.

She parted her hair down the middle. Talbur wanted it on the side, but the strands just wouldn't stay that way without a mess of pins. Sandis couldn't fit them into her hair the way the maid, Amila, did, but she didn't want to bother the woman with something so unnecessary. So she fixed it herself, pinning the locks framing her face back behind her ears.

A hot, clawed hand grabbed her shoulder, its touch charring her skin—

Sandis jumped and whirled around, the comb flying from her fingers. Her heart thudded hard against her ribs. Gooseflesh pocked her arms.

Alone. She was alone. Imagining things again.

Sucking in breaths so deep they hurt, Sandis hugged herself and slowly, carefully, turned back to the mirror. The woman looking back was wide eyed and pale. Lifting a hand, Sandis touched her shoulder. Pulled up her sleeve. The skin was unblemished, but she could *feel* the burns there. The touch of each hard, hot claw—

Kolosos.

She squeezed her eyes shut. Not Kolosos. She wasn't bound to him. The markings Kazen had painted on her skin before the botched summoning had long since washed away.

Twenty days had passed since she ran from his lair. Twenty days, and still she felt as if those marks had sunk into her skin.

Swallowing against her dry throat, Sandis sidestepped to the basin on her vanity and splashed her face with cool water, then hung over the bowl, waiting for her pulse to slow while droplets ran off her nose and chin. When she had calmed, she used a scrub made of some sort of cream and finely crushed pits from stone fruit. Talbur had told her to do it every morning. She didn't want him to be angry with her, so she did. Just like she applied the rouge and the kohl. She thought they made her look strange, but today they might help mask the pallor still clinging to her features.

She was grateful for the clothes.

As she did every morning, Sandis walked down to the dining room. Sometimes Talbur was in there; sometimes he worked in his study or at his single-story office deeper in the city. Today, he was absent, but there was a plate of tarts sitting in the middle of the lace tablecloth. Sandis sat down, picked up one of the delicate pastries, and sank her teeth into it. She was also grateful for the food, despite the guilt she felt eating it. How many people in this city had never tasted a tart? How many were skipping breakfast today, while she wore expensive clothing and makeup and ate finely catered food?

What were the other vessels eating? Was Alys all right? Had there really been no way to grab her and take her with them? Would she have wanted to come?

The injury to her arm had looked pretty bad. Maybe even bad enough to impact her ability as a vessel.

Sandis stared at the imprint of her teeth in the broken tart crust. She had no idea if the others wanted to risk escape. With the exception of Heath, who'd been killed in one of Kazen's attempts to summon Kolosos, none of them had spoken about it. They hadn't dared.

Heath.

Celestial above, he must have been so scared. So scared and so alone, just as she had been when Kazen had attempted the same with her.

Her stomach tightened, but Sandis finished the tart, regardless— she wasn't one to waste food. She considered eating another, if only to prolong breakfast, but ultimately stood from her chair and wandered the house, passing Amila once as she did so. So much space for so few people. Amila didn't even live here.

The house consisted of three stories, though only two were aboveground. The third was the basement, where Talbur kept his study.

Rone hated houses like this. Too short for roof jumping—

Stop it. But she didn't chide herself soon enough to avoid the hollow pang that radiated in her chest. Sucking air through her nose, Sandis filled her lungs to bursting, pushing away the unpleasant sensation. It worked, a little.

Wandering to a window, she peeked out to the street. The sunlight had a gray cast to it from all the pollution, even this far from the smoke ring. No one lurked in the bushes across the street. No one lingered in the windows. She was safe.

The strange feeling of being watched pressed into her hair. Sandis whirred around, heartbeat quickening. The kitchen and dining areas were empty. Nothing out of place. Yes, safe. She was awake. She had to be safe.

Needing distraction, Sandis sought to busy herself. She didn't have much to do during the day, a complaint she didn't dare voice. She was incredibly fortunate. She feared getting a job in case Kazen still searched for her, but Talbur wouldn't have allowed it, anyway. *"You work for me now,"* he'd said after first bringing her here. *"Only a few hours a week, and you'll have all of this. Not bad, is it?"*

It *was* only a few hours a week. But what started as simple filing had already shifted to delivering packages at night to darkly clad messengers who reminded her all too much of grafters. To walking into a bar with her bloodstained vessel shirt on under her jacket—Talbur had kept it—and revealing the Noscon letters of her script to a client who owed his dues. That one had happened just a few days ago. Sandis hadn't spoken to the man. She'd barely looked at him. Just lowered her jacket and turned her back long enough to let him know she was a threat. A weapon. Talbur's weapon.

He takes care of you, she reminded herself as she climbed back up the stairs. *He's family.*

She thought again of the other vessels. Would Kazen try to summon Kolosos again, into one of them? But Heath had died under the monster's brute strength. Kazen wouldn't waste the others. They weren't like her.

A low, otherworldly growl sounded in her ears. Pausing at the top of the stairs, Sandis shook her head, listening to the rhythm of her own too-quick breathing. *They're fine, they're fine, they're fine.* You're *fine.*

She stopped at the nookish library and picked a book she hadn't yet perused. She'd never had access to books like she did here. She was a slow reader, having had so little practice, but she *could* read, so she took the book back to her out-of-place bedroom and sat on the floor with it.

She picked her way through the words until the bell rang for lunch.

Sandis recognized the sound of Talbur coming home; it was easy to catch, as his home was always so quiet. First, the sound of two horses trotting up the cobbled lane, growing louder and louder before stopping without any call from the driver. Then the carriage door opening and closing—he preferred closed carriages—followed by the opening and closing of the front door. In her great-uncle's absence, Sandis had picked her way to page 30 of her book; it was a novel about a pirate who sailed the Arctic Ribbon. So far, not much had happened in the plot, and she'd accumulated a list of words she needed to look up. The list was longer than she'd like. As she stared at them, she thought it might do her well to begin practicing her penmanship. Good penmanship could get her a respectable job. Maybe.

The floorboards in the hallway creaked, and Sandis closed her book just as a knock sounded at her door.

"Come in." She sat up straighter and smiled when the young Amila appeared.

She curtsied, only briefly meeting Sandis's eyes. Sandis had tried luring the woman into conversation on multiple occasions, but thus far, the attempt at friendship had been entirely one-sided. "Mr. Gwenwig wants to see you in his . . . study."

Sandis rolled her lips together to fight a frown. Amila always said it like that, with the hesitation. *". . . Study."* Like she was afraid of it. But the study wasn't that much different from Talbur's office near the smoke ring, just better furnished.

Sandis nodded and rose to her feet. Amila skittered away, leaving the door ajar. Sandis took the first flight of stairs down, her fingertips trailing the polished wood banister, then circled around to the door leading to the basement. There were two narrow railings that sandwiched this flight, and she touched both of them as she descended the steep stairs. A large room with some sitting furniture and several stacks of boxes opened at the base of the well. Sandis had been told not to rummage through anything in it. None of the lamps were lit.

Why did her great-uncle always work in basements? In dark, cramped spaces filled with drafts and shadows?

Circling behind the stairs, Sandis approached the door to Talbur's study, which was kept locked when he wasn't within. She knocked.

"Come."

Sandis opened the door and stepped inside. The air was clean of cigar smoke, but the walls reeked of it, radiating the scents of old spice and ash. Talbur smiled when he saw her. Sandis smiled back.

"How was business today?" she asked, sitting in a chair opposite his desk.

"Fine as always. But it's tonight's business we need to discuss." He put aside whatever papers he'd been looking at and pulled out the ledger that lay beneath them. He flipped through the pages before settling on one. "I need another late night from you, but this shouldn't be too bad. The place is close by. The Rose Inn. You know it?"

Sandis shook her head.

"Ah, well, I'll draw you a map. You can't take a carriage straight there, but I'll have someone drop you off on Marcis Street, and you'll walk from there. You know the rules."

Sandis shifted in her chair, the brands on her back itching. "What . . . do you want me to do?"

Talbur's eyes locked on his ledger. "There's a chap there named Gint Dana. Not a pleasant fellow. Not the first time he's bailed out on his promises to good clients. He's a crook and a swindler, but he's not bad-looking."

Sandis tilted her head. Why did it matter how attractive he was?

Talbur met her eyes. "He's hurt a lot of good people. Left them in the poorhouse, really. People with kids."

Sandis frowned. "That's terrible." A lot of the men her great-uncle sent her after were terrible people. She didn't envy his job—broker work that required him to mediate between angry and hurt parties. Some of the people he worked with were high caliber and wealthy; others were darker and crueler. Men like Kazen.

But Talbur hadn't realized what he was doing when he'd dealt with the grafters. He hadn't understood who Sandis was. Not really.

Her stomach tightened.

"Yes, it is." He nodded. "And this one has gone too far."

"Can't the police arrest him?"

A smirk touched Talbur's lips, but he rubbed it away with his thumb. "Ah, no. They don't care about us poor folks. You know that."

Talbur was anything but poor. Sandis nodded anyway.

"Police won't help, and the government only looks out for its own." He shrugged. "But our Mr. Dana will be at the Rose Inn tonight. You'll need to be careful what you wear. I want you to blend in without being mistaken for an employee."

Sandis furrowed her brows. "Why would someone assume I work there?"

Talbur looked at her matter-of-factly.

She waited.

Her great-uncle sighed. "The Rose Inn has rooms reserved for more than sleeping, if you understand me."

13

Sandis was about to say she didn't, but as she opened her mouth, her great-uncle's meaning became clear. Her neck warmed. "Oh."

Her brands itched terribly; she readjusted in the chair. She didn't want to go to the Rose Inn if the women who worked there . . . did *that*. If she could be mistaken as . . .

Her mind flew through everything Arnae Kurtz, Rone's martial arts master, had taught her. Had she learned enough to defend herself if someone tried to attack her? But no one would go after her without speaking to some man in charge. A brothel wasn't a crime den, right? And she couldn't do *that*, not if she wanted Ireth to—

A pang stung her chest, and she curled in around herself. She didn't have Ireth anymore. No doubt Kazen had already tattooed one of the other vessels with the fire horse's name. If Ireth was bound to someone else, she would never be able to summon him again.

"None of that, now."

Sandis met his eyes. "Oh, no. I was . . . just thinking about something."

He didn't ask her what, and likely for the better. "Dana has fairly distinctive facial hair, and he's on the tall side. I have a sketch." He pulled out a charcoal drawing and set it on the edge of the desk, though Sandis didn't reach for it.

Talbur smiled. "This is very clever, this next part. Real clever. Look at this."

He reached into a cup and pulled out some sort of translucent film. It dangled from his fingers like a worm or small fish.

Sandis leaned forward and squinted. "What is it?"

"It seals over the lips." He held it up to his mouth, though didn't touch it to his skin. "Sucks right on. You can't even notice it. Just lick your lips and stick it on."

Sandis didn't know where Talbur was going with this, but the itching on her back grew so intense she finally gave in and scratched it.

"You'll wear this, and before you exit the carriage, put this on." He held up a tiny unlabeled tube about the size of Sandis's pinky. "Now listen here. Don't spill it, and put it only on the outside of your lips, over the film. Don't lick your lips afterward. You'll go into the inn, find Dana, and give him a nice, full kiss."

Sandis's stomach disentangled from the rest of her organs and sank in her torso.

Talbur set the tube aside. "In an establishment like this, such a gesture is commonplace. He'll accept readily, and after that, you can dispose of the film and leave. You'll be done before midnight."

Sandis swallowed, though it took three tries before she was successful. "Wh-What's in the tube?"

He shrugged. "Don't worry about it. Just don't taste it."

She knit her fingers together and squeezed. "Great-Uncle . . . is it . . . poison?"

Sighing, Talbur opened a drawer and pulled out one of his cigars. "It's not perfume." He chuckled like the observation was funny. With the cigar in the corner of his mouth, he continued, "Gint Dana has hurt a lot of people. Made a lot of deals. Broken promises, Sandis. You know what that's like."

Another pang echoed in her chest, and she felt this one all the way up her throat.

"He's been bartered with. Warned. Threatened. He doesn't care. He and his company need to learn to care. So yes, it's poison. But you won't get in trouble, my dear. It will take a couple hours for him to start feeling it, and by then he'll have been around too many women to tell one from another. It'll just look—feel—like he drank too much. And then we won't have to worry about him, hm? My clients will be so grateful. So relieved."

Sandis's mouth was dry. Won't have to *worry* about him? Then the poison was lethal? "But . . . that won't get them their money back."

He struck a match. "Maybe not"—he lit the end of the cigar and puffed—"but it gives the world a little balance, eh? You'll be compensated well, darling. Don't fret."

"I . . . don't want to be compensated."

"Really, Sandis? That's incredibly generous of you! But I'll take care of you, just as I said. We'll find something nice for you if you don't want the money."

He started rattling off various luxuries, but Sandis's mind lingered on the money. On the image of her holding her hand out as Talbur placed bill after bill on her palm, compensation for killing a man she didn't even know.

Just as Rone had held out his hand to Kazen.

Blinking to clear her eyes, Sandis coughed, the sound of which interrupted Talbur's endless list of compensation. "No, Great-Uncle." She tried to make her voice sound firm, but it came out brittle. She'd never denied him before. "I . . . I don't want to do it."

Talbur pulled the cigar from his lips and let out a puff of peppery smoke. "Pardon?"

She pressed her hands together before him, entreating him. "Please. Give me something else to do. I'll do it. But . . . I can't go there. I can't do . . . that."

She looked toward the desk corner where he had deposited the poison.

Talbur frowned. The wrinkles in his face deepened, making his nose look wider. His eyes narrowed. "You can, Sandis. And you will. We'll never be able to go to my country estate if we don't work together. Isn't that what you want? To leave the city and those grafters who mistreated you so? Dana is a big part of what's tying us here. No one can do this but you. I'm depending on you, Sandis."

Her throat constricted until she could barely breathe. Her hands went numb. She shook her head. "*Please*, Great-Uncle. Please don't ask me. I can't do it. I can't."

His dark eyes watched her a little too long for comfort. He dragged on his cigar and blew the smoke out slowly. Considered. "All right. I'll find another way. You may go."

Her stomach crept back into place, and a cool sigh passed from her lungs. "Thank you." She stood, smoothed her skirt, and turned for the door.

"Oh, and Sandis?"

She glanced back.

"Find somewhere else to stay tonight."

Her muscles went rigid. "What?"

Talbur began flipping through the ledger, nonchalant. "You heard me. My home is reserved for those who do as I ask. Team players, so to speak. If you can't cooperate, you can find another place to stay tonight. I'll see you in the morning."

Sandis was stone. She didn't move for a long moment, and all the while her great-uncle smoked and turned pages, smoked and turned pages. "But—"

"In. The. Morning."

He looked up at her, his eyes cold and hard. His tone was so final, like a knife.

Even Kazen had never cast her out of his home.

Shaking, Sandis hurried into the hallway. Paused at the base of the stairs. She'd been out in the night before. By herself, even. But that had been by choice. Facing the darkness now . . . she was so unsure. She had no one to run from. No one to guide her to a safe place. No one to wait for her.

It would be just her and the nightmares. And on the street, she'd have no white-painted walls to put between her and them.

She bit the inside of her cheek. Where would she go? Talbur would keep his word. She knew him well enough to be certain of that.

Shivers coursed up and down her limbs. Her chest hurt. She needed a glass of water. She needed—

But there was no time to comfort herself, no time, even, to think. He'd tell the servants to see her out. She had to hurry.

Her steps passed beneath her like air. Suddenly she was in her room, finding a bag, stuffing it with—What should she take? Food? He'd want her out by dinner . . .

She could return, grovel, apologize—

But she couldn't do it. She couldn't pretend to be a harlot and kiss a stranger, only to take his life. The thought spurred nausea like acid in her belly. Why would he ask her to do something so awful? If he cared about her, why . . .

Pressing her lips together, she grabbed a change of clothes and a jacket. It got cold at night. Then she hurried down to the kitchen. The cook didn't say anything to her as she took a few pieces of fruit and a roll. Sandis barely registered her own movements.

The porch. Would he let her stay on the porch? No, if he saw her there, he'd only be angrier. Oh Celestial, what was she supposed to do? She couldn't stay in this neighborhood. The scarlets always lurked in the nice neighborhoods at night, away from true crime, but they wouldn't tolerate her loitering or trespassing on another's property to sleep. She'd have to go farther out, toward the smoke ring—

A small mewl sounded in the base of her throat. She heard footsteps on the basement stairs. Talbur? She hurried out the back door and started walking with no direction in mind. Clutched her bag to her chest like it was a buoy, carrying her through the waters of a canal.

She trembled with a sob and swallowed it down until it ached dully at the base of her throat. Her parents had never let her and her little brother, Anon, outside after dark. Too dangerous. If only Anon were still alive, maybe he would know what to do. Despite being two years younger, he'd always been wise. He'd had an old soul.

She wiped her eyes and looked up, trying to find some direction. She could still go back and . . .

But the thought of doing what he'd asked . . .

She kept walking. Back in the morning, he'd said. Just one night. She could do one night, couldn't she? She could just keep walking. If she never lay down, she wouldn't fall asleep, and she wouldn't dream. She'd stayed up all night before; she could do it again.

Sandis pushed her knuckle into her mouth and bit down. She passed big house after big house. The sun was setting. If she waited until after dark, perhaps she could creep into a neighbor's backyard and huddle on the stonework. No one would see her, surely. But what if they did? The people here were so unfriendly. And if the police saw the marks of the occult on her skin, it wouldn't matter who her great-uncle was—they'd send her to Gerech. She'd die there. Even the streets in the smoke ring were better than that.

She'd just have to go to an inn. There had to be one close by.

Sandis's limbs slowed and cooled as she realized she hadn't packed the allowance Talbur had given her. She rechecked her bag, her pockets, praying to the Celestial as she did, but she found not a single kol.

Her breaths came too fast. She slowed, forcing air in and out of her lungs. She couldn't panic. This wasn't the first time she'd been out on her own. She'd survived a night on the streets before meeting Rone. Granted, someone else had helped her—a woman and her son.

If only someone would help her now.

There was Arnae Kurtz, Rone's old master, but she'd promised not to return to his hidden door, and she didn't think she could find it on her own anyway. That, and it was too far to walk . . .

Pausing, Sandis turned, looking around as the polluted sky took on shades of violet and burnt orange. She forced more air into her body. Clutched her bag. Sat down, right there on the sidewalk.

She couldn't. She wouldn't.

The sky got darker. The air colder.

She couldn't.

But she had to.

Chapter 2

Sandis's mind floated elsewhere as her feet picked their memorized path through the neighborhood. He wasn't far. A mile, maybe. He'd told her the address. Pointed the house out after following her on one of her deliveries. He always followed her. She never spoke a word to him, but he talked anyway. Sometimes. Sometimes he simply matched her silence.

Sandis moved slowly, stretching out the mile until it felt like ten. The homes here were nice, sizable like Talbur's. Most still had lights on. So long as the lights stayed on, it was okay for Sandis to take her time.

The mansion where Rone lived was still lit, too. One of the window wells to his basement glowed yellow. He never turned in early, but seeing that light was both a relief and a trigger for her. Her muscles loosened, but her heart beat quicker in a squelching kind of way. Like it was sick.

As she came around the house, toward the stairwell that led to Rone's door, she heard voices. She slowed even more and turned the corner.

Rone's door was open, spilling yellow light into the stairwell. His elbow was up and pressed against the door frame as he spoke to a woman who stood a few feet away from him. She was tall, with rare blonde hair almost as light as Alys's. The similarity hit her like a fist to the gut. *Alys, bleeding on the floor, unconscious and alone . . .* The lighting was poor, but the woman looked to be in her early twenties—somewhere between Sandis's and Rone's ages.

She was pretty.

Sandis stopped short. The heart-squelching began to hurt.

This was a bad idea. She couldn't stay here. She could go back to Talbur's, maybe see if Amila would let her into the wine cellar, just for the night. Talbur never went in there, she didn't think—

"Well, thank you," the woman said, tucking a lock of long hair behind her ear. So much longer than Sandis's. More feminine. She smiled at Rone. "I'm glad to hear it."

She started up the stairs, and Rone's eyes followed her before flicking to the left. To Sandis.

The woman glimpsed her, too, and offered a tight smile before passing on.

Sandis felt like a sewer rat.

She couldn't bring her feet to move, neither forward nor backward.

"Sandis." He said her name like she was a lost thing found. He moved away from the door frame and stepped toward her. Sandis retreated a step. Rone stopped.

He rubbed the back of his head. "Finally taking me up on those seugrat lessons?"

She didn't answer.

Sighing, Rone dropped his hand. "What's wrong?"

She swallowed. *Move.* Her legs were leaden and numb, but she managed to inch forward and not fall down the stairs. She clutched her bag. The acidic yellow light stung her eyes.

She slipped into Rone's flat. The air within felt too warm. The layout was a little peculiar, like the space hadn't been designed to be an apartment. A random table stood just inside the door. The kitchen lay all against one wall. There was a couch beneath the window, and a door that might have led to a bedroom.

Celestial above, why couldn't she just *pretend*? Why couldn't she just imagine that Rone's exchange with Kazen never happened? That they were just as they used to be? She so badly wanted to forget. She so desperately wanted to pretend.

Like you pretend with Talbur?

Gritting her teeth, she banished the question from her thoughts.

Rone came in behind her and shut the door. Looked her over. Ran a hand through his hair and sighed. "She's just the landlord's daughter."

Sandis took a step away from him, focusing her eyes on the far wall. "I didn't ask."

"Sandis, I—" He paused, looking surprised. That she'd talked to him? But then his gaze fell to her shoulder. "What's this?" He reached for one of the straps of her bag. She pulled it away from his touch. It was a mistake—heat laced her skin everywhere they had touched.

She cleared her throat as silently as she could.

"Can I . . . Can I stay here tonight? Please?"

When Rone didn't answer, she finally dared to look at him. His forehead wrinkled in the way it did when he was confused. His eyes looked so dark, so endless. His lips turned down.

He was going to say no. He was going to reject her, maybe save the space for the blonde woman, and she'd have to find somewhere else to stay.

His hand touched her back, right between her shoulder blades. His skin somehow burned her through her layers. He guided her to the couch, then pressed her shoulders down and made her sit. He sat next to her.

Elbows on his knees, he said, "Tell me what happened."

She shook her head. "It's just for one night."

"*Sandis.* Black ashes, if you're talking to me, then just *tell* me."

She clenched her fists over her bag. "He said . . . He said I couldn't stay there tonight." Her voice was quiet and too high. She rubbed her throat to loosen it.

"Talbur said you couldn't stay at his house."

She nodded, her gaze fixed to the floor.

He groaned. "God's tower, that man is a piece of sh—"

"Please don't." This was another of his refrains.

A growl sounded low in Rone's throat. "Don't what, Sandis? Say what you won't? He's manipulative and greedy. Slimy. All he wants is—"

"He's family." She lifted her eyes and met his. "He's my only family. He's all I have."

A flicker of something heavy crossed Rone's features, but it vanished too quickly for Sandis to discern it. Maybe it was just the lighting. Hugging her bag, she added, "Just for one night. I can sleep on the couch . . . or by the door. I don't mind, as long as I'm inside."

Rone pressed his head into his palms. "Hell, Sandis. Yes, you can stay. No, you're not going to sleep by the door. Why would I make you sleep by the door?"

She bit her lip, unsure of what to say. A few stiff seconds passed before Rone stood up and strode to his bedroom. He came back a moment later with two blankets. One he rolled up so it resembled a pillow. He set it on his end of the couch. Sandis stood as he unfurled the other across the cushions.

The last time they'd shared the same space like this, Sandis had fallen asleep in his arms.

Turning away, she blinked rapidly. She would not cry, not now. She had come so far. No tears would fall. Not after she'd worked so hard damming them.

Steeling herself, Sandis pretended to study the tiles near the door to buy more time. As she lifted her gaze, she noticed a letter on the shelf near it. She took a single step toward it. There was a red-inked stamp across its top she didn't recognize.

"What's this?" she asked. Who would be writing Rone, and at an address he'd lived at less than a month?

Rone turned to look, then crossed the room in three strides and picked up the envelope. "It's a letter from my mother." He ran his thumb reverently over the ink. "From Godobia. Picked it up from the post office."

Sandis clung to her bag a little harder. "I'm glad she made it."

Rone nodded. Stuck the envelope under his arm. "Are you hungry? I can make—"

"I'll just sleep. If that's okay." She wanted morning to come so she could go home. Maybe with everything that had happened, her mind would be too preoccupied for demonic dreams.

Home. The word felt twisted, but she tried not to dwell on that.

"Yeah. It's late." Rone blew out the lamp on the wall, then took a second one from its hook near the door and set it on the narrow table near the couch. He lingered for a moment before turning for his bedroom. He shut the door.

Sandis set her bag down and curled up on the couch, pulling the blanket up to her chin. She licked her fingers, opened the lamp door, and extinguished the wick with a sizzle. The soft burn against the pads of her fingers made her think of Ireth, and the thought carved another hollow space inside her.

Rolling over, Sandis pressed her face against the back of the couch as a hard lump formed in her throat, sore and relentless.

She pushed the blanket over her eyes for fear of staining the furniture.

Chapter 3

Rone leaned against his bedroom door, staring at the flickering lamp near the window. He should go back out there. Grab her shoulders and say, *Just* tell *me. Tell me what he did. What you did. Anything.*

Sandis was her great-uncle's special pet, groomed just the way he wanted her. Talbur was incapable of doing any wrong in her eyes. So what spat could have brought her to his door?

Was this the first time this had happened, or had Sandis been punished previous nights and chosen the streets over his company? But he would have known. God's tower, he'd watched that damn house so carefully he wasn't left with any time to check his drop-off sites. Not that it mattered. Without the amarinth, there was no Engel Verlad, thief for hire. Just a coward hiding in a basement, unsure what to do with his pathetic life.

He pulled out the envelope from beneath his arm. He'd hurried home to read it, not wanting to do so at the crowded post office, only to run into Lina, the homeowner's daughter. She'd inquired after the length of his stay, and he'd answered indefinitely—he'd stay in this basement until Sandis came to her senses and left Talbur. And if that never happened, he would never leave.

Or was that another lie he told himself?

Rone sat in the chair to the small desk in his room. Opened the top drawer and pushed aside the map he'd drawn from memory of Kazen's lair, though it was incomplete. He had to go back there eventually, and not just for his amarinth. But cowards weren't the most proactive people.

He drew out his emigration papers. The date, though written in small writing, glared at him from the top left corner. He only had eleven days left before he left Kolingrad behind to join his mother. Only a week and a half before this invaluable treasure in his hands became nothing more than scratch paper.

He folded the papers and stuffed them into the drawer, which he slammed shut. Leaning his elbows against the desk, Rone weaved his fingers through his hair. Eleven days, except he'd have to leave a few days before that to make it to the border in time.

Did Sandis want him to leave? She didn't want him to stay. Once upon a time, she would have told him to follow his dreams . . . but that was before he'd shattered hers.

But she'd come to him tonight. Spoken to him, even. That was a good sign, wasn't it? Or was her desperation mounting its peak?

Black ashes, did she hate him that much?

His eyes found the letter and lingered there. He'd had to do it. His mother would have died in prison without the bribe money, and those papers had swept her away from the influence of the wealthy family who had so harshly prosecuted her for Rone's misdeeds. It had been Sandis or his mother, and he'd come back for Sandis. They were both free now. It had worked out, in the end.

At the cost of Sandis's trust and his amarinth, but it had worked out.

Rone clawed at the envelope's flap and tore it open, letting the thick letter topple onto his desk. He unfolded it like it was water and he a man lost in the desert. The familiar handwriting was a balm to his soul, and for a moment, he didn't feel that constant iron ball rolling around in his stomach.

She started by expressing her concern for his behavior at the pass—his confession about being responsible for her arrest and his sudden, unexplained need to turn back. But she went on to talk about the journey through the mountains. She'd met up with a Godobian family who'd taken her under their wing, though they could hardly understand one another.

But it didn't matter, because when we arrived at their home, Teon's grandfather spoke perfect Kolin. His father had been a grain merchant and had taken him on many of his ventures. He spent ten summers in Dresberg! So I was able to tell him my story, and he relayed the information to the others. I left out Gerech, of course. I confess I leaned on the tale of your father to explain why and how I left. It would make sense, after all. Surely the Angelic could use his influence to get his estranged wife emigration papers.

Rone set his jaw and turned to the next page. His mother was always so . . . not kind, but nonchalant when it came to his father. Like they'd merely settled on a divorce, instead of him abandoning his family to further his religious career. Rone both admired and hated how easy that had become for his mother. Then again, maybe she only made it look easy, for his sake.

She went on to talk about her search for land—something small and nearby, so she wouldn't have to make new friends all over again. Apparently, she'd found a place one town over. A son had been looking to sell his mother's house after her death, a modest cottage attached to a modest farm. Rone's mother hadn't wanted to risk purchasing the farm, for fear she'd have nothing left to subsist on until she found work, but the man had been reluctant to separate them. Apparently, after some words with this grandfather, he'd agreed to sell the house with half the land and turn the rest into horse grounds. His mother had written this letter on her first day in the house.

I hope it reaches you—it's such a ways to travel. I'm not sure what the turnaround is for postal service across the border, but if I don't hear back from you in four weeks, I'll write again. With luck, I'll be seeing you in person by then!

But, Rone, you know what I want. That explanation you promised me. I worry about you constantly, and I need to understand. I've sorted through every possible story you could tell me, and yet somehow I know none of them will be close to the truth.

I look forward to hearing from you. Seeing you. In case you ripped this envelope, or it fell into a roadside puddle, here's the address to the house. I tried to draw a map on the back of this paper, but you know how terrible I am with things like this.

Love you.

Rone took a deep breath. Started again at the beginning of the letter and read through to the end. Turned the paper over and laughed at the map she'd drawn. Had she done it while in a carriage? None of the lines were straight, and he had a feeling the scale was inconsistent as well.

Setting the letter aside, Rone opened one drawer, then another, trying to remember where he'd left the stationery he'd purchased in anticipation of this very moment. He found it and pulled it out, along with the quill and ink the previous resident had left atop this desk.

He focused on the door, his gaze lingering as if, should he stare long enough, he'd be able to see through it to the sleeping form on the other side.

He started by dating his letter in the corner, but he set it back a week. Then he began to write.

Mom—
Yes, I owe you a story. I owe you an apology. A thousand times over. I hope you'll forgive me after you read this letter. If you can't, we can just pretend, like we do with Dad.

It started with theft; both my theft of the headpiece, which was pinned on you, and the theft of a treasure of mine by a woman named Sandis Gwenwig—

Chapter 4

Sandis ran.

The ground shuddered beneath her feet. The heat was unbearable, turning her sweat into steam. Her lungs burned; her legs burned. Only darkness lay ahead of her, impenetrable and foreboding, but she dashed for its heart. She had to escape. *Escape.*

The beast roared behind her. A sob erupted from her mouth, and she ran, ran, *ran.*

Ireth, help me! she screamed inside her head. But the fire horse didn't respond. He couldn't. He was gone.

Flames licked her shoulders. Sandis fell, skinning her knees. Looked back.

The red face of a bull lowered toward her, and she screamed.

"Sandis!"

The heat and the flames vanished all at once, replaced by blue-hued darkness. Water dripped from her hair and chin. Soaked her dress. She coughed as it trickled down her throat. Something grabbed her, and she jumped—but these were human hands. Familiar hands.

The shadows and shapes of Rone's flat came into focus. His silhouette crouched before her, his face lowered close to hers. A discarded cup lay on the floor beside him. Water still ran from the pump in the kitchen to her right.

She sat on the floor, half-drenched, not far from the front door.

Rone's breathing was nearly as heavy as hers. "Sandis?"

Sandis wiped water from her eyes with shaking hands. "I . . . What?"

"You were sleepwalking," he said, his voice low, panicked. "You were *screaming*."

Sleepwalking? Sandis had never done that before. Or if she had, she'd always gotten back into bed before waking up. That meant they were getting worse, didn't it?

Rone's hands ran down her arms. "You're freezing." He jumped to his feet and grabbed the blanket from the sofa, draping it over her shoulders. Sandis clutched its edges in fists, trying to coax her body to stop shaking.

He had been there. Kolosos. It had felt *so real*.

Rone knelt before her. "What happened?"

Pulling the blanket tighter around her, Sandis shook her head.

"Damn it, Sandis, don't refuse to talk to me now. I know you. I know this is *not normal*."

He might as well have punched her in the gut. He knew her because they'd been inseparable before he sold her back to Kazen. They'd shared rooms. Sleeping rolls, even.

He tucked some of her wet hair behind her ear. Sandis pulled back. Filled her chest with a deep breath, and then another. "It was just a nightmare."

"People don't need to be doused in cold water to wake up from a nightmare."

She wiped her nose on the blanket.

Rone sighed. Stayed silent for a full minute. Then asked, "How long have you been having nightmares?"

She swallowed, a sore lump pressing against the walls of her throat. "They're not always nightmares," she whispered.

"They?" He loomed closer. Sandis didn't have the energy to move away. Part of her didn't want to.

Her hold on the blanket loosened. "Since Kazen. Since we left."

Now Rone pulled back, grabbing his knees in his hands. Almost whispering, he asked, "What are you dreaming about?"

She flinched as though Kolosos's claws caressed her back. "Kolosos." Rone swore.

"It's fine." She dried the rest of her face. The ends of her hair. "It's just a dream."

Rone leveled his gaze at her. "You just said they weren't always nightmares."

Avoiding his eyes, Sandis glanced to the window. "What time is it?"

"It doesn't matter. We need to talk about—"

"What time is it?" she repeated more forcefully.

She could feel his frustration like the humidity before a storm. "Almost dawn."

Sandis stood and walked toward the couch, grabbing her bag. If she could keep her focus on the bag, on the shadows, on her route home, then she wouldn't have to think.

"You can't just run back to him." Rone followed her like a stray dog. "We need to talk. What else, besides the nightmares? Sandis." He touched her elbow; she tugged it free.

"It's nothing."

"It's not *nothing!*" Rone shouted, startling her. He grabbed fistfuls of his hair and nearly pulled it out by the root. "If you could have *heard* yourself, Sandis! Please. God's tower, just let me help you."

She whirled on him, standing as straight as her spine would allow. "I think we both remember what happened last time you helped me, Rone Comf."

The stray dog metaphor had been accurate. At her words, he looked like one, and she hated the way his sorrowful expression pricked her heart.

She pulled her bag onto her shoulder. Looking at the floor, she said, "Thank you for letting me stay."

She hurried for the door and escaped.

Once again, Sandis felt as if she didn't quite belong in the world. Like somehow, she was separate from everything.

Until Talbur's home came into sight. Then she felt very rooted, and very small.

But at least he wasn't Kazen. Inside these walls, Kazen didn't exist. The vessels didn't exist. Kolosos *didn't exist.*

She tried to keep her back straight when she knocked on the front door—Talbur had never given her a key. Amila answered and offered a sympathetic smile before letting her inside. Shaking jitters from her arms, Sandis swept up the stairs to her room, where she changed into her nicest clothes and washed her face the way her great-uncle had told her to. Parted her hair just so, put on her makeup. Her fingers trembled, which made the kohl a little difficult, but it worked well enough.

She frowned at her reflection and left, forcing herself to slip into the learned routine.

Talbur sat at the breakfast table, his plate empty despite an assortment of smoked meats and bread sitting on the table before him. He read the paper. Like he was waiting for her.

Sandis wasn't sure if she should apologize. If she should say anything. Watching him, she pulled out the chair opposite his and sat.

Her great-uncle lowered his paper. "Ah, Sandis. Good morning. I trust you slept well?"

She stared at him. Nodded. Lied.

He nodded almost jovially and folded the paper before setting it beside his tray. Picking up a pair of tongs, he helped himself to three links of sausage. "Glad to hear it. I hear you've been rummaging through the library. Found anything you like?"

This was it, then? Everything would be jolly and fine? *If only I were as good at pretending as he is.* Maybe she could learn something from him.

She mentioned the pirate book and reached for a muffin, warily, as if Talbur would swat her hand away just before she touched it. He didn't.

"I've got a full day today. Might be home late." He wiped his mouth on a napkin. "Might need to hire that Engel boy again."

Sandis forced herself to chew through the mention of Rone's alias.

"As for you, I'd like you to deliver something for me. Tonight, at the last work bell. Amila will set the package outside your bedroom door. I want you in the city when the bell hits, mind you. Chaos is always good for delivery."

Chaos was a good word for it. So many men, women, and children worked in the factories. The streets were thronged after the last bell. Sandis raised her eyebrow, trying to figure out how it could possibly be prudent to make a delivery at such a time . . . unless Talbur didn't want anyone paying attention to Sandis and her mystery package.

Her stomach clenched, and she had to force herself to swallow her last bite of muffin. Was it something illegal? Perhaps one of those off-limits boxes in the basement? What if Sandis was caught? Didn't Talbur know that vessels, whether they were in active use or not, were strictly prohibited and would be hanged if arrested?

Her thoughts must have painted her face, for her great-uncle added, "No worries, dear." He reached inside a pocket and handed her a piece of paper. "I have a very precise route drawn out for you. You can hire a carriage to bring you home. Here." He added ten kol to the paper— enough for one-way transportation.

Sandis unfolded the paper, which she recognized as a map of part of the smoke ring in District Two, and traced the thick black line that wrapped around factories and flats.

"Well?"

She nodded.

Talbur smiled. "There's my girl." He shoved more meat into his mouth, then grabbed a piece of poppy bread. "I'm off."

He left his chair pushed out and departed out the back door.

Sandis sat at the table a while longer, despite having lost her appetite. She stared at her great-uncle's chair, skewed to the right. The smell of the smoked meats, which had been pleasant before, suddenly invoked thoughts of Heath.

As she stood to leave, however, she glimpsed one of the headlines in her great-uncle's newspaper: "Disturbing Increase of Missing Youth Has Police on Alert."

She picked up the paper and read. Several children, ages ten to sixteen, had gone missing from their homes and places of work without a trace. The article profiled each one, giving a name and a description for each. It then went on to say two had been found but were "greatly disfigured, making it difficult for police to identify them."

Coldness formed a snowball in her stomach. Greatly disfigured *how?*

With brands? Or had they simply been turned inside out, like Heath?

Sandis pressed her palm over her mouth, sure she'd sick up. Ages ten to sixteen . . . good ages for vessels. She, Alys, Kaili, Rist, Dar . . . they'd all been branded in that age range.

You're jumping to conclusions, she chided herself. *You're seeing things that aren't there. Again.*

And yet she knew Kazen. Knew him as intimately as the sword she'd use to run him through.

But Rone had lost his amarinth. A Noscon device more powerful than any sword. If Kazen had it, then he still lived.

Sandis set the paper down and turned away. Paused. Picked the article back up and reread it, noting the author's name: Vetto Dace. There was no mention of grafters or the occult. No indisputable connection to Kazen. And yet . . .

She thought she felt a hot breath against her neck. She bit her tongue to keep from crying out and blinked tears from her eyes. She just wanted to be *safe*. Was that such a horrible thing?

Nausea rolled through her middle as she retreated to her room, newspaper still in hand. She closed the door behind her, then leaned against it and slid to the floor, her arms wrapping around her knees. At least this meant Kazen had moved on. That he wasn't looking for her anymore. Maybe she *was* safe.

Shame licked at her. Did the other vessels know the names of Kazen's experiments, or did they simply put their pillows over their heads when they heard screaming?

At least in her nightmares, she could run. The children couldn't, and neither could the other vessels. They were trapped behind that heavy, locked door, waiting for Kazen to torture them, test them. Waiting for Kolosos.

Sandis could hide all she wanted, but it wouldn't stop Kazen from his mission of madness. Sandis had slowed him down before. Could she do it again?

But Talbur wouldn't let Sandis leave. Part of her didn't want to. For all his fault, Talbur was family. Her *only* family. And she so desperately wanted a family.

But Talbur didn't want the same, did he? He wanted an employee. Someone to deliver packages. To scare men in pubs and kiss debtors in whorehouses.

A new revelation came to her. Had Talbur ever heard her scream in the middle of the night? If so, he'd never tried to wake her.

Sandis sat against that door for a long time, until her tailbone ached and her feet tingled for lack of blood. When she stood, she was light-headed and had to lean against the door until she felt solid again. Solid and numb. She recovered the bag she'd taken with her to Rone's. Blankly checked its contents. Ate some bread she couldn't taste. Moved to her closet, selected another dress, and folded it tightly. Placed it in the bag. Added a comb. The newspaper. Her allowance. She tried to count the bills, but her brain couldn't wrap around the math. She split the amount in two, putting half in her skirt pocket and half in her bag.

She reached for the pirate book. Paused. No, that wasn't hers. It would have to stay.

Down the stairs, to the kitchen. She didn't remember the journey, only opened the cupboards and took what she could find that was small and lasting. Packed the bag until it couldn't hold any more.

When? Should she leave now, or later, when it was time to deliver the package? If she left now, Amila or the cook might see her and say something. But they all expected her to leave tonight, for Talbur's errand.

She had a feeling he wouldn't miss her.

Brain dust.

Sandis recognized the stuff the moment she opened the package at the end of Talbur's street. It awoke a sickening nostalgia in her. Galt had often smelled of the drug. A lot of the grafters did. Never Kazen. She'd never seen him smoke, sniff, or drink. But the scent of burnt brain dust was just as common in his lair as the smell of cleaner from the "messes" the grafters tended to make.

Sandis closed the box and tossed it into the first garbage bin she passed. Newly emptied. The collectors must have come today.

The numbness hadn't receded, but the farther she got from Talbur's home, her bag strapped to her back, the colder she became. It was still summer, though the season was ending, and the blanket of smog that covered the city made it unnaturally warm. Yet the heat couldn't penetrate her skin. And so she shivered, her footsteps echoing dully against the cobbles. Others were out and about, but Sandis didn't heed them. She just kept walking. South, farther into the city. She had to . . . what was it? Yes, she had to find a landlord. She needed a space to rent . . . but would she find one so late? Would they ask for identification?

An inn. She could afford to stay in one for the night. And then she'd find a rental in the morning. A small space. Nothing fancy. Something cheap, on the opposite side of the city from the grafters. And then she could . . . what? What exactly did she think she could do? She was only one person, after all. It would be better, safer to hide. To change her name and find a job.

"Where are you going?"

The voice barely registered in her thoughts. She kept moving forward, footsteps thudding on the cobblestones. It occurred to her that she didn't know how to find an inn, either. She'd stayed in one once, but that had ended badly. She didn't remember seeing any nearby. Her great-uncle had told her where the Rose Inn was . . . but she couldn't go there. She knew of a boardinghouse deeper in the city, but it would take all night to walk there—

"Sandis." Footsteps quicker than hers thumped behind her. A shadow blocked the setting sun—it had already disappeared behind the wall, but its yellow rays reached up from the unseen horizon. "Hey. What's wrong? What happened?"

She paused. Looked up. Rone. Where had he come from?

She stepped around him and continued on her path. Some taverns and bars had rooms. Maybe she could ask for a pallet. That would be less expensive, right?

Warmth pierced through the chill, funneling up her fingers. She looked down. Rone's hand had seized hers. It took her a moment to muster the will to pull her hand away.

"Sandis. *What happened?*"

She blinked, looked at him. "I'm leaving."

"Talbur?"

Nodding, she started to walk again.

He blocked her. "Where are you going?"

She swallowed. "Please go." She couldn't do this right now. Couldn't talk or think. She could only *do*. A plan would come later.

"I'm not going to leave. It's almost dark. Where are you going? Do you need to stay over again?"

She tried to step around him. When she spoke, her voice was airy and tight. "I need a landlord."

Rone rubbed the scruff on his jaw. "I can help you find a landlord. In the morning. Just come with me, okay? You're . . . not yourself."

She blinked at him. Not herself? How was she not herself? He didn't even know her. Everyone who knew her was dead or trapped in a cell underground . . .

A pang punched her chest. Just below her shattered heart.

She feinted to the right, then stepped to the left to get around Rone. Continued moving farther into the city.

"Sandis." He walked beside her now. "No one will be open for business at this hour. The light is leaving."

Sandis tried to speak, but the only word that made it past her lips was "inn."

Rone groaned. "I don't think there's one near here. Sandis." He grasped her wrist. "Let me help you. Okay? If you want to stay at an inn, I'll take you to one. We can get a cab. I'll pay for it."

Pay for it.

With what money?

The money he'd gotten from Kazen.

The pang hit her heart, but it didn't slide away as it usually did. It radiated. Expanded, until it filled every part of her. Until the numbness burned away and all she could do was *feel*.

She was alone. Her parents and brother were dead. The other vessels were trapped. Rone had sold her. Talbur wanted to use her. She had no family. No friends. Not even her god wanted her.

She pressed a hand to her chest, wishing she could still feel the old connection to Ireth, even the slightest pressure or sliver of warmth. He'd been an abomination, but he had been *hers*.

"Sandis?" Rone stood in front of her again, cupping her face. "Sandis? You're shaking."

Tears blurred her vision. Pain sucked at her heart, deadening it. Everything beneath her skin was smoke and salt.

She'd always thought summoning was the worst pain a person could experience, but she'd been wrong.

This was.

This emptiness. This . . . nothingness. She wasn't in a place apart from the world; *she* was apart from the world. She had no ties, no relations.

No hope.

Her strength dissolved, and she crumpled right there on the side of the street, crying like she had when her father died. When she couldn't find Anon. When the slavers first kidnapped her. Sobs ripped through her body like saw blades. The sun's rays finally slipped from the sky, enveloping her in a darkness as absolute as the one inside her.

Rone's hands smoothed her hair. Pressed into her back. "What can I do?" he asked, low and soft. "I'll do anything to make this better."

"I—" The sobs shattered her words. "I-I have n-no one . . ."

Her tears pattered against the cobblestones like rain.

"You have me, Sandis. I promise. You have me."

But Sandis shook her head as the thorns bloomed and coiled around her heart. "I-I don't," she lamented. "I . . . n-never . . . did."

Chapter 5

The sewers and tunnels underneath Dresberg were a temple in and of themselves. Or, more accurately, a sepulchre. A dying place buried by invaders so they could build their new world on the ruins of the old. So they could form their new religion and classify the old one as heresy.

Hypocrites. Every last one of them.

Kazen always contemplated this when he went into the underground. Not the tunnels that pushed the city's wastewater around, but the old, man-made caverns that spiraled below them—down deep where the filthiest of men did their bartering. Where the grubbiest slags of criminals hid for fear of justice. For fear of the light.

It was a place where Kazen had found power. And where he still held it.

The rejects, the thieves, murderers, and addicts looked up at him as he walked a narrow path around grime that leaked from the sewers and puddles of groundwater. The wretches all knew who he was. He had lost much as of late, but he had not lost his reputation.

He followed the light of the lamps, the burning kerosene driving back the smell of rot and unwashed bodies. The cavern opened up, giving way to a high black roof where burning lights couldn't reach. A narrow stream flowed down one side of it, and men with wares or services to offer occupied the other side. There weren't many of them, but those who had set up blankets and tables boasted more weapons than they did limbs, daring anyone to cross them. He passed a man at a stone table topped with a tent cover selling legal documents for hefty prices. Forgeries, not the real thing—Kazen had a better contact for acquiring such papers. But documents were not his quarry today. Nor did he wish to do business with the Ysbeno slavers across the way. He had his own men for vessel collections, and they were already hard at work, finding him what he needed.

Today, he meant to make a profit.

His target stood behind a ritzy booth in the corner of the cavern, near the narrow stream that eventually let out into the Lime River. Four guards, well muscled and well armed, flanked his station. His rounded table showcased a variety of high-value goods, some of Noscon make, likely stolen from the wealthy or from museums around the country, if not fakes forged by modern hands. He had a small apothecary behind him as well as a chest of the brain dust Galt had so enjoyed.

Thoughts of his old assistant didn't so much as bend the rhythm of his step as he approached the booth. The guards eyed him, eyed their master, and stayed right where they were.

Siegen always trained his boys well.

The merchant wore a turban on his head to keep off water that sporadically dripped from the ceiling; a drop hit the brim of Kazen's hat as he set his bag on the table. The man was pale from spending so much time in the dark, but his rounded cheeks and stomach whispered business was doing well. Kazen expected no less from the likes of him.

"Selling today?" Siegen asked, gesturing toward the bag. "Or are you hoping I'll make that parcel a little heavier?"

"I've no need of your trinkets today." Kazen possessed a "trinket" far more valuable than anything Siegen could ever hope to lay eyes on, let alone sell. A trinket worth even more than what he had in his bag, thanks to the slip of a two-timing hire. That was what happened when one relied upon a broker instead of taking care of business himself. "I have something you'll be interested in."

"Surprise me."

Kazen removed the strips of gold, backed by a special kind of leather, from his bag. As he set them down, Siegen's eyes widened. "Is that what I think it is?"

Kazen did not smile at the huskiness of the merchant's voice. Not where the man could see.

"It is." He removed a few glass vials full of gold flakes flecked with brown and handed one of them to the shorter man, who held it up to the nearest lamp to study it. The merchant would take him at his word. Kazen was always honest in his dealings, where it mattered.

Siegen whistled. "I'm surprised, coming from you."

Kazen shrugged. "She wasn't useful to me anymore."

Siegen reached forward and brought the gold closer, studied it, and weighed it on a scale by his apothecary shelves. "I'll give you thirteen thousand kol."

"Let's not cheapen the merchandise, my friend," Kazen said, raising an eyebrow.

But Siegen shook his head. "You're not the only one dealing in remedial gold. I've had inquiries from above."

That surprised Kazen, though he didn't show it. Surely not Oz, the only other summoner who had clout in these parts. Then who? "Oh?"

Siegen shook his head and pulled out his money box. Two of his guards moved closer, as though waiting for Kazen to make a move. "Don't ask for details," the merchant said. "I can't give them."

"Don't presume I care to know, my friend." Kazen reached his hand forward. "The thirteen will do."

Siegen counted out the amount twice before handing the bills to Kazen, who counted them again to be sure.

After slipping the money into his bag and slinging the bag over his shoulder, he tipped his hat. "Always a pleasure."

Siegen nodded, and Kazen retraced his steps.

Even with so much money in his pack, no one dared intercept him.

Chapter 6

Rone's old flat was still under his name and hadn't yet been rented to anyone else. He'd paid for the entire month, and there was still over a week left. The apartment hadn't been ransacked, like his mother's had been, and as far as he knew, the grafters hadn't touched it.

Just to be safe, he sought out his old landlord first thing the morning after Sandis's breakdown in the street and asked to be switched to a different space. He had one available in the same building, but moving would mean forfeiting the rent he'd already paid on his old flat. Rone took the deal without question.

Sandis was . . . a ghost. Pale, except for the dark rings around her eyes. Fragile, like burnt paper. Mute as a cobblestone.

But she went without complaint into the new space. Sat on the floor despite the room's furnishings. Stared off into another world.

Rone retrieved his provisions from his old flat and made some oatmeal for her. She didn't touch it. Just sat and stared.

He, Kazen, Talbur . . . they'd done this. They'd broken her. The metallic ball in his stomach rolled back and forth, and Rone swore he tasted blood. As he sat in the silence of his new flat, he couldn't help but think, *Did Talbur let her go, or will he come back for her, like Kazen did?*

He glanced Sandis's way. Talbur was no summoner. Perhaps he wanted Sandis for his own reasons, but he couldn't use her the way Kazen had. Maybe this would truly be a clean break.

When Sandis fell asleep in the afternoon, Rone hired a carriage to his basement apartment in District Three to gather the rest of his belongings. When he got back, Sandis was awake. At least she'd moved to the couch. The cold oatmeal was gone, the bowl set on the counter beside his.

Rone dumped his clothes in the bedroom, trying to sort out what he could possibly say to her. Sorry your great-uncle is burnt slag? Do you want to talk about it? Are you somehow hungry again?

He sighed. Fortunately, the moment he stepped back into the living space, Sandis broke the silence for him.

"I want my own flat."

Her eyes weren't as sunken, and the tear-induced swelling had lifted, but her skin had no color to it. Her posture was rigid and unnatural. She looked like a doll half-painted.

"You can stay here, Sandis. You can have the bedroom. There's plenty of space."

"I want my own flat." Her voice had no inflection. "I can afford it."

"For how long?"

Her mouth pressed into a line. Rone shoved his hands into his trouser pockets. Tried not to audibly sigh. "I'm not your enemy, Sandis. I want to help you. Just let—"

"Then help me find a new flat." She stood and grabbed her pack.

"Now?"

She moved for the door.

Rone sidestepped and blocked her path. "We need to talk."

She shot him a dark glare.

He matched it. "Let's start with Kazen."

She shrunk back from him. "Kazen's dead."

Doubt squeezed her voice, making it a trickle of what it should be.

Rone rubbed his eyes, thinking. "I've looked a couple times around the place where he holes up."

Sandis took two retreating steps from him.

"The area is quiet," he pressed on. "Too quiet. Like the locals still have a reason not to trespass there. But none of them will talk to me. They won't even open their doors. I have to wait for them to come outside to harass them."

Hugging herself, Sandis said, "You should leave them alone."

Rone sighed. "No amount of cheap rent would convince me to live there."

"Not everyone can afford better," she snapped.

This is going well. Rone chewed on the inside of his lip. She wasn't ready to talk about it. At least she was talking to him. But the longer they waited, the stronger Kazen would get. The more likely he would succeed in raising Kolosos. Rone was invested in this now. Invested in Sandis.

He studied her. "Did you have . . . another nightmare while I was gone?"

She stiffened.

Silence grew between them. He shouldn't have asked. After a long moment, he turned toward the door. "Let's see if we can find you a decent space close by—"

"Do you know where the printing press is?"

He paused, hand on the doorknob. "Printing press?"

She focused on the window. "For the newspaper."

"Which one?"

"*Dresberg Daily.*"

"Uh, yeah." He shifted on his feet. "It's not far. Why?"

Lifting her chin, she said, "I need to talk to someone named Vetto Dace."

On the way to the printing press, Sandis gave him a brief explanation of the newspaper article she'd read about missing children; Rone tried not to be sick about it. There was no solid evidence linking it to Kazen, but if it meant something to Sandis, Rone would help her.

He didn't have any of his own leads on the man, besides. When Sandis's words ran short, his head began sorting through the contacts he'd made since obtaining the amarinth and taking on the persona of Engel Verlad. He generally avoided *really* dirty work, but he knew a few people . . .

Someone hit his shoulder as he passed, not even muttering an apology. The streets were crowded, as always, so it was nearly impossible to avoid everyone. Sandis shrunk from the strangers in a way she never used to, even if it meant moving closer to Rone. Her eyes darted left and right, left and right, and occasionally she looked over her shoulder. Rone couldn't blame her. He often found himself searching for Kazen's lackeys, too.

The scent of bread pierced through the city's stench, drawing Rone's attention to a bakery on the next corner. He smiled. "How about a cinnamon bun? You like those, right?"

She looked at him, then the bakery.

"I'll get you one."

She shook her head and trudged forward.

Rone almost had to run to keep up. "Sandis, I'm just offering to—"

"Where did you get the money for it, Rone?" The words were so soft he could barely hear them over the increasing press of bodies on the overcrowded street. "Tell me where you got the money."

A draining sensation dragged at his bones. He walked alongside her for a long moment before answering. "What do you want me to say, Sandis? Yes, it's left over from my mother's bail." *Bribe* was a more accurate description, but *bail* sounded more . . . legal. "Do you want it? Take it."

He reached into his pocket, but Sandis scoffed and hurried her pace. They hit another throng, however, and it forced both of them to slow.

They took a side street to one of many tall buildings clustered together. A boy hawked day-old newspapers outside one of them. After some searching, Rone found the appropriate door and walked in. A tight foyer greeted him, as well as two men at two parallel desks.

The older one addressed Rone. "What's your business?"

Rone wrung his hands together like he was nervous. "Uh, I've been summoned? By Mr. Dace? He wants a quote for a story . . ."

The man jerked his head toward an adjoining hall. "Up the stairs to the third floor, first right. Don't touch anything."

Rone nodded his thanks. Sandis shadowed him, ghostlike, as he followed the direction. Even her steps and breathing were quiet, like she was waiting for something unpleasant.

The first door they reached on the third floor was ajar, so Rone let himself in. Vetto Dace was a surprisingly young man who sat at a small desk in a small office with another journalist. He stood when Rone and Sandis entered, barely clearing five feet. Sandis had at least four inches on him.

"Are you Mr. and Mrs. Terrence?"

Rone blinked. He *had* been waiting to interview someone. "No," he answered honestly, putting his back to the other journalist, but the guy seemed absorbed in his own work and paid no heed to them. "I'm here to ask you about an article you wrote."

"From yesterday's paper," Sandis quietly added.

Vetto's gaze shifted back and forth between the two. A line of confusion marred his brow for just an instant, but he shrugged and sat down. "Which one?"

Sandis answered, "'Disturbing Increase of Missing Youth Has Police on Alert.'" She said it without hesitation, like it was a mantra she'd been repeating all day long.

Vetto nodded. "Not the kind of thing you'd forget."

"We're hoping you'd give us more information on it," Rone said.

But Vetto shook his head. "There's legislation about these things. Information the police don't want published. Details I can't print because they're too"—he paused—"gruesome."

"Because of the bodies?"

Both men turned toward Sandis. She shifted her bag on her shoulder. Swallowed. "That's what I need to know. The bodies. The article said they were hard to identify. Were they"—she cringed—"Were they inside out?"

Vetto blanched. Stared at her. Nodded.

Rone cursed. He had wanted Sandis to be wrong. Though he suspected Kazen was alive, he'd hoped to face a weakened adversary. He'd wanted this to be easy.

"How do you know?" Vetto asked.

Rone said, "Let's not get too personal." He almost put a hand on Sandis's shoulder, but he stopped himself halfway there. That wasn't going to help things. Not now.

Vetto retrieved a pencil and tapped it against his desk. "I can't tell you much. The names I was able to release were cleared by the kids' families. The others I couldn't get permission to include."

"Others?" Sandis croaked.

God's tower, there were *more*?

"Almost all the information is from interviews with the parents and a brief meeting I managed to get with Chief Esgar," Vetto continued. "He doesn't like journalists."

"Did he tell you anything else?" Sandis leaned over the desk in a pleading way that made Rone shrink into himself. "Was anyone seen near the bodies or associated with the disappearances?"

The journalist pointed his index finger at a newspaper on the edge of his desk. "I promise you, everything else I was told is in that article. Secrets make for good stories—I include everything I can that won't get me fired." He shrugged. "Maybe the police know more, but why would they tell me, or any other citizen, for that matter?"

If only to reassure Sandis, Rone asked, "But they're thoroughly investigating, right?"

Vetto laughed. "I doubt it. I had to remind Esgar about the case before he remembered what I was talking about." The laughter snuffed almost as quickly as it had started. Averting his eyes, Vetto said, "One of the corpses that turned up—he was from a wealthy family. They investigated that one until the body was returned home. The rest . . . well, you get what you pay for around here."

Sandis reeled as though he'd insulted her. She clasped her hands over her heart. The need to reach for her again nagged at Rone.

"Thanks." Rone offered a departing nod before leading the way out of the press building.

The noise of the city assaulted them when they passed the front doors and took the handful of steps to the road. The enormous buildings around them felt like prison bars, so densely packed that Rone couldn't see the wall, no matter what direction he looked.

Ten days left, if he were to escape this place.

Sandis walked away from him.

"Where are you going?" he called after her. When she didn't respond, he jogged to catch up. Her hands were curled into tight fists at her side.

"The Innerchord," she said before he repeated the question. "This is Kazen. Someone has to do something."

"We are doing something. Sandis, they won't listen to you. They won't even let you into the Degrata."

She paused. Moved to the side of the street as a wagon passed. Turned suddenly, staring at the building behind them with wide, terrified eyes.

"Sandis?"

She shivered. Hugged herself. "It's nothing."

Rone leaned against the wall, thinking. "The triumvirate won't—"

"I know." She pressed the heels of her palms into her eyes. Shifted away from him and began walking down the road again. Her shoulders were taut, her stride long and shaky. Rone followed her, a pace behind. He didn't say anything.

Who could help them? His mind searched for names.

Fran Errick had a decent network. Had once hired Rone to steal musket plans from Marald Steffen, a factory competitor. The same sorry lout who'd put Rone's mother in prison. But would Fran know anything that would help him? He was a sly son of a whore, but he didn't seem interested in the occult.

Thamus Dakis might know something. He was a scarlet, a policeman. Dirty, shady, and two-faced—the epitome of everything that was wrong in Kolingrad. The man had first tried to hire Rone to assassinate Chief Esgar, of all people, but Rone didn't kill. He'd do a lot of things, but not that. Though he'd turned down the job and the money, Dakis had come to him again, hiring him to sabotage an apothecary cart and bring two of its chests—*heavy* chests—to him. Apparently someone had failed to pay a bribe on time, so Dakis had decided to help himself. Rone had spun the amarinth and stopped the cart with his body.

The scarlets let the underground get away with an awful lot, but Dakis would help him if he waved enough kol in front of his face. And money was the one thing Rone had in abundance right now.

His final option was Jurris Hadmar. But Rone didn't want to ask any favors of the ex-mobster if he didn't have to. Hadmar . . . he wasn't aggravating, like Dakis. He was just . . . creepy.

Rising from the depths of his thoughts, Rone realized they were approaching the Innerchord.

"Sandis." He quickened his step. "Sandis, they won't listen."

The Degrata loomed over them, the tallest building within Dresberg's walls. Even from this distance, Rone could see the guards haunting it.

Sandis slowed. "We could sneak in."

"In the daytime? They won't be there at night." Rone stopped, and thankfully, Sandis did as well. Lowering his voice, he added, "The Degrata isn't like the citizen records building, Sandis. It's too guarded. Too many locks, obstacles. And I don't have the amarinth. Even if I did . . . it's just not feasible."

Sandis peered toward the Degrata for a long moment before heading east, toward the stone walkway that trimmed the Innerchord. Some of the city's only greenery lined the stones—rounded shrubs that looked like they could use some water and clean air. A few stone benches marked the edge of the path.

Neither of them sat.

Rone rubbed circles into his forehead. "This city is so wrapped up in itself it can't see the disease festering right under its skin. It's always been that way." He dropped his hands. "God, I hate this place."

Sandis folded her arms.

Rone slid his hands into his empty pockets. "If I had the amarinth, *maybe* I could sneak in there and leave a threatening letter. Or something." He growled. "God's tower, I never realized how handicapped I'd be without it."

Sandis peered toward the Degrata. "I wish you cared about me half as much as you care about your amarinth."

The half-mumbled words struck him like the back of her hand. He took one heavy step toward her, fire blazing anew. "Are you serious? I *gave up* the amarinth for *you!*"

She spun toward him, eyes bright. "No, you didn't. You *lost* it. And you wouldn't have lost it if you hadn't sold me off in the first place."

He laughed. Pressure built in his chest, and his throat wasn't wide enough to let it out. He'd *abandoned* his mother at the southern pass out of Kolingrad to come back for her. He'd risked his life breaking into the grafter hideout. Black ashes, he'd *fought a numen.* "I *lost* it," he enunciated each syllable, "because I *came back for you.* And I'm not the one who sold you off in the first place, sweetheart."

She turned away. "No. But you did in the second."

The accusation threw water on the flames. Rone stepped back. *What the hell are you doing, Comf?*

He sucked in a deep breath, held it, released it. Shoved his hands into his trouser pockets. It was oddly quiet. The crowds of Dresberg didn't mill through the Innerchord like they did the smoke ring. It was between hours, which meant no employees hustling to meetings, no bell towers chiming, no changing of the guard. There wasn't even the chirping of a bird or buzzing of a fly. Just silence.

Rone paced away from the bench, paced back, then finally sat on the stone seat. Planting his elbows on his knees, he said, "They were going to kill my mother. For something *I* did."

The silence continued. He didn't need to look over to see if he'd caught Sandis's attention. He knew he had it.

He interlocked his fingers, pulled them apart, folded his hands again. "When your great-uncle offered me the job, he showed me the orders with my mother's execution date. I had three days before they hanged her. I didn't know what else to do."

The quiet stretched longer before Sandis said, "I'm sorry." And then, "I wish you had told me."

Rone rubbed his eyes. "To what end? My hands were tied. But I came *back*, Sandis. I came back for you."

The sound of passing footsteps seemed wildly out of place in that moment. They weren't headed for Rone and Sandis, but his ears fixed on them so his mind would have something to think about besides the growing awkwardness suffocating him.

"I wish you had told me," she repeated. Rone looked up. She'd sat on the bench, too, but on the far end, close to falling off its edge. Her body faced the Degrata, but her head pointed toward the ground. Her knees bent together, and she absently played with her nails.

Rone sighed. "Sandis—"

"I would have volunteered."

The words lanced through his chest. "What?"

She shook her head. "If you had told me . . . I would have gone." She finally glanced up at him, and her walnut-colored eyes were so deep and sorrowful that for a moment, his heart forgot to beat. She dropped her gaze a second later, but the power of it lingered in the space between them. She might as well have shouted at him.

She went on, "You had done so much for me. I would . . . I would have asked for a day, to find him. Talbur." She rubbed her throat. "But I would have volunteered. I didn't know Kazen's plans for me then. Not entirely. So I would have."

Rone closed his eyes and set his jaw, clenching it until it hurt. When he finally released it, he said, "Don't tell me that."

"It's the truth."

"Sandis." He shook his head, then cradled it in his palms. "Please don't tell me that."

He'd assumed she'd run, because that's what he would have done. Then he'd have had to chase her, restrain her . . . It would have broken him.

God's tower. He'd treated her like a slave, hadn't he?

He'd taken away her choice, just like Kazen. Just like Talbur.

Rone stood and walked away from her, briskly, needing to clear his head. He couldn't do that with her so close.

When he started to get too far, he turned around and paced back, passing Sandis and trudging the other way until he was almost out of sight. Turned around again. He was nearly back to the bench when he stopped and set his hands on his hips, catching his breath.

He looked toward the Degrata. Focused on it. The past was past; the best thing he could do now was get Sandis the help she needed. That they all needed, if Kolosos was truly as big a threat as she feared. But these bureaucrats . . . they didn't care. The city could be burning, and they'd only care about how much it would cost them.

If the name Comf had carried any weight outside of the Lily Tower, they would have listened to him. He would have gotten past the desk. But family relationships meant nothing in Celesia.

Rone blinked. Turned his gaze east, toward the wall. From this angle, he couldn't see a single stone of the tower that lay just beyond it.

He cursed.

"What?"

Rone dug both hands back into his hair and pulled until it hurt. Cursed a second time, then a third.

Sandis stood.

"We can try one more person," he mumbled. "Someone the triumvirate would have to listen to."

Black ashes in the pits of despair. He really, *really* hated this place.

Chapter 7

Rone didn't bother with the official pilgrimage this time, merely tied a gray sash around his arm and Sandis's and headed straight for the Lily Tower. So what if he didn't enter with a big group of people? What were the priests going to do, fight him?

Well, yes. They would. There were some sizable priests inside the Lily Tower. They weren't all acolytes and old men.

When he got to the door, he looped his arm through Sandis's. She tensed, but didn't pull back. Pilgrims weren't contentious, and looking *together* would help the ruse.

Not long ago, Sandis had willingly touched him. Smiled at him. He still couldn't remember what her smile looked like, only that it had been genuine. Beautiful.

The ball bearing in his gut burrowed deeper even as he told the priestess at the door, "Sorry, I hope we didn't break any rules by leaving the tower. We wanted to see the grounds."

The grounds weren't much to look at, but the woman smiled regardless, not bothering to check the filthiness of his hems—a measure of religious hardship for pilgrims. She didn't recognize him. He didn't recognize her, either, so she must not have been on shift when he and Sandis had come over a month ago. She asked if they needed help finding their room, and Rone acted like he needed to recheck the directions. He described the room he and Sandis had stayed in on their last visit. She nodded and motioned them in. The high priest within greeted them with a smile.

Rone tugged Sandis toward the stairs. Before they reached the second flight, she withdrew her arm from his. He pretended not to notice.

They passed the second flight and trekked up to the third. The Angelic would have already given his speech to today's pilgrims. It was close to dinner—the kitchens were probably running overtime to feed both clergy and visitors. Rone highly doubted the Angelic dined with the rest of them. He was probably in that secret little space of his behind the communion room.

Rone's palms tingled by the time he reached the seventh floor. The communion room was the place pilgrims came upon completing their journey, so they could hear their special leader spout off some garbage about love and charity. The space was almost entirely white, save for the gray veins in the marble floor. A small stage sat at the back of the room, behind which hung gauzy curtains. Three people garbed in white stood on the raised area: two priestesses and a cleric. One of the priestesses held a broom and swept out the corners of the already pristine space. The other two talked quietly.

Not letting their presence deter him, Rone put a hand on Sandis's back to keep her close and marched for the curtains.

"Excuse me," said the priestess without the broom as she hurried toward them. "May I help you?"

Rone ignored her. Stepped onto the stage.

"See here, young man!" the cleric called, running after him. "The Angelic is very busy, you can't simply go in."

Rone reached the curtains. The cleric reached him. Releasing Sandis, Rone spun around and swiped out his foot, knocking the cleric off both of his. The clergyman's breath left him in one gust when his back hit the hard marble floor.

Rone pushed Sandis through the curtains and down the narrow hallway beyond it, at the end of which was a door. A locked door.

"Wait!" cried the pursuing priestess.

Rone leaned back and slammed his booted foot into the door, just beside the knob. It flung open and hit the doorstop inside with so much impact the wood shuddered.

The room was nothing special. Just as eye-burningly white as the communion room, but with a nice collection of circle-top windows with frosted glass to temper the sunlight. There was a desk, a set of drawers, and a well-made cot in the corner. No chairs, which meant no visitors.

Oh, and a plant hung from a little hook in the farthest corner of the room. How quaint. *Guess there are some living things Daddy cares about.*

The Angelic sat at his desk, poring over some book—scripture, maybe—and startled when Rone burst through his door. His aging face morphed from surprise to anger to bewilderment as he took in his estranged son's face. He'd likely thought Rone's most recent visit, when he'd come here to petition for his mother, would be his last.

Sandis slipped inside. Rone slammed the door shut on the priestess and managed to lock the now-loose handle.

The Angelic stood. "What is the meaning of—"

"Let's skip the pleasantries, Pops. I need you to listen for two damned minutes to what I have to say."

Beside him, Sandis muttered an apology and actually bowed. *Bowed.*

"You're kind of ruining the effect here," Rone murmured.

The Angelic folded his arms. "And pray tell, what effect would that be, child?"

"Don't act like you don't know my name." Rone's words zipped from his lips like darts. "Believe me, I don't want to talk to you, either, but you have the triumvirate's ear. Hell is about to be unleashed in Dresberg, and someone needs to do something about it."

He wanted to add, *You have to care about something, right?* But the barb wouldn't help him plead his case. He needed to be civil.

Yet this place stoked his fire like nothing else.

Sandis stepped up to the desk. "I'm so sorry. I didn't think we'd be so . . . abrupt. But we're here, and we need to talk to you. Please." She bowed again, clutching the newspaper, and Rone resisted rolling his eyes.

The Angelic pursed his lips. Shifted his attention from Rone to Sandis before sinking back into his chair. "If this is not of the utmost importance, I'll have you delivered to the police."

Sandis paled. "Sir, you remember me, do you not?"

He hesitated, but nodded.

"Do you read the papers?"

He scrutinized her. Nodded.

"There have been reports of missing children. Children who are the age . . . preferred by grafters. They're being killed." She set the newspaper on the desk.

"I am aware." He massaged his forehead. "It is incredibly unfortunate. I've had the clergy here pray for these lost souls and their families."

"It's more than that," Sandis persisted. "It's . . . summoning. Sir, Kolosos is a real threat. Kazen will stop at nothing to bring it—"

"Have you really burst into this sacred room to repeat the same empty warnings you've already delivered?"

Rone growled. "It's an office. Get off your high horse."

"Rone." Sandis pleaded.

Rone leaned against the door. It was silent on the other side—he hoped their pursuers hadn't run off to get backup. He hadn't really planned what he would do *after* sucking up to his father.

"I am certain that this"—Sandis gestured to the article—"is the work of Kazen, sir. That he's trying to find a vessel powerful enough to host Kolosos. It isn't merely a matter of the underground occult anymore. He's hurting everyday citizens. *Your* followers."

Nice touch, Rone thought.

His father sat down, then reached back and rubbed the base of his neck. After a long moment of silence, he withdrew his hand and laced it with the other before setting both on his desk. "I understand your fear, child. It is a natural state within all mankind."

Rone shook his head. "A sermon won't fix this."

The Angelic ignored him. "But as I said before, such evil as you speak of cannot be summoned into this world. It is not possible. The Celestial wouldn't allow it."

Sandis glanced to Rone, but this time there was no hardness to her features, only worry. "Even if that's true," she continued, "Kazen is hurting people. His brutality is . . . extreme." She shivered. Rone almost reached out to comfort her. Almost.

Now the Angelic looked at Rone. "And you've gone to the police?"

He withheld a snort. Had his father really lived outside the city for so long that he'd forgotten about its corruption? Rone could remember him complaining about the scarlets when he was only a high priest and still gave a slag about his family. "The police are crooked. We're too unimportant to be seen by anyone who matters. What we're asking is for you to call on your theological right to speak to the triumvirate. Press them to take action."

The Angelic considered this. Frowned. Sighed. Stood again.

"I assure you, I am staying informed on all current events. I will overlook your trespasses this time, but not a third." He looked to Rone. "Why don't you go downstairs and get something to eat before you leave. No one will question you."

Rone's shoulders went slack. "*That* is your solution? A promise to pray, and then bribe us with free food?"

Sandis set her jaw. "Please, sir. You have a voice—"

The Angelic pointed to a bellpull on the wall. "I will summon security if you do not leave. I am sorry I cannot do more."

Wouldn't do more. Had he actually expected his father to act like a human being? Yes, part of him had. Even though his father had refused to help his estranged wife when her life was on the line, he'd hoped this would matter to him. That the danger to the children—to the city—would shake him to his senses.

Sandis pressed her lips into a tight white line. Rone thought he heard retreating footsteps as she reached for the door, but when she opened it, the way was clear.

Rone scowled at his father and turned after her.

"She's one of them, isn't she?" The Angelic's voice was like hot, rank breath on the back of his neck.

Rone turned around. Took in his father's white-and-silver robes. "Go to hell."

He slammed the door behind him.

There was no one in the communion room when they left the office, much to Rone's surprise. He'd expected a small army of Celestial worshippers to pounce on him and Sandis, bind them up in pilgrimage ties, and throw them out the fourth-story window. But the place was empty and shockingly clean.

Sandis walked a few feet ahead. Before they reached the stairs, she peered over her shoulder. The pity on her face was stark as spent oil against porcelain. Rone looked away. They took the first flight in silence . . . until a woman in white stopped them.

The priestess who had chased them to the office. She looked as pale as her robes and stricken. She was alone.

Rone took two more steps to put himself between the woman and Sandis. Had she overheard anything? Surely she'd been too far ahead of them to catch the Angelic's question regarding Sandis. Had Rone messed up again by bringing Sandis here?

Oddly, the woman pressed her index finger to her lips and motioned for Rone and Sandis to follow her. They hesitated only a moment. She led them through the third floor and back to a winding, narrow hall lit with the same circle-top windows cut into every level of the tower. Rone glanced over his shoulder repeatedly, but no one followed them. Seemed the priestess didn't want company, either, for she searched the hall before slipping through a door.

Sandis looked at Rone, her eyes full of worry, but when he shrugged and stepped into the room, she followed right behind him.

He closed the door to a small library.

"This way," the priestess whispered, and she passed two rows of books before following a third almost all the way to the back of the room. The window there faced west, and sunlight poured in at Rone's eye level, forcing him to raise a hand against it or be blinded.

"What are you doing?" he asked.

"I overheard your conversation."

Rone bit the inside of his cheek, but the woman made no accusations. Instead, she crouched down and selected an old text from the bottom shelf. She brushed off a bit of dust from the worn cloth cover, and the motes danced in the too-bright sunbeams pouring through the windows.

"I know about Kolosos."

Sandis straightened. "You do?"

A nod, and the priestess opened the book. "All of us know *something* of the occult. You must know about your adversary if you're to protect mankind against it."

Sandis tensed. Rone finally gave in to the urge to touch her, putting his hand on her shoulder to let her know he was there. That he wouldn't let anyone hurt her. Rather, he *hoped* the touch conveyed that. At the very least, Sandis didn't shrug him off.

The priestess flipped to a page near the back of the book and turned the volume around so they could see it. Sandis leaned forward until her nose nearly touched the pages. The skin around her eyes tightened, and she set her jaw.

The text was handwritten in cursive. Sandis couldn't read cursive.

"What does it say?" Rone asked, sparing her the embarrassment of asking.

The priestess turned the book back toward herself. "'But as there is light, so there is darkness. Our god created the ethereal plane to separate evil from the world of men. In the depths of this evil lies its antithesis, called Kolosos. The very depths of hell swirl in its heart, and if any could look upon it, their flesh would melt from their bones, for they would look into the nakedness of chaos itself. Blessed be the Lily, who formed this behemoth's prison. Praise the Celestial, who saves mankind with its bountiful pity.'"

Sandis turned to stone under Rone's hand. He rolled his lips together. His father had drilled scripture into him since he could walk, but he'd never heard anything like this.

The priestess turned the page, and on the next leaf was a diagram of a circle. She pressed her manicured finger to its base.

"This is an astral sphere . . . a device of the occult used to navigate the ethereal plane." She shuddered, and Rone nodded, acting as though he were unaware of this information. "At its very base is written that name. *Kolosos.*" She emphasized it with a whisper. Shook her head. "To think that any mortal could be power hungry enough to seek that monster . . ."

She noticed Sandis's stricken expression and shut the book. "My child, forgive me. I've frightened you. But I lack the Angelic's confidence, may he live as long as time. That is a trial of faith I must endure. But . . ." She wiped perspiration from her brow. "I felt you should know. Few of our numbers read the old texts, believing it better to pretend the occult does not exist. But I fear it. I think we all should."

Rone nodded. "Thank you. We'll . . . take it into consideration."

That seemed to satisfy the woman. She slid past them and said, "Let me take you to the kitchens."

"Wait." Sandis held up both hands, halting the holy woman. "Thank you for your help. What is your name?"

The priestess smiled. "Not many ask me. It's Marisa."

"Would you . . . Could you convince the Angelic of the danger, on our behalf?"

The smile faded, and Priestess Marisa bit her lip. "I have little persuasive power to throw around, but"—she straightened a fraction—"I do think I could plant seeds."

Sandis notably relaxed, and Rone drew back his hand from her shoulder. "Thank you," Sandis said. "Any help we can get—"

"Of course. But"—her eyes darted over Rone's shoulder to the door—"let's keep it between us. Now, you must be hungry. Let me escort you—"

"To the front door, if you would," Rone interrupted.

She blinked. "The meals in the tower are complimentary."

"Thank you again," Sandis said, her voice strained, "but we would like to leave."

Priestess Marisa considered for a moment before nodding. Rone's stomach clenched with want of food when aromas from the kitchen wafted into the hallway, but he didn't slow. As he stepped out into the evening sun, he nodded his thanks instead of speaking it, and the priestess retreated into her cloister.

He and Sandis marched back to the wall. The guards at the gate, even at this distance, watched them closely. The setting sun pressed against his back as he walked, the heat tracing up and down his spine. He slipped off his jacket, carefully folding it so the amarinth wouldn't fall out—ah, but that was right. No amarinth.

He slung the jacket over his shoulder and kicked a rock sitting on the side of the narrow road as he walked. Silence hung between him and Sandis, but he didn't know how to fill it. Maybe he—

Prickles kissed the back of his neck, like he was being watched. He looked back and scanned the tower and the space around it, but saw no one.

Shaking off the feeling, he quickened his step to catch up with Sandis, but the prickling didn't cease. He surveyed the wall looming ahead of them. Must have just been one of the guards.

He rubbed his neck all the same.

They had almost reached the wall when Sandis said, "I hope Alys is okay."

Rone's step stumbled. "What?"

"Alys. She housed Isepia."

The one-winged she-demon who tried to kill me. I remember. "I'm sure she's . . . fine."

Sandis slipped into silence, twisting a piece of hair around her finger as she walked, but thirty feet short of the gate, she came to an abrupt stop.

Rone ran into her arm. He hadn't realized he'd been walking so close.

Sandis turned to him, the red sunlight turning her hair copper. Her eyes were wide, and in them he saw . . . hope?

"I know who can help us," she whispered.

Rone made note of the guards, who watched them but were still well out of hearing range. "Who?"

"Grim Rig."

For a moment Rone thought she was joking. But there was no mirth in her voice. No smile on her face. Only that glint of hope in her eyes.

She clasped her hands together. "He'll talk to us. I know where he is—Kazen took me there once. I remember . . ." A sliver of sadness crossed her face. "I remember a little of it. Grim Rig hates Kazen. And like you said, Kazen is still reeling. If we can make an alliance, we might be able to stop him. And we can save the others, too."

Rone swallowed. "The other vessels?"

She nodded. "And the children from the newspaper."

He didn't have his amarinth. He didn't have his backup.

He didn't have any better or safer ideas. And the hope in her eyes . . .

Hunching, Rone planted his hands on his hips. "You want to waltz up to a mob boss and ask him for *help*? Sure, why not."

He wasn't certain if she picked up on the sarcasm. Yet as he said it, he thought he saw the slightest twitch of her cheek. Almost. *Almost* a smile.

Perhaps this was a risk Rone was willing to take.

Chapter 8

Mobsmen were untrustworthy, but any fear Sandis might feel was eclipsed by budding hope, which she tended like a master gardener would his prize rose. This. *This* was what she had needed to do all along. To act against Kazen rather than merely run from him.

Stop Kazen, stop Kolosos. Infiltrate the lair, free the other vessels. She could finally apologize to Alys. Make everything right. Her great-uncle had not given her the warmth and kinship she'd hoped to find with the last living member of her family, but perhaps she could find that with Alys, Kaili, Dar, and Rist. They could be true friends, away from Kazen's rules and walls.

"Sandis?"

She blinked, the map on the floor coming into focus, followed by the undecorated walls of Rone's apartment, the old sofa that sank in on the far end. Rone sat across from her, watching her, a half-eaten bowl of soup in his hands. Hers was untouched, near her feet.

She tapped her finger on the map. "Grim Rig's stronghold is here, unless he moved it. But when you're that deep into the city, there isn't much opportunity to do so. And Grim Rig . . ." She pried at her memory. "All the mob leaders are prideful. Resilient. He wouldn't leave his space even after Kazen threatened or hurt him. He wouldn't want to look scared."

Vessels weren't supposed to remember what happened when they were possessed, but Sandis had begun to do so in the last six months of her bond with Ireth. Grim Rig was one of the memories she had partially retained. She didn't have the entire story, only glimpses of it, from up high. Though she'd never seen the fire horse with her own human eyes, he was larger than she was, and the flashes of memory she retained came from a taller perspective.

There was arguing, raised voices she couldn't understand. Galt was there. A charred body lay on the ground, and Grim Rig stood nearby, red faced, pointing at it over and over and over again. Jutting his finger toward the corpse and yelling. Pointing like doing so would somehow take the black from his comrade's skin and resurrect him. But not even the Celestial had power over the dead.

Her stomach churned. Thinking of Ireth's destruction made her queasy. It wasn't the fire horse's fault; Kazen, who'd kept Sandis's blood inside his own veins, had controlled him as surely as he did Sandis. Neither of them had been able to escape his grasp. Not then.

In truth, they still hadn't escaped.

She cleared her throat. "It will be guarded, so we definitely can't walk in. We'll need to state our purpose up front and make it interesting. Interesting enough that Grim Rig will want to see us at once."

"Agreed. We can't give Kazen any more time to regroup his resources."

Rone made a good point. Sandis didn't know where Kazen got his lackeys from, but it was smarter to attack sooner rather than later. They'd already waited long enough. And Sandis didn't want to lose her courage.

She glanced behind her, half expecting to see something there.

"We can use that." She pulled away from the map. "Like I said, Grim Rig *hates* Kazen. Kazen killed one of his men . . . I don't know who, but he was mad about it." In the back of her mind, that finger continued pointing, pointing, pointing. Ireth's fire had flared, Grim Rig had backed off . . . and then it was dark, and Sandis had woken up.

"So"—Rone set down his bowl—"we wave Kazen's weakness in front of this guy's nose and give him an opportunity he can't turn down. The location of the lair. Information about its layout and Kazen's present lack of employees." Rone tapped his nose with his spoon. "We can offer the money as added motivation. Surely Kazen keeps a safe on hand."

Sandis took in a deep breath. "Okay." But would it be enough? What if Grim Rig thought it was a trap? Or worse, what if he recognized her and decided he'd much rather kill her out of revenge than help her with her plan?

An idea struck her. "You could be my summoner."

His hand dropped. "Pardon?"

"My summoner. We can't just go in with a gift and a smile and expect him to thank us. These men . . ." She struggled for the words. "They're . . . vindictive. Cunning. They're not nice."

"Riggers aren't nice? Shocker."

Sandis gave him an exasperated look. "We have to have power, too. Grim Rig might recognize me. Maybe he'll decide what Kazen made Ireth do was my fault."

Rone frowned. "I didn't think of that. Maybe I should go in alone. I don't think he'll be happy to see you."

But Sandis shook her head. "No. You're strong, Rone—"

"Why, thank you." He flashed her a smile.

Sandis tried to ignore the twinge behind her heart. "—but you can't take down an entire mob. Especially without the amarinth."

His smile faded.

"He won't know I lost Ireth. He won't know you're not a summoner, unless Engel worked with him before?"

"No. But we probably shouldn't use that alias."

She nodded. "We'll need to go late. When Kazen attacked him, he approached the cavern from this side." She drew her finger along the map. Rone leaned forward and watched, listening. The look on his face assured her that he would do this for her. With her.

Part of her hated relying on Rone for something so delicate, something that could so easily be turned against her, just like before. But she didn't think she could persuade the mobsmen alone. A vessel was nothing without her summoner.

She said a small prayer in her head that their plan would work. If it didn't, Sandis would have nothing left, again.

For a startling minute, Sandis was lost.

She stood nearly in the center of the smoke ring. Despite the late hour, a few factories still ran, keeping their furnaces hot and smokestacks billowing. Between the pollution and the darkened sky, the street looked fuzzy and smelled like cigar butts. Every building here had at least one glowing light on its eaves, and the smoke pulled the light into stretched-out halos. The crowd was thinner now that the last bell had rung, but the streets were hardly empty. As she scanned her surroundings, someone bumped into her and continued on without so much as an "excuse me."

She *knew* it was this direction, and yet none of this looked familiar. It had been some time since Kazen had walked her to Grim Rig's hideaway. That little leather shop was new, wasn't it? Had that factory been expanded? Did the street always curve right here?

Rone kept his hand possessively on the back of her neck. Sandis had told him to do it. Told him how to speak, how to act, how to treat her—all on the off chance Grim Rig had eyes on this route. So far, he'd kept to the script, except when he asked, "This way?"

"Don't speak to me," she'd reminded him. Kazen had never spoken to Sandis on one of their outings.

"Yeah, but I don't know where we're going."

And neither, it seemed, did she.

Sandis swallowed. Continued forward, right down the center of the street. And—there! She recognized that grouping of lamps. Four of them, forming a sort of plus sign, or a diamond, depending on how you drew the lines. The entrance to Grim Rig's hideout was just under that . . .

Trying to keep her lips from moving, Sandis said, "The boarding-house. Just around the corner. A set of stairs in the back leads into the basement. That's how we get there."

Rone's fingertips pressed into her neck as he guided her. Sandis desperately wanted to see where they were going and who might be on those stairs, but she had to keep her head down. Act passive. Act like a vessel.

When had it become so difficult to be what she was?

A shadow passed over the lamplight. "Sniffing up the wrong alley, bud."

The voice was low, like it came from a big man. Sandis raised her eyes just enough to see his shoes, which were so polished Rone's chin reflected in them.

"I don't think so," Rone replied, his tone hard and deep. Almost like it sounded when he talked to his father. "I'm right where I need to be."

There was a brief pause. "Is that so?"

Rone shifted, like he was looking the man up and down. "You his secretary? I need to speak to your boss."

Another pause. "I don't know you."

"A pity."

The softest growl came from the man's throat. He must have gestured to someone, because a new person came up the stairs, his shadow mixing with that of the first. Sandis saw the underside of his nose in his equally polished shoes.

"You know this guy?" the first asked.

But the second replied, "Who's the girl?"

"If you don't let me have my say, I'll show you," Rone threatened.

Another pause. There was a shift in the light reflecting off the men's shoes, like they'd exchanged a look. Finally, the second murmured, "She looks like . . . doesn't she? The hair."

The first stepped over, fully blocking the stairwell. For a terrifying moment, Sandis thought they wouldn't let them pass. "What's your name?"

"Jase Kipf," Rone answered.

Another pause. Did the name sound fake? But it shouldn't—Jase was such a common name, and there had been a grafter named Kipf in Kazen's retinue. No, the pause wasn't for the name. The name was perfect.

To his comrade, the first Rigger said, "Go check. You two, wait here."

The pressure of Rone's fingertips increased on Sandis's neck. She forced her head to remain down.

After what felt like an hour, but could have been only a few minutes, the second man returned, huffing. "Take him to the wait while the others get ready. Count of eighty."

That meant a side room where Sandis and Rone would hide their time while Grim Rig and his fellow mobsmen armed themselves. Sandis shivered. Had this been a bad idea?

Rone pushed her forward, and they went down the long set of cement stairs, following the first man. Sandis saw the back of his head—he was surprisingly tan and had a shaved scalp. Enormously broad shoulders. How had Rone mustered such a confident tone in front of such an intimidating figure?

They were never left alone; the large man guarded them in the "wait," which was barely larger than the room Kazen used for solitary confinement. He checked both Sandis and Rone for weapons; Sandis froze when his hand reached up her shirt and passed over her brands. There would be no doubt as to what she was now. She only hoped he didn't check Rone for the same brands. After all, all summoners had once been vessels. Even Kazen had given up his body to a numen at some point, only to later slice a long scar down his back so no one could ever use him that way again.

Sandis counted to eighty in her head—the number the man had been given—but nothing happened, so she counted again. Then a third time.

Finally, a rhythmic knock sounded against the door. Sandis heard the clicking of a gun and stiffened. Rone's hand went clammy against her skin—or was that her skin sweating against his?

"Come on." The man opened the door and gestured them out. The end of his barrel flashed in Sandis's peripheral vision.

They went down another set of stairs—Sandis remembered these. The man then guided them through a maze of corridors, some of which she was certain they crossed more than once. Finally, they stepped into a large room; the door was guarded by two more men with very large, very shiny shoes.

Rone pressed Sandis forward until they stood in the middle of the room, which was covered by a long maroon carpet. Peering up through her eyelashes, Sandis saw the space was filled with at least two dozen people—all men, except for one woman in the corner, whose lips twisted into a mean scowl. All of them wore black. All of them were armed.

Three forward-facing chairs sat at the front of the room, almost like thrones. An older man, a little younger than Kazen, sat in the middle one. "Jase Kipf, we meet at last," he said. "I've heard of you from some of my . . . colleagues. Though I can't say I'm impressed."

Sandis had guessed right on the name, then, unless the speaker was playing them. She lifted her head a little more to get a better look at the man. He was dressed well, his suit hugging his thin waist and broad yet bony shoulders. His pale hair was cut close to the scalp.

Grim Rig. He looked exactly as he had in her memory, pointing at the charcoal corpse.

He looked right back at her, his eyes hard as marbles.

"We all have our ways of getting things done," Rone said, and Sandis felt him shrug. "But you, my good man. Let's talk about what *you* can do. I want to make a deal."

Grim Rig laughed. "You want to make a deal, yet you didn't use any of the normal messengers, and you brought *that thing* into my home?" He waved his hand—or Sandis thought he did—and the weight of two dozen aimed guns pressed into her skin. "I'll shoot you down before you utter a single Noscon word."

Rone lifted his hand, and Sandis took the opportunity to straighten a little. He held his hands out in mock surrender. "My good man, I would not expect you to hire me without a pistol in your pocket. Do you expect me to meet with you without a weapon of my own?"

The scent of smoke—no, sulfur—filled Sandis's nose. She tensed, feeling heat bloom across her back, as if someone held a lamp too close to her skin. But no one stood by her other than Rone.

She bit down on the inside of her cheek. *Not now. Not now. Celestial help me.*

It's just a bad dream. A bad, waking dream.

"That *weapon*," Grim Rig continued, "has been a menace to this place in the past."

"Mm, yes." He sounded so frighteningly calm, just like before, but he shifted his hand. Could he feel the heat in her skin? *Please, no.* If Rone could feel it, then it wasn't all in her head. "So I've heard."

Grim Rig snorted. "Not even in chains."

"Oh, she's very well trained. Sit, pet." Rone squeezed her neck.

Sandis forced herself to sit. Fold her legs beneath her. She squeezed her eyes shut and prayed. *Go away. Go away. Go away.*

A few men chuckled softly. At her? Or had Rone said something? The scent of sulfur slowly receded. Sandis's back cooled.

"You know her previous owner, I presume?" Grim Rig asked.

"I know what his nose feels like under my knuckles, yes."

Sandis's skin prickled, but Grim Rig smirked at the joke. "Is that so?"

Another shrug from Rone. "Kazen is quite fond of his vessels, and it turned out, so am I. We had an argument."

Grim Rig barked a laugh. "And you got out alive? You expect me to believe this story?"

A few gun hammers cocked, though one of the men sitting beside Grim Rig mentioned something to him, and the mobster's expression relaxed. Mobsmen and grafters ran in different circles, but even they must have heard about grafters infiltrating the city, looking for something. Or, rather, someone.

"Do *you* expect *me* to put my neck on the block just to lie to you?" Rone sounded angry now. "The fact of the matter is that I have her, and he doesn't. But I'm not done with Kazen, and I have a feeling you're not, either. So let's strip him of what he has left, shall we?"

Grim Rig paused. Glanced to the corner, then back again. "Explain."

"I know where Kazen's lair is."

"We know as well."

Sandis carefully leaned against Rone's leg. *He's lying,* she tried to tell him.

"Why do I not believe you?"

Grim Rig set his jaw. "So what? You want to tell me? If you know Kazen, you know it will be meaningless. That man is unassailable."

"I know far more than that. But if you want to hear it, tell your minions to lower their weapons."

The mob leader tapped his fingers on the armrest of his chair. After a few seconds, he nodded, and the tension in the room lightened a fraction as his men pointed their barrels toward the floor.

Rone rolled his shoulders back and popped his neck. "That's better."

"Explain," Grim Rig demanded.

Rone ruffled Sandis's hair. "My little prize here isn't the only quibble I've had with Kazen. I'm, hmm . . . a little *upset* with him. And I have it on good authority that Kazen is weak right now."

Grim Rig raised an eyebrow. "Weak? Sick?"

"Oh"—Rone laughed, and it rang false in Sandis's ears—"he's in splendid health, I'm sure. But he recently went on a bit of a goose chase and lost some men. A lot of men."

The man in the chair to Rig's right leaned over and whispered something once more. Surely the Riggers knew Kazen had hired Straight Ace's men. Was that what they spoke of, or something else?

Grim Rig turned back to Rone. "And you know this how?"

"Because I killed some of them myself. As did little dearie here." He rubbed her head like she was a good dog, but the truth behind his words bit at her like fleas.

Yes, she had killed some of them. Both when Ireth had turned her body into explosive flame and when she'd been cornered at Helderschmidt's with a rifle. She didn't *regret* those deaths, not truly, but before her escape, she had never—unpossessed—so much as hurt a person, let alone killed one. Celesia preached against murder. Were she not already an abomination, would the Celestial condemn her for those deaths?

Rone pulled his fingers from her hair. "I know where he is. I know his numbers are poor, and I know he's down at least two vessels, possibly three."

Sandis's breath hitched. *Alys.* But Rone was only fibbing. He had no idea what condition the vessels were in.

It had been just an arm wound.

"If you want revenge, my good man," Rone carried on, "now is the time to get it."

A few whispers rose up around them. Speaking over them, Grim Rig said, "And what is the endgame, Jase? What benefit do you get from this?"

"Revenge, the same as you." He rubbed his scruff. "And our mutual friend has something of mine, and I'd like it back."

Sandis perked. They hadn't discussed the amarinth at all in their planning. A worm wriggled its way into her gut. Was *that* why Rone was helping her? To retrieve his amarinth?

She didn't have much time to dwell on the idea before Grim Rig responded, "Something of yours. Care to elaborate?"

"It's small. It's sentimental. It shouldn't be a problem for you. The fact is, Kazen is desperate and floundering. If revenge doesn't suit your palate, then perhaps something else will."

The man to their right whispered, "Vessels."

Panic raced up Sandis's spine. No, Grim Rig couldn't have the vessels! Mobsmen didn't deal in the occult. That was what distinguished them from the grafters. She forced her breathing to stay even. Grim Rig could have all the treasures he wanted. But he couldn't have Alys. Kaili. Rist. Dar. No one could own them after this.

Her brands itched. They felt so solid, so *there*, like she was a part of them and not the other way around. She thought she could feel a hot claw—or maybe a hoof—run down her back, and she shuddered.

The man on the right continued to talk. Sandis concentrated as hard as she could and thought she heard him say, "Probably has *that gold.*"

What gold?

Maybe this had been a bad idea.

"I'll tell you where the lair is. I'll even give you the layout, but in return, I need your men and a promise that my *trinket* will be returned to me. The rest is yours."

Grim Rig frowned. "Tell me what the trinket is, and—"

"Agreed."

The word flew in from the corner of the room, from the woman with the small, tight lips. She strode forward, just as tall and broad as any of the men. She'd been holding the rifle attached to a strap across her chest, but she slid it to her back as she approached the carpet.

"We'll take your deal, Jase Kipf. But I choose the day of reckoning."

Sandis rose to her feet, confused. Rone turned back and forth, splitting his attention between Grim Rig and this newcomer.

Then he whistled. "You're Grim Rig, aren't you?"

The whole room laughed, the woman included. Once the volume died down, she said, "Grim Rig was my husband. Kazen burned him to a crisp months ago with this girlie you have at your side."

Sandis's lips parted. The corpse . . . *that* had been Grim Rig? And now this man, the one on the "throne," was a decoy for the mob boss's . . . wife?

Sandis found herself in a strange sort of awe.

"We follow special regulations now," the woman said, squaring her shoulders. "Your information seems sound to me, and I know what that bastard did to Straight Ace's numbers. He'd only depend on the mob if he was desperate or playing at something. Now we know it's the first. Do you accept my terms?"

"Do you want the slaves?" Rone countered. "You'll be demoting yourself to Kazen's level if you do."

The woman raised a thin eyebrow—brows that seemed too small for the rest of her face. She glanced at Sandis. After too many heartbeats, she answered, "If the loot is good, then no."

Rone nodded. "It will need to be soon. I don't want to give him much more time to recuperate."

The woman's hard eyes scanned the room, seeming to touch every face within it. "Very well. Tomorrow night it is."

Sandis and Rone didn't emerge from the Riggers' maze until just before dawn. The smoke towers turned the predawn light a pale brown, which made Sandis think of the sewers. She was exhausted, yet incredibly awake. They'd spent the rest of the night drawing and tracing maps, making plans . . . Grim Rig's wife, whom everyone called Sherig, had even asked Sandis's opinion near the end. Sandis had lived with Kazen, after all.

Rone kept his hand on Sandis's neck until they left the smoke ring. When he let go, he wiped both hands down his face. "We need to go to bed if we're doing this tonight. I can't believe . . ." He shook his head, not finishing the statement, but he didn't need to. Neither of them could believe what had transpired below that boardinghouse. Sandis was incredibly grateful for all of it.

He turned toward her. "Are you all right?"

Her steps slowed. "Just tired," she answered.

But Rone shook his head. "When we were talking in there . . . you looked like you'd seen a demon—"

"I didn't." She pushed past him.

"It hurt, Sandis."

She stopped.

Rone caught up to her. Buried his hands in his pockets. "It hurt to touch you."

She whirled toward him, stomach sinking. She stared at him, at the sincerity and worry etching his eyes. He had felt it. He had *felt* it.

Not a dream. Not a dream.

Sandis dropped into a crouch and lowered her head, trying to find air.

"Whoa, it's all right. You're in one piece." Rone crouched next to her right in the middle of the street. Touched her shoulders. "See? Cool as spring rain."

Sweat grew sticky in her elbows and knees. "It touched me," she whispered.

Rone tensed. "What?"

"Kolosos." She closed her eyes. *Inhale, exhale.* "Before you came that day . . . I felt it. In the back of my throat. In my hair, my skin. I felt that monster coming. Kazen failed, but I *still feel it.*" Her throat closed around the words.

"Oh, Sandis." He moved closer to her.

She stood suddenly, putting distance between them. Her head spun for a moment, anchorless. Kazen. She had to focus on Kazen. The only way to stop Kolosos was to stop him. Destroy the summoner, lock the beast in the ethereal plane forever.

She would destroy him.

Sandis focused on the cobblestones. On Rone's shoes. On pushing back the fear and the confession. "I need something. I'll pay, but I'm not sure where to go."

Rone didn't answer for a moment. "Anything, Sandis. Just name it."

"A gun," she said, looking him directly in the eyes. "I want my own firearm."

Chapter 9

Seven days. The number presented itself in the back of Rone's mind as he crouched on the half-sunken rooftop of an abandoned apartment building. Its demolition had likely been postponed because the grafters lived in these parts. Whether they bribed inspectors or threatened them didn't matter. They were here, and one wrong move would land Rone and the others either five stories down into a rotting basement or with a bullet in their heads.

His legs began to ache from crouching, and his mind wandered. *Seven days,* it whispered. Seven days and one night until his emigration papers expired.

His mother was waiting for him. Had she received his letter yet? He doubted it.

Cold fingers with long, blunt nails spidered over his neck. He shivered as Sherig lowered her head to his. "If you're wrong, you're dead."

Rone shifted, pulling out of her grasp. "Kazen has nowhere else to go. He's here." *Please, please, please let him be here.* He wasn't sure he could weasel his way out of this one.

Unless he's actually dead. But that was too much to hope for.

Sandis crouched at his other side, her chin hovering above the edge of the roof as she peered into the darkness. A cool wind tousled her hair; she didn't seem to notice it. Rone wanted to smooth it back, tuck it behind her ear. He didn't move.

Footsteps below. They all tensed, including the two Riggers huddled close to Sherig. One of them pointed a gun at the top of the dilapidated stairs that led to the street. Sandis balanced on her knees and reached back for her own firearm.

Rone had purchased the sleek rifle that morning. It was a high-end firearm polished to a dull silver gleam. A small scope perched atop it. It could fire seven rounds before needing to be reloaded.

Sandis had been adamant that she buy the gun herself, though even with Talbur's allowance, she wouldn't have been able to afford this model. She also didn't have identification papers, a requirement for legal firearm sales. Even so, she'd been reticent to let Rone buy the gun for her and peeved when he wouldn't let her pay him back. She didn't give up the fight until Rone pointed out that if she spent all her cash on a decent firearm, she'd be completely dependent on him for living expenses. It stung a little, knowing *that* was what had persuaded her. Being forced to stay close to him.

Once they defeated Kazen, and Rone could somehow guarantee that she'd be all right . . . he could go. After that, he wouldn't have a reason to stay.

Seven days.

Footsteps neared, and the faint sound of a buzzing fly thrummed over them. Everyone lowered their weapons. That buzz was a signal from one of Sherig's scouts.

The scout's shadow added to the darkness of the roof, and he carefully picked his way toward them, careful to circumvent rotted boards. Crouching in front of his boss, he said, "The entrance is there. Only two guards watch it. I didn't see or encounter any others within a three-block radius."

Despite the lack of light—the half-moon was covered by polluted clouds—Rone saw Sherig's eyebrow rise as she turned to him. "We might be friends after all, Jase."

All I ever wanted. Let's celebrate. Rone simply nodded.

Sherig spun her fist in a circle near her shoulder, a signal to begin moving out. A stricken expression crossed Sandis's face, and she reached forward and touched Sherig's elbow. "Don't hurt the vessels," she reminded her. "Please."

That was the first place to strike—the vessels' room in the main hall of the lair. Kazen kept his vessels locked in there, every one, at night. If they could get to that room first, they could keep the vessels away from their summoner. Kazen wouldn't be able to use them as weapons.

Unless Kazen already had one with him. They had no way of even knowing if he was home. A risk, but one they'd all agreed to take.

Sherig swatted her hand away. "I'm not that coldhearted. I get how it works. I know the uniform—open back. What do you take me for?"

Sandis didn't reply.

The mob mistress and her followers toed their way to the stairs first. It was part of the deal; Grim Rig's men would enter first, overwhelming the place with their sheer numbers and taking out any lingering grafters . . . as well as getting first dibs on any valuables they found. Sherig had begrudgingly agreed to let Rone look through any gathered treasures for his "trinket," but with luck, he would find it himself. On Kazen's fresh carcass.

They just had to shoot Kazen sixty-one seconds after they found him.

Sandis turned back toward the road below them, her rifle at the ready. She was supposed to snag any escapee grafters. The Riggers presumed she'd do it as a blazing stallion, but given that Ireth was gone and Rone wasn't actually a summoner, she would instead serve them as a sniper. Two Riggers had set up with rifles at the ready in adjacent buildings. Rone couldn't see any of them through the night's cloak.

Slowly, gracefully, Sandis pushed out her firearm's lever, readying a shot.

They waited. Rone's legs cramped more. After several minutes, a single muted light gleamed on the road below. Shadows rushed together like bandits converging on a carriage, only the carriage was Kazen's front door.

The gunshots erupted seconds later.

Rone scanned the dark streets below them. No movement.

"Let's go," he whispered, and Sandis quickly uncocked and shouldered her rifle and followed him to the stairs. She was eager to get inside the lair. Rone was eager to end this, though he felt entirely too mortal without the amarinth. His palms sweated as he clambered for rotted railing and picked his way to ground level.

Under the thrall of the coming fight, he felt as if the street itself propelled them to the lair's entrance. He barely noticed the two guards bleeding on the broken cobbles beside it. He wanted to step between them and Sandis, to spare her the blackish gleam of their wounds, but her focus was so trained on the rifle now raised to her shoulder she didn't seem to notice.

Havoc reared its ugly head inside.

Sherig's men were *loud*—Rone heard them long before he saw them. Gunshots and voices, even triumphant battle cries, echoed between the narrow walls of Kazen's lair. He nearly tripped over a body coming down the ramp to the entrance. Another corpse lay a ways ahead; Kazen really was short on men. Sandis shied away from it and nearly collided into a grafter thrown from an adjoining hallway by two Riggers. The grafter's face was so smashed and bloodied he was barely discernable as human.

Sandis bolted ahead of him, gun at the ready.

Rone froze for just a second, unsure if he should go after her or follow his gut. He chose her, but there were so many mobsmen in the hallways, already looting rooms, he lost track of her. He yelled her name, but he could barely hear his own voice.

Gunshots up ahead. The battle wasn't over, not yet.

Gritting his teeth, Rone charged forward, his memory unfolding a map of the place as he went.

The summoning room was dead ahead. He would start there.

The vessel room was just past a dying man and the two Riggers kicking him. Sandis averted her eyes, not wanting to relish the war she had instigated. Another shot sounded far away, followed by a hoarse cry. Zelna? But Sandis could feel no pity for the woman who had so often trussed her like a turkey for Kazen's feast.

Sandis's heartbeat doubled when she saw the open door to the vessels' room, its dead bolt unlocked. Several Riggers were inside, attempting to herd the vessels out like sheep. For a moment, Sandis felt completely disoriented—the first person she saw was an unfamiliar boy of no more than thirteen years of age, wearing common clothes. But her eyes shifted to Dar, defending himself with a chair in the corner, and she remembered the newspaper article. This boy was one of the kidnapped children. Thank Celestial he was all right.

And Dar . . . he was alive. And Kaili and Rist, who fought against the mobsmen's manhandling. They fought, but they were uninjured. Sherig had kept her word.

"They're not here to hurt you!" Sandis cried, shouldering her rifle and pushing through.

The vessels' eyes shifted to her, shock written across their features. "Sandis?" Kaili asked.

Relief bloomed inside her at the sight of their hale faces, except . . . "Where's Alys?"

They looked confused. The Riggers continued to push them toward the door.

Sandis ran up to Rist. "They're only trying to get you out of the lair so Kazen can't use you! Go with them! *Run!*"

Rist froze in his fight against the Riggers. He glanced to Kaili. Dar dropped his chair.

Kaili reached out for the boy. He took her hand, and she shoved Rist out the door in front of her. Dar bolted after them. The Riggers followed, though there was no longer any need to usher the vessels toward the exit. Within seconds, the room was empty.

Sandis turned around and readied her rifle once more. Alys. Where was Alys? What if Kazen had her and they had to fight Isepia? Alys had been bound to the one-winged numen when Sandis last saw her. *But facing Isepia is better than fighting Kuracean or Drang.*

The sentiment did little to ease the sickness spreading through Sandis's gut. If Alys wasn't here, Sandis couldn't free her. This was a one-chance deal with the Riggers. If she couldn't save Alys—

Solitary. She hadn't checked solitary.

Sandis sprinted from the door, only to stop as three mobsmen barreled past her. After they passed, she made her way down the sterile hallway that curved toward the grafters' quarters. Solitary was the first door on the right, also locked from the outside with a long sliding bolt. It stuck when Sandis tried to move it, so she grabbed it with both hands and threw her weight into it.

The bolt whined, metal on metal, as it slid open. She pushed her shoulder into the heavy door, its hinges creaking.

Someone sat inside, in the middle of the cot. He flinched before lifting a hand to block the light from his eyes.

He?

Sandis balked for a moment, until another gunshot spurred her to life. She stepped inside the foul-smelling room, if only to protect herself from the ruckus outside. "Who are you?"

It wasn't until she came closer that she saw the unnatural pallor to the man's skin. Sweat beaded on it. His fingers trembled. When he stood, he retreated back a step, then blinked rapidly. Pale-blue eyes surrounded by pale freckles. A thick rope of strawberry-blond hair hung over his shoulder.

Her lips parted. He wasn't Kolin. He was Godobian. She'd only ever seen Godobians in the markets near the Innerchord—merchants who came to Dresberg in the summer to sell their wares. Had Kazen even abducted foreigners? And how long had this man been here? He looked . . . awful.

"Who are you? What's going on?" His voice was a choppy tenor, but his words and accent were both solidly Kolin. He lowered his hand. He was a couple of inches taller than Sandis, and she guessed him to be about a year older. His eyes darted between her and the open door, and his shoulders sagged in what looked like relief.

"No time to explain." She rushed forward and grabbed his wrist. "You need to leave. A mob has infiltrated the place."

"M-Mob? But—"

"Hurry." She pulled him into the hallway. He didn't resist. "Go."

He hesitated, wide eyes looking her up and down. "Y-You're Sandis."

The declaration startled her. "How do you—"

But the man shook his head and hurried from the room, pulling Sandis with him. A man in black came around the corner, and the Godobian teetered back with so much force he nearly pulled Sandis to the floor.

"He's on our side," she assured the Godobian, grabbing his arm to steady him. The blue-eyed man paused, while the Rigger pushed past him to see what treasures could be found in the solitary room. He frowned and hurried down the hall.

Toward Kazen's room.

"Go," Sandis pleaded, and followed the Rigger. They *had* to get Kazen. She'd go mad if they didn't stop him. Her freedom was so close.

But the Godobian stuck to her side. "Kazen?"

The name spiked fear down the center of her chest. "Is he alive?"

When the Godobian nodded, Sandis felt both hope and fear. Hope that she could end this torment, fear that the summoner would only magnify it. Or that he'd elude them altogether.

Sandis picked up speed, running as fast as her legs allowed. Was it too much to hope the Riggers had already cornered and captured him? Kazen was always prepared for everything, but surely he'd never considered an all-out attack from the local mob.

Kazen's suite was at the very end of this hallway. She'd never been inside it. She jumped over a fallen grafter. A few of the bedroom doors were open, their spaces being raided. The Rigger in front of her ran to a closed door, seemingly desperate to discover treasure of his very own.

Sandis slammed into the door at the end of the hallway. Locked.

The Godobian who'd followed her paused a few paces from the door and worried his hands.

"Move." She pushed him aside and readied her rifle, aiming it at the lock.

The shot jarred her shoulder. The blast rang in her ears. Lowering the gun, Sandis kicked open the door.

A panel in the wall swung shut just as she did.

Sandis stared at it for half a second. A hidden door. A hidden passageway.

He was escaping with Alys.

"There!" she cried to the mobsmen in the hall, running for the panel. So long as Kazen lived, she would always be waiting for him. Always looking over her shoulder. Always moving through each day in fear. Always have these nightmares . . . and Kolosos might still be summoned to destroy them all. She couldn't let that happen.

She dug her nails into the seam in the wall and wrenched the panel open. The tunnel was narrow and short, and she pushed her way through it. She heard the Godobian yelp behind her, but she didn't stop to check on him. Ten feet in, the space suddenly widened into a hallway. From the light coming through the door, Sandis saw a flash of Kazen's coat and a bag over his shoulder.

No blonde hair. No Alys. No Isepia.

She pulled her rifle forward, cranked it, and fired.

The shadow ahead of her dropped, and almost instantly she heard a familiar whirring sound, faint and fairylike. The amarinth. It floated of its own volition, until its golden loops hovered above the grafter's shoulder. Kazen's spidery hands reached up to snatch it.

A shout behind her grew louder as it neared. Sandis turned just as the Godobian charged ahead of her. His body collided with Kazen's, sending the amarinth flying. It was only then that Sandis saw a second, third, and fourth glimmer of gold, all coming from the Godobian's exposed back.

He was a vessel, just like her.

But Sandis didn't have time to dwell on the discovery. Kazen was immortal for the next minute.

As they fell to the floor, Sandis bolted toward them, following the whirring sound. Turning her rifle around, she batted at the amarinth with its butt, sending the artifact flying toward the start of the passageway. She couldn't stop it from spinning, but she could at least get it out of Kazen's reach.

The two men grappled with each other. Kazen grabbed the Godobian's braid and wrenched it back, then planted a hand on his forehead.

He was trying to summon on him.

"No!" Sandis shouted, and she cocked the lever on her rifle and shot again. The lighting was bad, and her fingers shaky, but the bullet pierced Kazen's cheek, passing through without leaving a spot of blood. The amarinth's magic still held; Kazen was the last one to touch it.

But Sandis had four more bullets, and Kazen's time was ticking.

She had to end this *now*.

The impact of the shot forced Kazen to relinquish his hold on the vessel. Sandis fired again as he scrambled to his feet, but this time she missed. She expected her old master to turn his relentless gaze on her. To demean her, fight her. She'd seen him fight Rone. He knew seugrat. She wouldn't win against him if he got past her gun.

But Kazen sprinted away, vanishing into the darkness.

"No!" Sandis shouted at the same time a familiar voice yelled, "What's this?" from the passageway entrance. Sherig. Celestial bless her arrival! For a moment Sandis thought she referred to the amarinth, but the mob woman climbed right past it, blocking the dim light from the room.

"Kazen is getting away!" Sandis shouted as Sherig and her mobsmen pushed their way past the narrow neck of the passageway.

"*What?*" Sherig barreled forward, nearly trampling Sandis. The Godobian was still picking himself up; Sandis grabbed him under the arm and pressed him against the wall as Rigger after Rigger poured into the tunnel, cutting off her chase with their own. Her mouth moved in silent prayer that their speed would outmatch Kazen's. A gun fired up ahead, but whether from Sherig or from Kazen, Sandis couldn't be sure.

When the last man darted through, Sandis released the vessel and headed for Kazen, only to notice the Godobian didn't follow. He leaned against the wall and trembled, though Sandis saw no injuries on him. But she didn't have time to help him. Kazen was so close. He was on the run. They nearly had him—

The vessel crumpled in on himself, afraid.

Shouldering her rifle, Sandis grabbed his wrist and dragged him through the tunnel. Whatever terrified him, this passageway seemed to magnify it. Her feet slammed on the tunnel floor, but she urged her legs faster, faster.

She and the others would never be free as long as Kazen was alive.

The tunnel darkened to pitch. Sandis didn't slow, but her companion mewed like a sick cat. The path turned, and Sandis clipped her shoulder on a corner and stumbled to her knees. Hissing through clenched teeth, she forced herself up and found a moldy wall. Afraid there might be stairs or other impediments ahead, she continued at a slower pace. She couldn't hear the Riggers anymore. Releasing the Godobian, she charged ahead. Kazen was more important. The Riggers had a better chance of killing him than she did, but she couldn't step back and leave the task to them. She had to ensure their success. And she had to find Alys.

The heavy air grew lighter, and finally Sandis saw the passageway tilt upward toward a square of light, where a door had been thrown open. She stumbled out of a different rundown building, nearly falling onto several lines of broken barbed wire glinting in the light of an exposed moon. She stepped over the wire. Readied her gun.

Silence.

No! Where had they gone? Had Sandis been so slow? Or had she missed a branching of the pathway?

She ran out into the narrow street between this building and the next. Saw a man in black. She recognized him as one of the mobsmen who guarded the Riggers' hideout.

"Where did they go?" she cried.

He shook his head, even as another Rigger ran through the next intersection, as though searching for something. "He vanished!" The first mobsman spun around. "We were right on his tail . . . This place is a godforsaken maze."

Sandis's heart thudded against the back of her tongue. No. *No.* He didn't get away. He didn't . . .

She turned around, retraced her steps, and ran down another narrow street littered with broken cobbles. She nearly rolled her ankle stepping on one. Three Riggers converged ahead of her. "Nothing," one said, and both his companions cursed.

Nothing. Even with an army, they hadn't caught him.

If Sandis had only been faster. If she hadn't stopped to see the vessels or check solitary, she would have reached him in time, surely.

Sandis fell to her knees. Clasping her hands together, she prayed, *Please, Celestial, let them stop him. I know we're bad people, but Kazen is worse. He'll summon Kolosos or kill more children trying. Please stop him.*

Please protect the others.

Please let Alys be safe.

Heat burned around her calf, as though a fiery hand grabbed her leg. Sandis jumped and fell onto her backside, kicking. Nothing was there. Only the empty alleyway. Tears pricked her eyes. "Leave me *alone*!" she screamed.

Footsteps sounded behind her. Grabbing her rifle, Sandis leapt to her feet and spun around.

The Godobian vessel from before held up his hands and stepped away from the barrel. It rose and lowered with each of Sandis's heavy breaths. Just the vessel. Just a person. Kolosos wasn't here.

They stared at each other for several seconds before he said, "I-I won't hurt you." He swallowed. "Th-Thanks for . . . getting me out. I . . . I don't like tight spaces."

Sandis lowered her gun as her wits came back to her. It was no wonder he looked so sickly, then, between the tunnel and solitary. Why he'd been so afraid.

The vessel reached into his pocket and pulled out something. He tossed it toward her, the metal glinting in the moonlight.

Sandis caught it in one hand and immediately recognized it. The amarinth. Did this man know what it was? Surely he wouldn't have given it up so easily if he did. Yet all of Kazen's vessels had heard of it at one time or another.

A little bit of reassurance. Safety. Shoving her strapped gun behind her, she clammed it between both hands and let out a long breath. "Thank you."

Safety. All wasn't lost; there was still something in that lair that gave her safety. Needles and ink that could fix the broken name at the base of her neck. Her citizen papers. She ached for them.

The man turned and looked down the road. He ran his hands along his braid over and over. "Did they get him?"

Sandis shook her head. "I don't . . . know." She hadn't seen all the Riggers. Hadn't seen Sherig. Maybe there was still hope, but Sandis couldn't feel any. "You should go. Get a head start. Just in case."

She trudged back toward the hidden exit.

"Wait!" The vessel lunged out and grabbed her arm. "You can't go back in there. They might be your allies, but it's chaos. They're already fighting over the goods in Kazen's room. I-I heard them."

"I have to go back." She pulled from his grip, but his clammy fingers were like vises. A tendril of panic traced its way up her neck. "You don't understand. I have to find Ireth." He would know what to do, even if Sandis couldn't understand him. If she could just *feel* the numen there, with her, maybe he would drive away Kolosos's touch. He could cure her, comfort her.

He let her go. "Ireth?"

She stepped over the barbed wire.

"*Sandis.*"

She paused.

"You already found him." He clutched his braid. "Ireth is bound to *me.*"

Chapter 10

Rone broke away from his guard and pushed open the door to Grim Rig's "throne room" himself. The Riggers had made quick work of Kazen's lair, descending upon it like a swarm of locusts, leaving as quickly as they'd come. It was already dawn again, yet Rone had come from the grafters' hideout with even less than he'd gone in with.

"Where is Sandis?"

His shout stirred the attention of half the mobsmen in the room—considerably fewer than before, but then again, Sherig's guards hadn't insisted Rone wait for her to assemble her small army this time.

The mob boss sat in the chair at the head of the room, looking over a ledger. She waved a hand, and her men went back to counting out their earnings and bantering with one another. She then stood and strode across the room, dismissing Rone's guard with another gesture. She obviously no longer considered Rone a threat, especially without his vessel in tow.

Sherig may have been one of the most powerful women in Dresberg, and not only because she had an infamous mob at her beck and call. She was nearly twice as thick as Rone and a couple of inches taller. Most men would likely cower at her sheer size. Rone, however, held his ground.

She pulled a flask from her belt. "Thirsty?"

Rone moved to bat the offering away, but she was quicker and pulled it from his reach. "I half want to punch you in the gut, Jase, since Kazen got away."

Rone's stomach dropped. He *had* gotten away, then. Words rolled over each other as they raced up his throat. "Where is Sandis?"

Sherig shrugged. "She didn't come back with my boys. Figured she was with you, but maybe she ran off with the vessels."

His skin prickled like he'd just jumped into a cold bath. "She's not here?" He was too stunned to curse.

Kazen had escaped. Sandis was missing.

God's tower, the summoner had taken her. He'd taken her *again*, and Rone had allowed it to happen.

His body warped from cold to hot. He grabbed fistfuls of hair.

Sherig slapped him on the back. "You look like you're going to hurl." She pointed to a corner. "There's a bucket—"

"Did you see Kazen?" He whipped toward her, grabbing her sleeves. "Did you *see* him? Does he have Sandis?"

Sherig laughed. "Vessel means a lot to you, eh? No, he took off on his own." She looked away and frowned. "Bastard."

Relief hit Rone so hard he nearly lost his footing. They'd gotten separated was all. Kazen wouldn't have risked coming back for her after making his great escape, would he? He'd be caught . . .

His stomach squirmed.

Sherig shrugged again. "You can look around, but believe me, I know each and every time one of mine brings a woman in. Especially one as pretty as her."

Rone set his jaw. Turned on his heel and headed for the door. Paused. "I take it you've filtered through all the loot personally?"

"That I did."

"Did you see a fist-sized trinket with a pearlescent center, surrounded by three skewed golden loops?"

Sherig raised an eyebrow. "Something like that I would remember. Afraid you're out of luck."

Rone nodded once and pushed his way back to the street just as the first work bell tolled.

He had to find her. He had to find her *now*.

She was armed, he told himself as he wandered the dilapidated ruins outside Kazen's lair and noted a few bullet holes in the buildings. The place was incredibly quiet. Dead. He'd already picked through every lane and alley, but he had to be sure.

She was armed. Kazen couldn't have grabbed her, if he even saw her.

Sandis was faster than the old man—or she had been when they'd chased each other through the city the night Rone had taken a bullet to his hip. But if the man was so slow, how had he outrun an entire mob? Had he stowed away a horse somewhere? Had he taken a vessel with him and used a numen?

Sandis. She'd done nothing to break her script. Kazen could have summoned on her, forced her to come along . . . but if Rone's understanding of the occult was correct, it was a bit more complicated to summon a numen into an unbound vessel. Not something Kazen could do on the fly.

He doesn't have her.

Maybe she'd finally run away. Not from Kazen, but from him. She'd freed her friends. Perhaps she'd decided to take refuge with them. Maybe the idea of depending on Rone had hurt her a little too much.

The ball in his gut burrowed down, and Rone pressed a hand to his belly to ease it. The ache radiated up to his chest.

His legs were like marble pillars when, in midafternoon, he dragged himself back to his new flat in his old building. His body ached all over, begging for sleep, but his mind was spinning in nonsensical circles. Should he check the cathedral? The local police? What if she'd been arrested? He had money for bail, if they hadn't discovered what she was. He could—

The door creaked when it opened, and Sandis looked up from the couch.

"Rone!" She stood. "You won't believe what—"

He crossed the room in three strides before engulfing her in his arms and burying his face into her hair. Relief trickled down his body like autumn rain. Exhaustion fled.

She smelled like butter, rain, and smoke. It was intoxicating. How had he never noticed before?

"R-Rone . . . I c-can't . . . breathe . . ."

He let her go immediately, only then realizing what he'd done. He took a step back, then another, giving her space. Her cheeks were flushed. Had he really squeezed her that hard?

"I didn't know where you were." The words came out too fast. "I thought you might be dead, or that Kazen had . . . I don't know. You weren't with Sherig—"

Movement from the corner of his eye made him swallow the rest of his words. He looked over to see another man standing there, wearing *his* clothes. His shirt, anyway. It was a little too long and too tight in the waist—the guy was both shorter and stouter than Rone. He was notably Godobian, and—

Rone blinked. "I know you. You were in the lair when I went . . . the first time." He'd run into him, and the man had pretended not to see him.

The Godobian looked him up and down. A small smile tugged at his mouth. "You were pretending to be a grafter." The smile fell. "Life was hell after that."

"This is Bastien," Sandis said, gesturing to him. "He's one of Kazen's vessels. My . . . replacement."

Rone looked between the two of them. "Replacement? Then—"

"I bear Ireth's name, yes," Bastien answered. He started playing with his braid like it was his pet cat.

"Oh." Rone didn't know what else to say to that. "Thanks for not ratting me out."

Bastien nodded.

Sandis smiled. *Smiled.* He hadn't seen a real smile from her for so long, and yet now it felt like a knife to his gut. A rusted knife, slowly twisting.

She was smiling at Bastien.

Rone rubbed his dry eyes and cleared his throat. "The rendezvous was at Sherig's place."

A pause. "Did they decide that?" she asked.

"*We* decided it." He dropped his hand. "I thought something horrible had happened to you."

Sandis rubbed her shoulder. "I don't know if I could find it from—"

"And there weren't three dozen other guys you could have followed?"

Sandis's expression darkened.

"I-I'm going to use the privy," Bastien announced, and he scuttled down the hallway. Already knew where it was, apparently. How long had they been here, while Rone frantically searched architectural graves for some sign of her?

Sandis picked at the waistband of her dress. "Bastien and I—"

"I'm guessing Bastien couldn't find his way into the city, either."

Her nostrils flared. "*Bastien* spent more years underground than I did, Rone. So no, I don't think he could have. We came here. Look, you found us."

"I've been sick all morning trying to find you!" Rone gestured toward the window, in the general direction of Kazen's lair. Why was she getting mad at *him*?

"People weren't exactly going in and out single file. I didn't know where you were. I was trying to follow Kazen, and Sherig was there—"

"You didn't know where I was because you ran off."

Her ears reddened. "To *help* people, Rone! That was the whole point of this! To rescue them and to stop Kazen."

"And that worked out splendidly."

Sandis threw her hands into the air. "What do you even want, Rone? Your business is done with me. It has been for a long time." She pushed past him for the door.

The tautness in his shoulders evaporated. "Sandis—"

"My papers weren't there." Her voice squeaked around the words. "But this was." She reached into her pocket, yanked her hand back out, and chucked something at him. He caught it with one hand and nearly dropped it.

The amarinth. The *amarinth*.

Sandis wrenched open the door.

"Sandis, wait."

"I need some air." She slammed the door behind her.

Rone took a deep breath and closed his eyes. *Nice one, Comf. You're a moron.* He looked down at the amarinth in his hands. He should feel better about getting it back. And he did. It was just . . . he shouldn't have gotten it this way.

Falling back onto the couch, Rone balanced the artifact between his thumb and pinky and spun it with his index finger. The loops rotated around each other, void of magic. It had already been spun today.

Kazen had gotten away, all right.

Next time, it wouldn't be so easy.

If Rone pressed himself to the wall, he could see Sandis out of one of the dingy windows. She hadn't gone far. She hunched over the rusted railing of the balcony, staring down into the street. This flat was only two stories up, so it didn't even have a good view, but she stayed out there a long time.

He turned away and made something to eat. Only then did Bastien come out of the privy.

"I'm guessing you're hungry," Rone said without turning around.

"I had some bread, thank you."

Rone pulled the diminished loaf out of the cupboard. "I see that."

He heard the vessel drop onto the couch. The ensuing silence was awkward.

"I've got some raisins," Rone said.

"Do you think they'll look for us?"

He paused. "Kazen or the Riggers?"

Bastien looked at his knees. "Both?"

"I don't think so." He couldn't guarantee that, but this guy seemed especially jumpy, and Rone would rather he not piss himself with worry. These floors were a pain to clean.

He put the raisins back onto their shelf.

"Raisin' the raisins."

Rone crooked an eyebrow. "What?"

Bastien shrugged. "It's a joke."

Rone hesitated before saying, "That . . . was a really bad joke."

He started manhandling his braid again. "I know."

Quickly losing interest in the conversation, Rone smeared the last of his butter onto a piece of bread. He took a bite and studied the guy. He was closer to Sandis's age than his. Maybe nineteen? No older than twenty. For some reason, that made Rone feel slightly superior.

That, and he could definitely kick this guy's ass if he wanted to.

"You don't see a lot of foreigners around these parts," he noted.

Bastien dragged his toe across the carpet. "I don't remember Godobia. I vaguely remember my parents."

Rone thought of his own mother. "You miss them?"

"They're the ones who sold me."

"Oh." He took another bite of bread. "That's rough."

Bastien gave him a pointed look that made Rone feel like a stranger in his own flat. Granted, it hadn't been his flat for very long.

He swallowed. "You can rummage through the cupboards if you want. I'm going to take a nap."

Bastien nodded.

"Keep an eye on her."

He nodded again.

Bread still in hand, Rone strode into his bedroom and closed the door. He heard Bastien open the front door and tried not to think of the Godobian and Sandis together, alone, out there.

Rone plopped down in his desk chair and set his food on the desk's corner, ears pricked for sounds of Sandis. He doubted Kazen would try to reclaim Sandis at this point, but he wanted to play it safe. He certainly wouldn't be able to sleep so long as she was exposed, so he might as well find some way to stay busy. Opening a drawer, he retrieved his emigration papers. The tiny date in the corner stared back at him.

Seven days. He still had time. Plenty of time. She clearly didn't want him here, so he *should* leave. Soon. Just not . . . yet.

Slipping the papers away, Rone snatched up his meal and shoved it in his mouth before lying on his bed and kicking off his shoes. He stared at the ceiling, feeling the ball in his stomach draw slow circles, around and around, always in the same direction.

The front door opened again, shut. Bastien was saying something too quietly for Rone to make out. His body sank into the mattress, his eyelids wavered, but his attention focused solely on the room beyond his door.

Their plan had failed. But Rone still had cards he could play. Engel did, anyway.

It was time to pay a visit to the police. More specifically, to crooked Thamus Dakis.

Sandis shifted on the couch, glancing periodically at the bedroom door. Her emotions danced into knots inside her. Anger at Rone's accusations. Surprise at his worry. Sadness that she couldn't talk to him, the way she might have, before. Half of her wanted that door to open. The other half wanted to bar it shut and set a match to the entire flat.

The thought of fire brought her attention back to Bastien. He'd shown her Ireth's name on the back of his neck, printed just as it was on hers, minus the missing corner. But of course the fire horse was bound to someone new. Kazen wouldn't let such a powerful numen go unchained. Ireth was sitting right next to her . . . yet he was just as far away as before. She had no connection to him anymore . . . and neither did Bastien. At least, not like the one Sandis had once possessed. When she'd asked if he *felt* Ireth—the warm pressure of his presence—and experienced dreams about him, he'd given her a confused look, much like the other vessels had done. Things like that just didn't happen. Not for them.

"They didn't talk to me much," Bastien said, picking at a cuticle as he spoke about the other vessels. "I mean, as much as they talked to each other."

Sandis shook her head. "I wish I had given them a meeting point. Anything." It had all happened so fast; she'd wanted the others to be free. And they had gone. There was that, at least. And yet . . . fear wasn't the only reason none of them had tried to run off before. They had nowhere to go but the streets. Sandis had only felt empowered to escape after finding Talbur Gwenwig's name in that gold-exchange record. She had thought she'd found salvation.

Thinking of her great-uncle now made her heart ache. But there was a strange comfort, knowing he was still out there. If she returned to him, would he be happy or angry?

"I wouldn't worry about them."

She refocused her attention on the Godobian. "What makes you say that?"

He shrugged, elbows on his knees. "Dar is so independent. Fearless. Big. He'll find a job or something soon. Rist and Kaili seem to be closer than anyone. I bet they're together, figuring things out. They might have family in the city. Did either of them ever mention . . . ?"

Sandis shook her head. "I don't know anything about their families." Except that wasn't true. Alys had told her about her background once. She'd lived with an aunt in a town west of Dresberg. Then she'd gotten very quiet, like whatever had happened during her capture was too sad to voice. Sandis understood. It had taken her a long time to mention Anon to anyone.

"Alys?" she tried. "She wasn't with the others."

Bastien's lips formed a thin line as he considered. "I haven't seen her in . . . four days, maybe? But I'd been in solitary for . . ." He shuddered. "I-I don't know. A little over a day, I think."

Four days? But she'd gone as long without seeing one of the others before. Depending on Kazen's work schedule or his punishments. *She's fine.* "Why were you in solitary?"

He frowned. "Kazen was pretty ruthless with me. I don't know if that's how he was with all his recruits, but if I stepped even a little out of line, it was solitary. Sometimes for three hours, sometimes three days." He closed his eyes for a moment—perhaps the memories were too strong. Sandis hated solitary, too, but mostly because it was dark and lonely, not because the space was tight. "Dar said he used to have an assistant who dealt other punishments, but Kazen got rid of him."

"He killed him."

Bastien blinked. "I-I'm not surprised, honestly. He killed one of my old master's men when they traded me. I don't know exactly what the bargain was, but they got into a big fight right there in the hallway. It was . . . terrifying."

That perked Sandis's interest. "In Kazen's hold?"

He nodded.

She remembered a fight drawing Galt out of his office before Ireth was taken away from her. A fight that had left her handcuffed to his desk, allowing her to find Talbur's address and her own citizen record, which she'd foolishly left behind and now was lost for good. Could that fight have been between Kazen and Bastien's old grafters?

"Kazen went back on part of the deal," Bastien continued. "Oz wasn't happy about it. But Kazen never did keep a contract."

Sandis knit her fingers together. "I hope she's okay. Alys."

"Me, too. She was nice. She talked about you. I mean, they all did, from time to time. The one who got away. The one who broke Kazen."

"Broke?"

Humor glinted in Bastien's blue eyes. "Apparently he was much more levelheaded before you walked out on him. You could say you really sanded him down."

"I . . . what?"

"You know." He twisted the end of his braid around his index finger. "Sandis. Sanded."

Sandis almost smiled at that. She would have, if only Kazen had been killed, captured, anything. But he was still out there, somewhere. Hurting, yes, but nothing could keep that man down for long.

"You're sad."

She looked back over at Bastien. "I'm worried. He's going to find a way to summon Kolosos, I know it." She'd told Bastien about Kolosos earlier, after they got back to Rone's flat. Not about the visions, the nightmares, but the facts. The things she understood. Bastien had confirmed that newcomers came in every now and then, went into the summoning room, and never came out. There was a lot of screaming at night, but Bastien had assumed that was normal. *Normal.* Had their lives really devolved so much?

"Do you know where he might go?" he tried.

Sandis shook her head. "He had allies, I know that. But . . . he only used me with his enemies. Always at night. I only remember small pieces of it, and sometimes nothing at all."

Bastien nodded his head in agreement. He *understood.* He knew the pain of summoning. He wore brands identical to hers. He'd lived under Kazen's roof. Not as long as she had, but he understood her better than Rone ever could.

She glanced to his door again, then away. "Maybe he'll go back to the lair and we'll get a second chance."

The thought of stepping into that summoning room, even with Kazen long gone, raised gooseflesh on her arms. They were silent until Bastien sat up straight and grabbed his knees with his hands. "You're brave. Y-You could fight him."

Sandis shook her head. "How can I fight him if I don't know where he is?"

"With . . . me. With the others, if we can find them."

Her skin prickled as she looked at her new comrade, at the honesty lighting his freckled face. "What do you mean?"

"I mean you're eligible to be a summoner."

Sandis's lips parted, but no sound passed them. She stared at Bastien, her mind churning until it caught like a cocked gun hammer.

She'd never considered that before. She'd summoned on *herself*, yes, but never on another.

A summoner.

She met all the qualifications. All summoners had to be vessels first, even if just for one possession. It connected them to the ethereal plane. They needed to know the spells, which Sandis did. She didn't have an astral sphere, but Bastien, Alys, Dar, and Rist were already bound, and Sandis thought she knew the symbols for a few other numina to summon into Kaili.

She could be a summoner? Summon *Ireth*? The idea of taking Bastien's blood and pumping it into her own veins made her hair stand on end, but she'd be using Kazen's own weapons against him.

"I don't . . ." She tried to find words. "I don't know the meditation." Meditation was what aligned the summoner's spirit with the ethereal realm, allowing him or her to call down numina from one plane into the other.

"I do."

She blinked.

"I know it from watching my old master. He wasn't . . . as hard as Kazen, I guess. Or maybe he was just hard in different ways." He shook his head. "I could teach you—"

The door to the bedroom swung open, and Rone, circles under his eyes, stormed into the room. "No, Sandis. Please don't."

Sandis's spine instantly straightened. "Were you spying on us?"

"Spying? I am literally one very thin wall away from you." He gestured to the room. "I don't exactly have to try."

"It wouldn't hurt her," Bastien tried.

No, she thought, *but it would hurt you.*

Rone ignored him and walked to Sandis, crouching in front of her so they were level with each other. "Sandis." His voice was softer now, but strained, like he wanted to yell but couldn't. "You're afraid of Kazen using you? Then *break* it." He stood and half ran into the kitchen, grabbing a paring knife from one of its drawers. He returned, crouching in front of her once more, and held its handle out to her. "You'll be free of them if you just break the brands. Just one of them. They'll never be able to use you again. It won't stop you from . . . summoning"—he took great discomfort from the word—"so you'd get the best of both worlds."

A tremor coursed through her arms. She looked at the knife, at Rone. It wasn't the first time he'd made the suggestion. "I-I can't. Ireth—"

"Ireth isn't yours anymore."

Sandis felt tears sting her eyes. Bastien's gaze burned a hole into the side of her face. She couldn't meet it.

Ireth hadn't finished telling her whatever he'd been trying to say. There were clues she was missing. Something *important.* What did he know about Kolosos? And she . . . she *missed* him. Missed the ever-present burn in the back of her throat or throb just beneath her skull. The promise that she was never fully alone.

Ireth had been true to her until the very end. And now a true monster had replaced him. Yet she wasn't bound to Kolosos, so the numen should have no connection to her.

Was it all in her head?

Rone felt your skin burning.

"Sandis." Rone took one of her hands with his. "I want you to be safe. This is how you'll be safe. Even if you want to . . . summon. But you won't be *used* anymore."

She swallowed. *Why do you want me to be safe* now? she wanted to say, but not with Bastien sitting right there. So she just shook her head, and Rone sighed and pulled away, taking his warm hand with him.

She and Bastien watched him trudge back to the kitchen and toss the knife onto the counter. "About earlier. I shouldn't have taken this victory from you. I didn't mean to be so . . ."

"Malevolent?" Bastien tried.

Rone glared. "Let's go with cross."

Sandis nodded, and Rone's shoulders relaxed. Sandis knew his expression well. He was thinking about something. She didn't like it.

"I'm going to go talk to one of my contacts," Rone finally said.

She rolled her lips together. "Contacts. Engel?"

He nodded. "A crooked scarlet. Might have an idea where Kazen likes to hide."

Sandis massaged a knuckle into her tightening belly. "Maybe it would be better to lie low for a while longer. Make sure we're safe."

Rone scoffed. The sound both agitated her and curled her stomach into an even tighter ball.

Closing her eyes, Sandis took a deep breath, filling her chest, all the way up to her shoulders, before letting it out. "Be careful."

Rone studied her face a moment. "Keep the door locked."

He slipped into his room and grabbed a packed bag—the same one he'd toted around before, when he'd helped Sandis run. Before he'd . . . stopped. Slinging the bag over his shoulder, Rone strode out the door and shut it firmly behind him. Following his path, Sandis locked the door.

Silence floated about the flat for a long minute.

"The meditation," Sandis whispered, turning to Bastien. "How would I start?"

Chapter 11

Kazen had lost it all.

His assailants had been Grim Rig's old gang; he was sure of it. He should have destroyed them when he'd killed their boss. And that impudent Godobian . . . had *she* let him out of his cage?

Sandis. Sandis. *Sandis.* Kazen absently drew her name on the slick stone beneath him near the mouth of the dark market, where he had fled. The closest lamp was a hundred feet away and around a corner, leaving him a glimmer shy of complete darkness.

It rankled him to think how differently all of this could have played out, had he been a little swifter when Sandis had been chained to the summoning-room floor. Had he killed Rone Comf himself instead of sending incompetent men to do the job.

Choices, choices, choices. Somehow, he kept making the wrong ones. This had not been a problem in a very long time.

His long fingers curled into fists, which he smashed down onto her invisible name. His lair, gone, and his valuables with it. His amarinth, gone. His vessels, gone. All he had left was the truth. He'd make them all see it soon enough. He'd unravel the lie and make the entire country choke on it.

Sandis. Yes, if only he'd been swifter. He'd have his monster, he'd—

Kazen sat up, his back rigid, his body feeling thirty years younger. Could he possibly . . . ? It was an option, yes. Oh yes. If he did that, if the child's body wasn't ruined, he could have his Kolosos and his revenge—without the chase. Yes, *that* would do wonderfully.

Kazen picked himself up off the stone, ignoring the dampness of his clothes. He brushed his tailored jacket with moist palms and held his head high, his plan stitching together at the forefront of his mind.

Yes. First, he'd visit his accounts and withdraw the money he needed.

Then the hunt would begin.

Chapter 12

Rone assumed Thamus Dakis still worked in District Four—the eastern slice of Dresberg that housed Helderschmidt's firearm factory, Arnae Kurtz's flat, and the dilapidated neighborhood where Kazen and his grafters operated. He passed over the northeast canal and swung by the library, hopping on the back of a passing cart to hasten his journey to the police station.

The station was a two-story cube built of cinderblock, its windows thick and double paned. One in the back had bars—the sole window of a temporary holding cell for prisoners. The building's front door was heavy but unlocked, permitting the common man to walk in and file complaints to the deaf ears behind the too long, too tall desk to the left. Just beyond that desk was a set of cement stairs leading upward. Rone had reached their base when one of the men in scarlet uniforms jumped up from his chair and said, "Halt!"

Halt. Like he was a soldier. Rone quickened his step and took the stairs two at a time, emboldened by the amarinth in his pocket. The scarlet bolted after him, drawing a pistol from his belt. Rone took a sharp turn onto the second floor and immediately grabbed the second doorknob on the right, swinging it open.

To his relief, the piece of slag he'd been looking for sat at his own desk. The man jumped up suddenly. He'd been sleeping.

Rone wasn't surprised. But Dakis was, when his eyes found him.

"I'm here to see him," Rone said, letting a northern accent slip into his voice. "Calm down."

The policeman chasing him had a face nearly as red as his uniform. He didn't lower his gun.

Dakis's beady eyes shifted from Rone to the scarlet. "It's fine, Tad. Let him be."

The scarlet holstered his gun but held his place. Rone slipped into the office, shut the door in *Tad's* face, and locked it.

Thamus Dakis hadn't changed at all since Rone last saw him, save for somehow looking slimier. He was in his late forties and small in stature, his mousy brown hair cradling his ears like it feared the baldness on top of his head.

Dakis folded his fingers together, stuck them behind his neck, and leaned back as though he owned the world. "This is a surprise. Desperate for hire?"

Something about the scarlet's tone made Rone want to knock a few of his teeth out. Could he get away with that? Probably, considering the kol in his pockets.

"I need information." Squaring his shoulders, he closed in on the desk. Some of Dakis's smugness drained from his face.

The policeman sat up. "I owe you nothing, Verlad. I pay my fees."

Yes, you're a good little cad. "Then I'll pay mine." He took a stack of kol from his pocket and dropped it on the desk. Dakis's eyes glittered like newly cut diamonds, but when he reached for the cash, Rone dropped his fist onto it. "I'm looking for a man named Kazen."

Dakis frowned. "Is that a given name or a surname?"

"Doesn't matter. It's all I have." Rone studied his face. "I think you know who I'm talking about."

"Hmm." Dakis folded his arms. "What does a nice chap like you want with grafters?"

Rone picked up the cash. "I'm paying for answers, not for questions."

Dakis shrugged. "I haven't heard a lick about him for a month. If you're wanting something recent, you've reached a dead end." His hand darted out like a viper, trying to tug bills from Rone's grasp. He succeeded with a few.

God's tower, the man was a rabid dog begging for scraps.

"I don't believe you."

Dakis met his eyes. "You don't have to."

Rone hunched over the desk, but Dakis didn't cower. "You expect me to believe you didn't hear a single gunshot yesterday? That you didn't see an army of mobsmen infesting that dilapidated southeast square of yours in the middle of the night?"

Dakis barked a laughed. "No! Really? Hmm." He rubbed his chin. "But even if I had, I wouldn't have."

Rone glowered.

Dakis sighed. "My good chum, did you know that men scramble to work on my force? That they request District Four more than any other in the city? Specifically that southeast corner?"

Rone said nothing.

Dakis folded his hands under his chin, a smile tempting his lips. "They *fight* for it. That dark, dreary, disgusting spot overrun by slag. Why? Because of the kol. Do you have any idea how much money Kazen pumps into our coffers to keep my men from snooping around? To keep his roads and buildings full of holes?"

Heat churned at the base of Rone's throat. "Too bad you weren't there last night, then. Use your head, Dakis. If I'm looking for Kazen, he's on the run. Which means he won't be around to make his usual bribes."

The policeman's jaw slacked. "I . . . see. And you've no leads."

He cursed inwardly and straightened. "I didn't come here for tea."

Dakis's hands formed fists and thudded into his desk. "Damn."

So the louse really didn't know where Kazen was. What a waste of time. Rone pocketed the rest of his kol save a couple of bills, which he let float to the desk.

As Dakis leaned forward to collect them, Rone asked, "Do you know my real name?"

Dakis lifted his head. "What? No—"

"Good." Rone swung a right hook hard into the scarlet's cheek, knocking him off his chair.

He vanished out the door before the man had a chance to get back up.

Sandis sat in the small hallway that stemmed off the main room in Rone's flat. It led to the privy and a closet, nothing more. The curtains were pulled shut, smoky midday light pouring around them, giving the place a grayish hue. Rone had left some time ago to get food and supplies, wanting to head out between work bells so the crowds wouldn't be so bad. He'd told her twice to lock the door behind him, then tested the knob once she'd done so.

But Sandis wasn't supposed to think about any of that. She wasn't supposed to think about anything. Focusing on the back of her eyelids, she cleared her thoughts.

Bastien sat across from her, guiding her through the steps of meditation. He'd said it would take more than a couple of practice sessions. Still, Sandis wanted to get started right away so she could finish the journey sooner.

They'd purposefully waited until Rone left to start.

Right now, she focused on her breathing. Drawing air in slowly through the nose, releasing it quickly through the mouth. "My old master always thought of the sky," Bastien said quietly. "Like he was breathing in part of the sky and discarding it, over and over again, until it disappeared, and the ethereal plane was exposed."

Interesting. No, don't think. She forced her mind to clear. Inhaled again, trying to imagine herself outside, and not under four stories of flats. Tried to imagine herself breathing in gray sky. She coughed at the thought of the pollution filling her lungs.

Try again.

Stars. She imagined herself atop the Lily Tower, outside the city, where the pollution was a little thinner. The sky wasn't gray, but black and endless, dotted with tiny winking stars. She breathed in, and the glowing specks rushed into her, tickling as they fluttered through her nostrils and down into her lungs. She expelled them quickly and inhaled again, sucking in more stars. A little bit of the black. Another inhale, another piece of the sky torn down. Behind it . . . yes, if she squinted, she could imagine a crystal wall. Dark blue and hard, like glass. Could that be the ethereal plane? But was it really something so physical, looming above them like a second heaven? Or was it more spiritual, haunting the very streets Sandis walked?

She wanted to reach for it, feel it beneath her fingertips—

A knock sounded at the door.

Sandis opened her eyes, the gray of the apartment engulfing her, the visions of stars and crystal vanishing. She felt too heavy, like she'd woken from oversleeping, or eaten too much.

Bastien turned, looking down the hall. The knock sounded a second time. He stood.

"Wait." She lunged forward and grabbed his pant leg. "Rone wouldn't knock on his own door."

He stiffened. "Do you ever have visitors?"

She shook her head. "I don't think so." Who could be at the door? A neighbor? A scarlet?

She stood, leaning against the hallway wall. Crept past Bastien and peered into the sitting room.

The knock didn't sound again. A solicitor? She couldn't imagine who—

The door burst open, ripping the dead bolt from the wood. Sandis shrieked. For a split second, she thought Rone stood there, filling the doorway and glaring coldly at them.

But this wasn't Rone. He was too tall, too thin, with skin so pale it glowed white, and short hair darker than the night sky. His eyes were black orbs of tar.

He looked at Sandis, then at Bastien, who stood beside her.

He moved like wind.

The man stood in the doorway one moment, and the next he was in front of Sandis, close enough for her to catch the mingled scents of dust and cigar smoke. His hand flashed forward, whiplike, grabbing her wrist and wrenching her arm behind her back. Pain blossomed in her shoulder. Leaning back, the ghostly man sent a solid kick into Bastien's stomach, throwing him into the wall.

"No! Stop!" Sandis screamed, even as her shoulder burned. This wasn't one of Kazen's men, was it?

The man pulled down on her arm until she doubled over. He landed a knee to her gut that made her see stars and spit up part of her breakfast. For a moment she was weightless; then a bony shoulder pressed into her diaphragm. He was picking her up. He meant to take her.

Bastien barreled into the stranger's back, knocking both him and Sandis to the floor. Sandis landed hard on her still-bruised shoulder and rolled until her back hit the couch. She blinked, trying to gain her bearings. Bastien, she had to—

The stranger was already on his feet, moving like a dancer. Bastien was a stone pillar, and he, water. He stood in front of Bastien one moment, then appeared behind him the next, grabbing the Godobian's braid and jerking his head back. Bastien yelped, his hands going for his hair. The stranger released the braid, crouched, crooked two fingers on each hand, and struck Bastien twice in the hip. Bastien's leg immediately buckled, as if the bone had simply vanished. His shirt hiked up in the fall, revealing the edge of his script.

After half a second's hesitation, the stranger grabbed Bastien just as he had grabbed her and threw the Godobian over his shoulder, showing only a little strain at the weight.

He was going to take Bastien.

Bastien, not her. But then why . . . ?

She didn't have time to think about it. Sandis flung herself across the floor, barely managing to grab the stranger's ankle before he could reach the door. She didn't trip him, only made him stumble. The tall man's black eyes dropped to her, calculating.

Through the far wall, a neighbor shouted, "You okay in there?"

Bastien's fists beat at the stranger's back. The slender man crouched and spun, breaking Sandis's hold while gaining momentum. He released Bastien, sending him flying into Rone's bedroom door. The wood buckled under the impact.

The stranger lunged for Sandis.

"No!" she screamed, kicking out, managing to land a heel on his cheekbone. All it did was turn his narrow face slightly to the left. He grabbed her under the arms; she knotted her fingers in his hair and pulled.

Two strikes, just like he'd done to Bastien, only under her right arm. The limb tingled and went numb, like she'd slept on it all night, cutting off the blood. It fell uselessly to her side.

"Help!" she cried as the stranger again lifted her and kneed her in the stomach. Her air left her. Her pulse radiated around the blow. Before she knew it, she was on his shoulder again. Bastien groaned, but he wasn't getting up fast enough.

The stranger stopped abruptly. Using her left arm, Sandis pushed herself up just enough to see why.

Rone stood in the doorway, two bags of groceries at his feet. "I don't believe we've met," he said.

He sped from the door frame and collided with the stranger, and Sandis found herself falling face-first into the carpet.

The impact jarred some life back into her arm, but she could do little beyond twitch her fingers. A foot stepped on her hair as the two men shuffled deeper into the room, fists and feet flying. Sandis rolled back toward the couch, nausea pressing into her bruised belly like someone stoked it with a bellows.

She lifted her head and glimpsed a woman in a smock peeking through the doorway. The woman—the neighbor?—then widened her eyes and fled. Rone threw a punch at the stranger's head. The stranger ducked and spun, kicking out. Rone evaded the blow, but the stranger repeated the maneuver with his other leg, and this time he struck Rone in the ribs. The space was small; Rone hit the wall and winced, but pushed off and threw himself at the taller man, landing knuckles to his stomach.

"Watch out for his hands!" Sandis croaked. She tried to push herself up, forgetting about her numb arm, and teetered onto her left hand. The stranger's heel kicked her neck as he evaded another one of Rone's blows. She reeled back, coughing and stumbling on her awkward limbs. Pain spiraled into her head.

Her pinky brushed something hard. Her rifle case. She tried to move the fingers on her right hand, even as the stranger flew over the couch and struck the window, shattering part of it with his elbow. Her knuckles bent just a little more, especially her pinky, but the limb was still heavy and useless.

She grabbed the case with her left hand and slid it out from beneath the couch, fumbling with the locks. Her father had always told her firearms should be stored separately from their ammo, lest an accident happen, but Sandis hadn't unloaded the gun. Not when she might need it at a moment's notice. If the last seven weeks had taught her anything, it was always be ready.

She heard a cry and looked up. Bastien knelt on the floor, blood dribbling from his nose. Rone and the stranger fought around him, moving so quickly they blurred. They seemed to strike and block at the same time. Rone ducked from one blow, only for the stranger to slip behind him and send an elbow into the inside of his shoulder blade. Rone fell.

Sandis's right hand twitched, still useless. She grabbed her rifle by the barrel and set its butt against her knees, trying to hold it in place with her chin. She half hugged the thing and cocked it—

She heard the *snap* before she saw it—the stranger's foot slammed down on Rone's knee and overextended it until the joint shattered and the bones popped apart. Rone's scream deafened her.

She didn't hear the rifle go off, only felt it. The recoil thumped against her jaw and into her skull, setting a match to the headache already flourishing there.

Scarlet bloomed on the stranger's left arm. He paused over Rone, who writhed and hissed and tried to reach for his leg but couldn't for the pain. The stranger touched his shirt sleeve and brought his fingers back, almost . . . *curious*, at the blood.

He raised his dark gaze to Sandis, then shifted it to Bastien. Lifted his injured arm. Flinched.

Then, swift as the wind, he soared toward the open door and disappeared.

Sandis crouched, her own arm tingling like it was stuffed with needles, the rifle still clutched in her left hand. Her breaths raked up and down her throat, and her pulse sounded in every part of her body. She heard distant voices around her—more neighbors, people on the street? She was outside of herself, floating away—

Rone groaned.

She dropped the rifle and leapt to her feet, pain and nausea forgotten. His leg was bent at a terrible angle, and the amarinth had been used too recently to be of help. He kept trying to reach—

"Rone?" She knelt at his head. He squeezed his eyes shut and bared his teeth. She grabbed his face with her left hand. "Rone, stop moving. Stop!"

He swore through his clenched jaw, then swore again.

Outside, a police whistle blew, the sound sending gooseflesh cascading over Sandis's body.

One of the neighbors had called the scarlets . . . or perhaps patrolling officers had heard the gunshot.

Sandis let one of Rone's favorite words pass her lips. Before her thoughts caught up with her intentions, she found herself on her feet and rushing out the door, onto the balcony. No neighbors were near, probably wanting to get away from the ruckus, but several people had gathered on the street below. Among them, Sandis spotted two men in scarlet uniforms, the image of a sailless boat pinned to their shirts.

"That way!" she shouted, pointing in a random direction. "He went that way! Please, hurry! He's wearing all black!"

The neighbors turned to look at her. The scarlets hesitated only a moment before running in the direction she'd indicated. It wouldn't get rid of them for good, but it would give her time.

Shaking, Sandis rushed back into the flat and slammed the door shut as best she could on its bent hinges. Her gaze shot from Rone to Bastien.

"You'll have to hide," she told the latter. "Tuck in your shirt. And Rone—" She looked at him, at his set jaw and pallor. It made her stomach and heart sick. "I don't think we can get you to a hospital without someone learning too much."

Bastien came over, his hand and lip stained with blood. He favored one leg, but the other worked well enough to keep him upright. His shoulders quivered. "W-We have to set it."

"God, no," Rone spat, blinking tears from his eyes, only to squeeze them shut again. "A few hours . . ." He was close to hyperventilating. "A few hours and—"

"A few hours until what?" Bastien looked green. He didn't know about the amarinth.

"Look in his room, in his bag," Sandis said, trying to keep her voice even while her heart rampaged in her chest. "See if he has bandages. I think there's pain powder in the cabinet by the privy. Go!"

She wanted to send him to the market, but Bastien was still trembling, and his red hair stood out like a flag. And what if the stranger had friends?

You can do this. You can do this.

She had to move Rone.

She inched toward him, her right palm tingling as feeling slowly returned to her arm. She wiggled her fingers experimentally and found she could also bend her elbow a little. Swallowing hard, she said, "Bastien's right. We have to set it."

Rone's face was pale and moist, his pant leg spotted with crimson. "Just . . . a few hours . . ."

"You're going into shock." One of the boys in her line at the firearm factory had gone into shock after accidentally shooting himself in the foot. She knew what it looked like. Knew what it felt like—that same cold, pain-laced confusion had swallowed her after Kazen burned gold deep into her skin. Reaching over with her good arm, she wrenched a pillow from the couch and shoved it under Rone's head. She was fairly certain she could set the leg. All Kazen's vessels had been taught basic wound treatment. Sandis now suspected the lessons had been in case Kazen got hurt, not one of them.

After she set the leg, she would have to move him and hide the blood before the scarlets got back . . . or before more showed up.

She touched his thigh.

Rone groaned and flailed, then bit down on a scream. "God's towel, Sandis!"

"I'm going to smash that gun into your head if you don't *stop moving!*" she hissed back. "The police are outside. If they don't see you, or this"—she gestured to his mangled knee—"then they can't force me to take you to the hospital."

Bastien came back in with a roll of bandages. He looked between Sandis and Rone several times before dropping them on the floor.

Turning back to Rone, Sandis asked, "Do you have anything to help with the pain? Whiskey? Laudanum?"

Rone pressed the heels of his hands into his eyes. He didn't answer. To Bastien, Sandis said, "Check the kitchen." Then, biting her lip, she prodded Rone's ruined knee. His good knee came up and nearly socked her in her bruising chin. She bent her right elbow, testing it. Full feeling had returned to the limb, though it ached where the stranger had jabbed her.

She carefully put both hands into position. Her hands were relatively small and Rone's leg relatively thick, but she thought she could do it—

She grabbed his leg and jerked it into place, hearing a sickening *pop* when she did so. Rone said nothing.

He'd passed out. All for the better.

"Help me move him," she said as Bastien returned empty handed. "Then hide."

Cool, smoky air filtered in through the broken window. Sandis lit a lamp to chase back some of the darkness. The scarlets *had* returned, *three* of them, only moments after Sandis and Bastien dragged Rone's body into his room. Sandis introduced herself to them while Bastien hid in the privy. Assuming Rone legally rented the flat, she gave her name as Sara Comf—her mother's first name, Rone's surname. Surely the scarlets would be thorough enough to at least verify his name, unless they deemed the attack an unworthy cause. For once, Sandis hoped they would shirk their duty. She told many truths and a few lies, and thank the Celestial, the scarlets announced they wouldn't come back until morning to further their investigation.

Sandis didn't want to be there when they returned.

After the police left, Sandis set Bastien to watch over Rone while she ventured out for bandages, a variety of liquors, and some packets of powder from an apothecary. Fortunately, with the city so thickly populated, she didn't need to go far. She took a bit of the medicine herself, to counter the ache that radiated from the large bruise over her stomach.

She wrapped and elevated Rone's leg as best she could, but the swelling was terrible. She placed the amarinth on Rone's chest and watched it rise and fall with his breaths, willing it to reset. They would have to explain to Bastien, who slumbered in Rone's bed, in the morning. A person didn't just heal overnight like Rone was going to. And he *would* heal. The injury was not grievous enough to kill him. Not before dawn.

"Rone." She gently prodded him. "Rone, try again."

His eyes fluttered open. He exhaled, the smell of whiskey permeating the air. She'd given him as much as she could as often as she could, hoping to dull the pain. He'd broken his leg helping her, after all. And Bastien.

He felt around. Sandis guided his hand to the amarinth, which he spun lazily. Nothing.

She sighed.

"Thank you"—his voice was soft and groggy—"for . . . finding it."

Sandis set her hands in her lap. "I was in the right place at the right time. Bastien helped."

"Ssstill."

"I know it means a lot to you."

Groaning, Rone tried to roll over. Sandis pushed his shoulder down to keep him on his back. He didn't resist. "Bastien . . ." He laughed, though it was more of a sad, drunken chuckle than true laughter. "M'Mom's in . . . Godobia."

"I know." Then, hoping to distract him, she asked, "Is she well?"

"Think . . . so. I'm . . . still here."

"And you'll be here until the amarinth resets." She glanced toward the bedroom. It didn't matter if Bastien overheard, in the end.

Rone muttered something she couldn't decipher. "Go to sleep, Rone. I'll wake you up in a bit."

". . . piss pot."

"What?"

"Your great-uncle. He's . . . a piss pot."

Sandis rolled her eyes. Studied her lap. "At least he never pretended to be anything else."

His half-lidded eyes rolled toward her. "S'not fair."

Plucking up the amarinth, she set it back on his chest. "What *is* fair, Rone?" Her throat tightened. She swallowed and took a deep breath, in long and out quick, like the form of meditation Bastien had taught her. "You . . . You were my savior." There was barely any voice behind the words. "And you took me right back to him. Kazen. You knew what kind of man he was. You knew what he would do, but you didn't give me a choice. I really . . ." She hugged herself and stared at the floor. "I really thought . . . you and I, we had—"

She stopped, noting the sound of his breaths, long and drawn out. He'd fallen asleep again. Sandis wilted beside him. She couldn't blame him. His skin was hot with fever, and his belly full of drugs and liquor. Reaching up, she brushed hair from his forehead.

His slumber, the darkness, the silence . . . for a moment, they made it easy to pretend. Pretend they'd left Arnae's house and found Talbur, that she had convinced her great-uncle to pay the bribes to release Rone's mother, and everything else had fallen into place. Pretend her heart didn't beat in two separate pieces, and that Rone cared about her the way he cared about his mother and his amarinth. That maybe he did the things he did solely out of affection, and not out of guilt.

She was tempted—*so* tempted—to curl up next to him and lay her head on his chest, just for a moment. He would never know, and she could imagine them back before it all happened, in Arnae Kurtz's secret room, enveloped by darkness and hope.

It was the last time she remembered being happy.

Her eyes burned, and she banished the memory, knifing it like a butcher would a pig. Looking at Rone, thinking these thoughts . . .

Celestial, make it stop hurting. I'll do whatever you want if you take it all away.

This new assailant could only have been hired by Kazen. His fighting style . . . it was seugrat, wasn't it? Just like Kazen's style of fighting. Was this stranger a new hire or someone Kazen had reared himself, someone he'd stowed away where the vessels couldn't see?

Part of Sandis wanted to give up and flee. She'd never seen Rone beaten so badly. She was scared. But even if she quit, she couldn't leave Dresberg. She didn't have the identification that would allow her passage.

No, Sandis had to fight. And not because she was trapped by her lack of papers. Because Kolosos—

She turned, sure the shadows shifted the moment she thought the monster's name. Celestial above, it was waiting for her. Waiting for her to close her eyes. Waiting for a moment of weakness.

Shaking her head, Sandis dug her fingernails into her palm. She needed to think. Plan. Fight.

The stranger . . . he'd wanted Bastien, too. Not just her. Did Kazen think Bastien strong enough to host Kolosos, or did he simply want Ireth back? *Or both.* She shivered.

Maybe Rone wasn't strong enough to fight this new man, but a numen was. Ireth was. Sandis needed to stay focused. Become a summoner. Find the others.

Win.

That soft breeze wafted through the window again. This time it smelled like sulfur. Smelled like the bull from her dreams. A bull with claws and cracking red-and-black skin, narrow, glowing eyes—

"Rone." She jabbed him between ribs. "Rone, wake up. Try again." *Please don't make me be alone right now.*

He stirred. She poked him again. Picked up his hand and put it on the amarinth. Held it there until the fingers gripped.

He groggily spun the thing.

The center glowed faintly, and a soft whirring filled the room.

Chapter 13

It was almost dawn. Another night had passed with little sleep. Sandis was beginning to think she'd become a nocturnal creature, like the rats that skittered about on the streets between trash heaps.

A rat. It felt like something Kazen would call her.

They'd left Rone's flat two hours ago. Now Sandis trudged up the stairs behind Bastien to their next temporary home, her limbs aching for rest. Rone was already fishing in his pocket for a key. She'd never been to his mother's flat before, but apparently his contract for the place hadn't terminated yet. She knew he wanted to leave Kolingrad for good, but even if Kolosos weren't a threat, he couldn't without emigration papers. Sandis and Bastien . . . they couldn't even leave the city. They could try to smuggle away on a caravan, like they'd done briefly after their pilgrimage to the Lily Tower, but surely they couldn't stow away *two* people. And Sandis wasn't about to abandon her new friend—or the old friend he carried with him.

The thought made her remember her great-uncle's promise to bring her to his country estate, but she managed to push the thought away before the ensuing sadness could take root. At least Rone was healthy again, though he still wore the trousers with the bloodstains on them. He pushed the door open with his elbow.

"And it really heals him in a minute?" Bastien bent close to her ear.

She nodded. "It prevents injury, even injuries sustained before it's spun." Sandis considered the mystery of the amarinth as she stepped through the threshold of the flat. Truly, it was a working miracle, yet it had been created by the Noscons, the same people who worshipped the occult Celesia so vehemently protested. Bastien had recognized the word, *amarinth*, when she'd first mentioned it, but he was still incredulous that one actually existed.

Sandis wondered how the Noscons had made such a contraption and why they hadn't created more of them, since Rone's amarinth was incredibly useful. Then again, maybe they'd taken all their trinkets with them upon leaving Kolingrad, before Sandis's ancestors had ever settled it.

The flat was larger than the apartment they'd abandoned. Maybe even bigger than Rone's basement up north, but perhaps it was just more . . . square. The front room expanded off to the right for a living area and off to the left for a kitchen that fit a decent-sized dining table. Behind that was a hallway and a bedroom. There was a bit of clutter, a few drawers on the floor and some broken glass. Thieves had ransacked the place, leaving little behind.

But at least the grafters had never come here.

She ran her hand over the dining table, pulling back when a small splinter bit the underside of a knuckle. Rone closed an open cupboard and came toward her. He paused, awkward, watching her a moment too long.

Sandis forced her shoulders to relax. "We should rest."

Bastien said, "Should one of us keep guard?" He eyed the door while wringing his braid.

"Even if he knew where we were, he's not coming for us anytime soon. Not today." Rone kicked the front door shut anyway, then sidestepped to a window and peeked out onto the street. They were in a nicer neighborhood—not like Talbur's, but better than before. A good ways from the smoke ring.

Sandis rolled her lips together. Did Kazen know where Kaili had gone? Rist? Dar? Alys? Did this stranger intend to go after them as well, or had he targeted Sandis and Bastien because they were stronger vessels?

But Dar could host a level-seven numen, too. Was there a reason Kazen had, so far, spared him?

"You've always been special, my dear girl." Kazen's voice crawled through her memory like a half-crushed insect.

Sandis hugged herself. She had to find the vessels. They could only fight Kazen together.

"Take the bed," Rone said, hands shoved into his trouser pockets. "Red and I will sleep out here."

Sandis shook her head. "I'm the smallest. I should—"

"Sandis." Rone gave her a pointed look, his dark eyes free of mirth. "Take the bed."

Biting the inside of her lip, Sandis nodded and padded back to the small bedroom. The bed was nothing special, though its blankets were flung about as if someone had been looking for something. She grabbed one of them, cocooned herself in it, and lay down.

She fell asleep within minutes.

"When I left, I went straight to the bank," Sandis said, cradling a hot mug of tea, trying to forget the red light and shadows that had pocked her slumber. "If I'd run without a purpose . . ."

She and Bastien sat across from each other at the dining table in Rone's mother's apartment, trying to figure out where to begin their search for the other vessels.

"No one survives without a job," she added.

Bastien nodded. "They'd have to get work. Smoke ring is the best place to do it."

"Unless they think Kazen is coming for them. I never stayed in the same place because of that." She leaned close to the tea, letting the steam warm her nose, and allowed herself a quick glance at Rone. He was reading something in the sitting room, his back toward them. He still wasn't happy with Sandis's plan. But Rone's happiness didn't matter. Couldn't matter.

"Would they know he's alive?"

Sandis hesitated, then shook her head.

Bastien rubbed his chin. "They could just break their scripts. Why would he pursue vessels with broken scripts?"

Sandis paled. "But if they broke their scripts, I can't summon with them." That was the plan, wasn't it? Drooping over her tea, she added, "But it would be good to help them either way. Good to have allies."

Bastien wove the end of his braid through his fingers. "You could . . . I mean, w-we could start back at the towers." He swallowed, obviously at odds with his own suggestion. "I mean . . . that abandoned neighborhood over Kazen's holding. It's . . . towery."

Sandis nodded. "Makes sense. We could find clues to where they went, or where Kazen went—"

"That's a bad idea."

They both looked over at Rone, Bastien turning in his chair to do so. Rone blew loose curls from his forehead—he needed a trim. "If Kazen is gone, no one is paying off the scarlets to stay out of that place. They'll be looking for their own cut, probably. Other grafters might be snooping around, too."

Bastien said, "Maybe it's been long enough—"

"It's only been two days. And by the time it *has* been long enough. You'll find nothing useful." Rone's tone was sharp and insistent. "Do you have any idea what sort of bounty Grim Rig has on his head?"

"Grim Rig is dead, right?" the Godobian countered.

"I strongly doubt they know that, or care." Rone tossed the paper he was reading onto the threadbare couch. "Even with corruption, the police will do their jobs for bounty money. They're going to investigate the hell out of that place and be suspicious of anyone snooping around. Give them one glimpse of what's under that shirt, and you'll be sweating it out in Gerech while they tie the knot on your noose."

Bastien blanched.

Sandis's stomach tightened. "Rone."

"Do I lie?"

Pressing her lips together, she shook her head. "Then we won't start there."

"You shouldn't start anywhere, not with that freak after you." Rone shuddered. "I felt like I was being watched, before. When we left the Lily Tower. Wonder if it was him."

"You did? You didn't tell me." Sandis's grip on her cup tightened.

"You didn't ask."

He looked at her, and she looked at him. The air was almost too thick to breathe.

"It's fine." Bastien coiled his braid around his head. "We're not ready for the others yet."

Sandis finally took a sip of her tea, letting the bland hot brew warm her gums before swallowing. "I wonder how long it takes." Mastering the meditation, she meant.

"I'm not sure. My old master was already a summoner when I met him. Depends on the person, I guess. And the soul."

She nodded. "Might as well try."

Bastien offered her a weak smile. "You'll get there. And we'll find them." He reached across the table and clasped her wrist, since her hands were still snug against her cup.

Rone scoffed and moved toward the door. "I'll be back."

Sandis stood, pulling from Bastien's touch. "But—"

"I'm going to find out who this slag is. He knows seugrat. There are only so many who teach it." He wrenched open the door and, without looking at her, said, "Do *not* leave the flat. Slide the bolt after me. If you hear anything, go out the fire escape through the bedroom window. There's a manhole at the bottom of it."

He shut the door and was gone.

Sandis's back was sore from sitting so erect on the floor, doing the breathing and mind exercises Bastien had related to her. After rolling her neck, she leaned against the edge of the sofa and sighed.

Bastien sat cross-legged, his head tilted slightly to one side, his braid hanging over one of his ears. Before Sandis could ask what he was thinking, he said, "Do you ever wonder where they come from?"

She slouched, stretching her spine. "Who?"

"*What*, I suppose. The numina."

Sandis tucked a piece of hair behind her ears. "The ethereal plane."

Bastien shook his head. "But *where* do they come from, *really*? Why are they there? Why is the ethereal plane there? What is it like? Have you ever wondered?"

A small smile tugged at her cheeks. "I can't say I have."

"I've wondered." Bastien brought his legs in front of him and hugged his knees. "I've stayed awake at night, wondering. The numina, the ethereal plane . . . the amarinth now. I wonder about that."

"Me, too."

"Even us," he continued, "Where did *we* come from? This earth we live on? The stars?"

Sitting up straighter, she said, "The Celestial."

But Bastien shook his head. "Can't be."

"Why not?"

"The Celestial is only what, three centuries old? The world is much older than that. The Noscons alone are so much older."

"He wasn't *invented* three hundred years ago." Sandis's brows drew together. "That's just when our people started worshipping him."

His face softened. "I'm sorry. I didn't think you were a believer."

She shrugged. "Most Kolins are."

He shrugged back. "Most Kolins aren't like us."

Frowning, Sandis reached over her shoulder, her fingers brushing Ireth's broken name. Reaching a little farther, she touched the smooth, leathery edge of her highest brand.

"Why do you care about him?"

She pulled her hand away and glanced to the door. "Rone? I don't. I mean . . . no, it's—"

Bastien laughed. "I meant Ireth."

"Oh." Her cheeks warmed. She pressed her palms into her knees. "It's hard to put in words. He was . . ." She pressed her lips together, considering. "If I weren't a Celesian, I suppose he would have felt like a god to me."

Bastien cocked his head in the other direction. "That's interesting."

Sandis rolled her lips together. "I suppose it is. I don't know. I don't think about things in the way you do. He was always there, even when Kazen wasn't. Even when I couldn't feel any heat or pressure, I just . . . knew. Sometimes I felt what he felt. I knew he . . . cared."

Knew he loved me, she wanted to say, but something about that seemed too personal to share with him.

"It was never like that for me." Bastien frowned. "Bonded or not. Even with Ireth. Just nothing, then pain, then nothing again."

"I was bonded to him awhile."

"I was bonded to Grendoni for almost five years." He ran a hand down his braid. "Do you know him?"

Sandis shook her head.

"He's a six, I think. I've been told he looks like a goblin cat." He crooked his fingers to imitate cat ears. "His head is half his size, and he has big tusks on his lower jaw." He moved his fingers to his face to illustrate. "Big eyes and tail. My old master made a deal with another summoner who wanted Grendoni, so he unbound me a few months before he traded me to Kazen. I never felt his presence, even when he was summoned. I was always just . . . dead." He settled his hands in his lap. "I wish I knew what it felt like, to have that sort of bond."

Ignoring a twisting in her chest, Sandis murmured, "Maybe you'll get it, in time."

"Maybe." He sounded doubtful. Then, silently, he studied her, looking at her like she was a book he'd like to read, though given his background, Sandis was fairly certain Bastien *couldn't* read.

A few moments after his gaze became awkward, she asked, "What?"

"You're doing well. Really well," he answered. "Maybe, since you're so close to Ireth, it would work."

A chill passed through her, but a small flame deep in her core slowly burned it away. She didn't dare ask if he meant what she hoped he did.

When he spoke, his words were like balm to a burn. "You could try summoning on me, Sandis. Bring Ireth here. If it works, it might allow you to connect to the ethereal plane without as much practice."

For a moment, she couldn't speak.

Her throat swelled. Her pulse danced up and down her neck. Her limbs tingled like her arm had after the stranger had struck her shoulder. Nearly a minute passed before she worked up enough spit to swallow.

"I . . ." Her voice was quiet as falling snow. "I don't want to hurt you, Bastien." He dangled a carrot in front of her—a juicy, golden, heavenly carrot—but Sandis knew firsthand how utterly painful it was to be possessed. Like every fiber of your body was lit on fire and pulled apart or doused in flesh-eating acid.

He smiled. "I don't mind."

"That's a lie."

He laughed. "Maybe a small one. But, Sandis." He crawled closer and took her hand. "You rescued me. You're my friend. You're nicer than others have been. And what you say about Ireth . . . I'm so curious. It only hurts for a moment."

A moment that scars you forever. Her fingers trembled. "Bastien—"

"It will make me a little hoarse."

Sandis blinked, not understanding what he . . . oh. She rolled her eyes. "It will make you a *big* horse."

Bastien grinned, but let it fade. "Do you *want* to?"

She frowned.

He waited.

Hesitant, Sandis nodded. She wanted to grab his collar and scream, *Yes, yes! I want to so badly! I'll do anything! Let me see him!* But her more reasonable side said, "It might not work."

"Then you have nothing to worry about."

Standing, Sandis spun and glanced at the windows. "Here?" Rone had asked them not to leave the flat, and indeed, it was probably the safest place for the transformation. If it worked—*if* it worked—Bastien would be unconscious for hours afterward, and she didn't think she'd be able to carry him very far.

"I guess." Bastien looked at the ceiling. "There's enough space. He shouldn't light anything on fire unless you tell him to, right?"

Sandis bit her lip. Moved to the window near the door and adjusted the curtains, making sure no light passed through them. Bastien followed her lead, checking all the other windows.

Bastien moved into the kitchen and emerged with a knife. Returning to Sandis, he held it between them. Only then did Sandis realize what he intended.

Of course. She didn't need his blood to *summon* a numen, but to control it. Kazen had used a tube and a hollow needle to transfer her blood into his body, which was undoubtedly more efficient, but she and Bastien didn't have anything like that. Ireth might not *need* to be controlled, and yet . . . it was a risk neither of them could take.

"Pick a body part," Bastien said.

"Um." She held out her right hand.

Bastien snorted. "You want that hand disabled for the next couple days?"

She swallowed. "How much does it take?"

"Not a lot, I don't think." He considered. "Not for just one summoning." He handed her the hilt of the knife.

Pushing it back, she said, "I'd rather you do it."

He didn't press the request, merely pushed up her sleeve so her forearm was exposed, then did the same for himself. He grimaced, hesitating. Perhaps he didn't handle blood well, but before Sandis could recant her request, the knifepoint dug into the top of her forearm. She winced, but in truth, it didn't hurt that much. A strange sort of eagerness pulsed through her veins, drawing her attention away from pain.

Bastien made a similar shallow cut on his own arm, then awkwardly twisted to press the cuts together, his arm on top.

Sandis searched his eyes for the stifled fear so often hiding there. "Are you *sure*, Bastien?"

His pale irises flicked to hers. The fear was there, but faint. "Do you want me to change my mind?"

She shook her head. He held their arms together a little longer before pulling back. They had some bandages left over from Rone's earlier injuries, but the cuts weren't bleeding terribly—Bastien hadn't made them deep. Vessels worked better the fewer scars they had. Oddly enough, the deep scars trailing the length of their spines didn't count.

Stepping back, Bastien guided her into the front room, where there was the most space. He pulled off his shirt—he wasn't trim like Rone and Dar, or thin and wide like Rist. He was stout, with extra flesh over his chest and waistline. Despite his years of captivity, he had never wanted for food. His freckles began to fade at the base of his neck and floated like snow to his shoulder blades before disappearing entirely. His golden script, branded in large, looping Noscon letters down his back, was an exact replica of her own. Though the gold leaf charred into his skin was hardly natural, it seemed to flow with his flesh as if it had always been there. He pushed his braid back, and the strawberry-blond hair covered two-thirds of it.

He hesitated, wringing his shirt—Rone's shirt—in his hands. "What should I do with my pants? I'll, uh, ruin them."

Sandis bit her lip, considering. If this had been someone else—Rone, for instance—it would have been more awkward. But Bastien was a vessel. He was probably used to being stripped before a summoning to preserve his clothing, something Kazen had often made her do, too. And while Bastien had become a fast friend and desperately needed a confidant, he didn't make her nervous the way Rone did—had—in similar predicaments.

Sandis moved to Rone's mother's room and retrieved a blanket. She handed it to Bastien, who tied it under his ribs. A moment later, he kicked his slacks and undergarments onto the sofa. Then, a wry smile pushing through a countenance that had begun to lose its courage, he bowed to her like she was some sort of politician—presenting his forehead. "Go ahead. Hurry, if you would. Tell me everything when I wake up."

Sandis stared at his hairline, where the ginger locks met his freckled forehead.

"Thank you," she whispered, and she pressed her hand to his forehead, offering a prayer to the Celestial that this would work. She needed this like she needed air.

She pictured Ireth in her mind. Or rather, imagined *him*, since she'd never beheld him with her own eyes. She whispered, *"Vre en nestu a carnath. Ii mem entre I amar. Vre en nestu a carnath. Ireth epsi gradenid."*

A strange energy struck the center of her head and flowed down her arm and out of the hand touching Bastien's forehead. A bright flash burned her eyes.

Sandis wrenched back and turned away, blinking tears from her vision. Shadows swirled before her, dancing beneath her feet and across the walls.

Heat tickled her skin, followed by the *shush* of blown breath.

Raising her head, Sandis looked back and forgot herself.

He stood before her in the flesh, bright and unyielding and so much *more* than she'd pictured. His ears brushed the ceiling. His eyes were night without stars, his fur—skin?—like polished graphite. Near-white light encircled his breast like heavenly feathers. Red and orange fire brushed his long face and neck, broken only by magnificent and deadly horns—four altogether. Two pointed up, two pointed forward.

Staring up at him, she felt so small and insignificant. It took all she had to stay standing. Something ballooned inside her, threatening to snap her ribs and split her skin. Not in a painful way, but a very . . . reverent one.

It finally pushed against her throat hard enough to move her voice into her mouth. "I-Ireth?"

The numen lowered his head and hoofed the ground before reaching its muzzle toward her.

Sandis placed shaking hands on either side of it. Heat almost too intense for touch raced through her arms and into her shoulders, settling in her chest with such familiarity it brought tears to her eyes.

Words abandoned her. *I missed you. I'm sorry. I failed. What can I do?* But those phrases all seemed too human, too pathetic. Tears streamed down her cheeks, and Ireth dulled his fire and pressed his large nose against her breast.

Weeping, Sandis hugged his muzzle to her and cried against his forehead.

Ireth mewed softly back.

Chapter 14

Despite the overcast sky, Kazen wore his hat pulled low over his eyes. The uneven cobblestones underfoot did nothing to hinder his stride. Towering buildings stood like sleeping sentinels to either side of him, surveying the crowds at their feet. The people skittered like insects, buzzed like insects, toppled over one another like mindless, pathetic insects.

Soon, very soon, Kazen would wake them from their buggish stupor. All he needed was a little more searching, planning, doing. He would get what he wanted, one way or another.

Kazen lifted his head at a dull flash at the edge of his vision. A young woman in a janitorial uniform tried pushing her way against the flow of foot traffic. The aura was slight and could only be seen by those trained to notice them. An open spirit, one that reached beyond the body and wasn't trodden down by the pain of existence. There were so few of those in this city. Kazen's eyes followed her, his mind calculating.

Too old. Not yet thirty, no, but more likely than not she'd had children. Birthing damaged a body beyond repair. Even if he were wrong, she'd only hold a three at best.

But he wouldn't find what he needed on these streets.

He paused in the middle of an intersection, peering up at the pollution-choked sun.

Oh yes. He should start there. Yes . . . that would do nicely.

Pulling his hat down farther, he turned left, never once brushing against the throng.

Chapter 15

Rone moved swiftly over the rooftops of Dresberg—too swiftly for a man whose amarinth had not yet reset. His toe had slid on the last jump, and he'd barely made the one four leaps earlier. He hadn't given himself time to judge the distance properly, and he wasn't in the part of town where he'd previously hidden boards and rope for easier travel.

He was sidetracked, his thoughts getting away from him.

Dakis had been an aggravating dead end. If any of his contacts knew where Kazen had fled to, it would be Jurris Hadmar. The man had worked in Straight Ace's mob in his youth and had hired Engel on two occasions—once to steal jewelry from one merchant cart and plant it in another and once to deliver a man to them.

Rone never knew what became of either of those jobs, those people. He hadn't felt bad about the work then. But it itched now. He was getting soft.

But even back then, Hadmar had bothered him. He was a sketchy guy with too much underneath the skin, not unlike Kazen. He kept things simple, didn't ask questions, and paid on time, but he wasn't the sort of person you wanted to double-cross.

He also wasn't the sort of person Rone wanted to approach for a favor. But with this new hire of Kazen's—Rone winced, remembering the sound his leg had made when it snapped—Rone was on edge. They all were. He wanted to end it.

He wanted to stop pretending he didn't hear Sandis whimpering whenever she slept.

But Hadmar wasn't his quarry today.

He finally stopped atop a factory where two men in work uniforms were smoking cigarettes. An industrial pipe billowing smoke hid him from view. Not a great place for a break, considering the air quality, but Rone needed to rest his legs before jumping again, or he'd be self-made roadkill on the cobblestones six stories below. Grabbing his foot, he stretched out one thigh, then the other. Wiped sweat from his forehead.

He shouldn't care this much. God's tower, he shouldn't care this much. She would never forgive him. He should turn around right now, pack his bags, grab his emigration papers, and go. His mother was waiting for him. Maybe he could even beat his letter, get there first. He had six days left. Still enough time.

The image of his mother in her small Godobian cottage entered his mind. Her hair was neatly pinned back, as she usually wore it, and she held his letter in her hands, reading it with a slight frown on her thin lips. Then the door would burst open, and he'd shout something stupid like, "Honey, I'm home!" and then she'd yell at him and hug him, and they'd do dull, safe, homey things until it was time to turn in. Day after day, year after year.

It wasn't the worst future he could imagine.

Despite the smoke, the smell of Sandis clung to his nostrils. And Sandis aside, he was partly responsible for this mess. For the ghosts she jumped at, too. He couldn't walk away. Not yet.

He rubbed his eyes and turned away from the chimney. Rather than make the jump to the next building, he searched for the stairwell the smokers must have used to get up here. He found it and, not bothering to conceal himself, took it down into the factory. A cotton factory. Sandis's father had worked at a cotton factory, hadn't he?

Why did he remember that?

He took the stairs down to street level. The air here felt cooler. He slipped off his jacket. Walked with his head down, his eyes searching. No sign of grafters, but that didn't shock him. No sign of the man who had thrown Sandis over his shoulder like she was a sack of flour.

The assailant had been ready to leave with her. Why? The thought made Rone's blood boil.

Next time he'd rip the bastard's head right off his shoulders. Maybe then Sandis would forgive him.

More likely she'd be offended by all the blood.

Rone turned down a side street out of habit. It had been a few years since he'd cleaned these gutters, but his feet knew where to go, even if his head was in an entirely different space. He crossed the road to a different street, this time looking over his shoulder as he went. Not searching for anyone specifically, but making sure he hadn't drawn any attention to himself. He rounded a block twice just to make sure, then, because he was such a *good person*, he approached the flat from the front instead of from the brick wall in the back.

He pounded his fist on the door four times. Waited. Pounded three more.

The second the latch gave, Rone pushed his way inside.

He nearly got fingernails in his eyes in exchange for his bold entrance, but Arnae Kurtz, his old seugrat master, had enough control to stop before striking. Shutting and bolting the door, he said, "You are the densest man in my acquaintance, Rone Comf. I told you not to come back here. You endanger—"

"A man who knows seugrat attacked me yesterday," Rone interrupted, pausing in the middle of the sitting room. He thought he heard a sound behind the wall in Kurtz's small kitchen, where his secret room lay, but he didn't pay it any heed. Whatever refugee had taken up with him wasn't Rone's business. "Tall." He held his hand a few inches above his own head. "Skinny. Weirdly pale. Dark hair, dark eyes."

Kurtz folded his arms across his broad chest. "Dark hair and dark eyes? In Kolingrad? That certainly narrows it down."

Rone glowered. "The sarcasm is not appreciated."

"Neither is your attracting attention to my flat."

"I wasn't followed. And the grafters have been dealt with." More or less.

Kurtz raised an eyebrow. "Go on."

"Narrow face. Sharp shoulders and elbows." Despite his healing, Rone could still feel all the bruises those sharp joints had pounded into his skin and muscle. The cracking of his knee still echoed . . .

Shaking his head, Rone drew on his memory for more details. "Quiet. Didn't speak at all. *Really* dark eyes. Black as tar." He sighed and almost sat in the closest chair, then turned at the last minute, changing his mind. "He found the flat where Sandis and I were staying, along with one of her friends. A vessel friend."

Kurtz's arms fell from his chest. "Another?"

He dismissed the inquiry with a brusque wave of his hand. "This guy kicked my ass. *Hard.*" Rone took a deep breath. If Sandis hadn't shot him . . .

Kurtz frowned. "Then how . . . oh yes. I remember."

Rone merely nodded, knowing Kurtz referred to his amarinth. "Does he sound familiar?"

Kurtz rubbed his short gray beard and paced the width of the room before settling on the sofa near the front door. "He's not anyone I trained. How old?"

"Thirties."

Kurtz shook his head, and the movement somehow made exhaustion swallow Rone whole. He finally dropped into that chair.

"I am not the only master of seugrat in Dresberg, though I admit it's a dying art." Kurtz clasped his hands over his knees. "I'm sorry, but the man doesn't sound familiar." He paused. "That good, eh?"

He'd suspected as much. Kurtz was choosy with whom he taught. Surely this assailant wouldn't have passed the test.

Kazen knew seugrat. And he'd be more than happy to have a stone-faced maniac under his tutelage. Yet Rone had a hard time believing Kazen would have waited this long to use such an impressive asset. That pale-faced stranger had been far more competent than any of the grafters who'd been sent after them. Perhaps the guy had merely been on a different job and unavailable.

"I thought I was dead," Rone confessed. "I *honestly* thought I was dead."

A trickle of the fear he'd felt right before the man shattered his knee—the moment Rone knew he'd left himself open—traced down his spine like the finger of a corpse. He shut his eyes for a moment and planted his elbows on his knees. When the sensation faded, he said, "He wanted her."

A brief pause. "Sandis?"

Rone nodded. "He was trying to take her away. Apparently, he went for Bastien, too—the other vessel. I'm betting he switched because she was lighter."

Silence glistened between them. Kurtz shifted on the sofa, drawing Rone's attention to him.

He looked disturbed. His wrinkles deepened; his bottom lip curved into a deep frown. "I wonder."

Rone straightened. "Wonder what?"

"Both vessels? Hmm."

Standing from his chair, Rone snapped, "Wonder *what*, old man?"

Kurtz didn't react to the jab. He stared ahead in thought. "Have you heard of remedial gold?"

Drawing his brows together, Rone answered, "No." But his memories flashed back to Sherig. Hadn't she used those words?

"Old wives' tale, or so I thought. A special kind of gold sold on the dark market for far more than the worth of the metal. Believed to have medicinal properties. What, I'm not sure."

"And what does this have to do with Sandis?"

"It has everything to do with Sandis." His master's dark eyes finally lifted. "Remedial gold is stripped off the backs of vessels."

Rone's stomach clenched. He took a step back. Swallowed. "The . . . brands?"

Kurtz nodded. "I don't know more than that, so don't ask. This is something I heard from a cleric a long time ago." He rubbed his beard again. "It's a thought. If you've truly eliminated the grafters as a threat, then that might be what motivates your man, especially if he wasn't picky about which vessel he took. A man could live comfortably for the rest of his life off a single flayed vessel."

Flayed.

Rone stared wide eyed at Kurtz and pressed a knuckle to his lips to keep from retching as his mind pictured too vividly what the process might look like.

Could Kurtz be on the mark? Could that be this bastard's purpose?

It wouldn't matter, then, if Sandis cut the brands or not. Gold was gold. The image of her lifeless body lying on some table, the skin on her back missing—

Rone swallowed bile. "I'll keep that in mind." He started for the door. Paused. "Do you know anyone else in the city who teaches seugrat? Who might be able to identify this guy?"

Kurtz stood and shook his head. "I'm afraid the only one I'm acquainted with went to Gerech some time ago. I doubt he's still there."

Rone set his shoulders. "Thank you."

"Thank me by not sending me to the same place, hm? I love you like a nephew—a *nephew*, mind you, not a son—but so long as you're involved in the things you're involved with, you can't keep coming to my door. I won't be so hospitable if you do it again."

Rone extended his hand, and Kurtz took it. An unspoken promise, and silent thanks.

Wrenching open the door, Rone swept back onto the street, keeping his head down until he reached the main thoroughfare, his stomach still unsettled.

Remedial gold. The idea haunted him as he trekked back through the city. Not on rooftops this time, but following the uneven lines of the cobblestones, occasionally moving over for a carriage or wagon. The idea that people actually *bought* it . . . Surely they couldn't know where it came from. But if they didn't, why would it sell at so high a price? And on the dark market, no less?

Sick bastards. As far as Rone knew, there was nothing special about the gold brands on Sandis's back outside of giving her the ability to be possessed. Were people so twisted? Did the Celestial's worshippers really spit on the occult, then turn around and wear it around their necks, their wrists? Could they pretend not to believe in the Noscon blasphemies, only to spend their coin on gold stripped from the skin of vessels?

Rone pressed the heel of his palm into his stomach, worried he was going to be sick.

Wood planks—a temporary fence—forced the road to bend inward to accommodate construction where a building had just been torn down. Likely its replacement's walls would be so close to its neighbors not even a rat could squeeze between them. Everything in this godforsaken city was cramped and bloated, and it worsened by the year. Rone sneered as he moved around the fence.

A flare of black hair caught his eye.

It shouldn't have. Nearly everyone in Kolingrad had dark hair. But he paused at the sheer *blackness* of it, his heartbeat accelerating, the back of his mind screaming, *The mercenary.* The one who'd snapped his leg like a piece of chalk.

Cringing, Rone stepped back, ready to fight—knocking over a woman in the process—but it wasn't the seugrat-trained man at all, just a construction worker carrying a heavy beam on his shoulder, while another man held up its back end.

But Rone didn't move. He stared at the man, his black hair pulled back into a short tail. He was tall and lean. He looked . . . familiar.

A memory tugged at Rone's mind. Sandis running off in Kazen's lair. Rone pushing through the sea of mobsmen in hopes of finding her—a small group of people pushing right back, dressed neither like grafters nor Riggers. They'd worn beige shirts just like the one Sandis had worn upon their first meeting. She'd refused to take her jacket off because the shirt opened in the back, revealing her script.

Vessels. And Rone could have sworn one of them looked like that construction worker.

Rone tucked closer to the fence, letting the crowds in the street push past him. Someone cursed him out for getting in the way, but Rone ignored the comment and stared harder at the man with the beam. The worker stumbled a little—he was strong but inexperienced with the labor. *New.* Hoping for a better look, Rone pushed along the fence, squinting past it. The man was fully clothed—no chance of checking the skin on his back for golden brands. But if Rone could see his face, maybe . . .

The two men moved the beam down a slight slope. The man in question turned slightly, giving Rone a glimpse of a broad forehead and a narrow face, eyes a little lighter than Sandis's.

It was him. Rone was sure of it.

After checking for the foreman or police, Rone jumped the short fence and ventured onto the construction site, staying out of the way. He circled the area until he got close to that hill, then pressed against a small storage unit, probably full of nails, tools, and the like.

He waited.

About ten minutes passed before both construction workers came back up, perhaps to retrieve another beam. Rone's gaze homed in on the black-haired man. He looked to be a couple of years younger than himself and had a stoic cast to his expression. Granted, Rone would be pretty emotionless, too, if he had to spend his days working construction.

As the two men neared, Rone coughed and muttered, "Kazen."

He'd hit the mark. The dark-haired man stiffened and looked around, while his companion continued on without him.

Rone stepped forward, putting himself in plain sight. He raised his hands. "I'm not a grafter. I'm friends with Sandis," he said, and the black-haired man's eyes narrowed. What were their names again? He knew Alys—she'd tried to kill him multiple times in her numen form. And . . . Heath. No, he was the dead one. Rist?

The vessel glanced at his fellow worker's retreating back before stepping behind the storage unit beside Rone. "Who are you?" he asked, his words quick and hard. He puffed out his chest, trying to look intimidating—and in all honesty, he was. In looks, anyway. But knowing what cloistered lives vessels led, Rone suspected this guy likely didn't have much clout when it came to fighting. "What do you want?" the man pressed.

"Rist, right?" Rone tried.

The man stepped back, surprised, but said, "My name is Dar."

Dar. If Rist was the turtle crab, then Dar was . . . Rone hid a shudder. That wolfy thing that had been there the day he'd turned in Sandis. Huge, snarling, long clawed.

Rone checked their surroundings before speaking. "Like I said, I'm a friend of Sandis's. She's looking for you guys."

Dar softened a fraction. A very small, barely noticeable fraction. "She freed us. But Kazen—"

"Kazen is the reason she's looking for you. She wants to gather you, act as summoner." Rone still didn't like Sandis blatantly putting herself in harm's way, but if Sandis wanted to try it, and Dar was right in front of him . . . he might as well help. "She thinks you could take a stand—"

Dar held up a hand, stopping him. "It doesn't matter."

Nearly whispering, Rone added, "There's a numen named Kolosos—"

"It *doesn't matter*," Dar insisted. He snorted. "Summoner. If any of us could manage it, she could. But I'm useless to her. I cut my script the moment I got out of that place."

Rone paused a moment, then slowly, mechanically, nodded. Of course he had. Perhaps that was the reason for the earlier falter—an incision not yet healed. From what Rone understood, it didn't have to be particularly large to do the job, but it also never hurt to be thorough. It's what Rone would have done—made himself useless to Kazen. Made it so he couldn't be used that way ever again.

It's what he wished Sandis would do, even if it only saved her from *one* of the men trying so desperately to hurt her.

Just as Rone had hurt her.

"We split up, but my guess is the others have done the same." Dar's eyes bolted to the right, checking for listeners. "They'd be stupid not to." He rubbed sweat from his forehead. "I should move on. If they fire me, I'm a dead man. Don't look for me again."

And with that, Dar stepped away from the storage unit and jogged toward the temporary fence, where his companion stood beside a pile of wooden beams. They were too far for Rone to hear what they said, but it didn't matter. Dar's script was cut. He was useless as a vessel, though the golden brands printed into his back would forever mark his enslavement.

Pushing off the storage unit, Rone headed toward the construction, then climbed over another fence toward a sad-looking building of flats. He needed to get back.

When he told Sandis the news, he hoped she wouldn't blame the messenger.

Chapter 16

Sandis sat on the floor of Rone's mother's flat, legs tucked under her. A single candle burned against the growing darkness outside; she didn't want to waste resources by lighting more. She also didn't want to disrupt the strange reverence that drifted through the room—or risk that someone outside the curtained windows might catch a glimpse of the flames burning on the other side of the glass.

She and Ireth had not been able to communicate in words; he couldn't speak, and Sandis could only assume he understood her.

Regardless, they had been together once again, and though they were not bound, Sandis had never felt closer to her numen. She'd stayed with Ireth a long while, murmuring her apologies and stroking his leathery nose. Ireth had let her tears sizzle against his dark skin and pressed warmth into the coldest recesses of her soul.

Bastien now lay supine on the floor, the blanket covering him from chin to toe. It was singed on one edge. The Godobian would likely be unconscious until morning. Sandis smoothed loose tendrils of hair from his face as she watched his chest rise and fall.

Oh, how she envied the name tattooed into the base of his neck, and yet gratitude filled her to bursting. How could she ever repay him? How could he have let her, practically a stranger, elicit such pain from his body, just so she could see a numen she had a completely bizarre attachment to?

The lock in the door clicked. A coil of relief rose in Sandis's chest when Rone stepped inside. He'd been gone awhile. Despite the joy she'd taken in her meeting with Ireth, worry had been steadily building in her chest, more each hour, almost to the point of pain.

Rone's brow was tight, his movements distracted. Something was bothering him. But the expression dropped from his face the moment he turned and saw her beside Bastien. His eyes rounded, almost child-like, his forehead creased, his breathing hitched, his shoulders drooped.

Why?

Sandis pulled her fingers from Bastien's hair. "What happened?"

His umber eyes shifted from Sandis to Bastien. "I could ask you the same thing."

Licking her lips, Sandis stood and settled herself on the edge of the sofa. "I summoned."

Rone's eyes narrowed.

She smiled. She'd *summoned*. "He let me. I . . . I met Ireth."

A faint whistle passed Rone's lips. He walked into the small sitting room and sat on the sofa's armrest, close to her. "I'm shocked the flat isn't burned to a crisp."

"A numen can control its abilities."

"Or you can, anyway." He nodded to the scabbed-over cut on her arm.

Placing a hand over the shallow wound, Sandis nodded. "He was beautiful, Rone."

Rone eyed Bastien. "He's terrifying."

She blinked. "When did you . . . ?" *Oh.* The weight in her chest doubled. After she'd been traded back to Kazen, the summoner had invoked Ireth to control her. Rone must have seen the numen then. Shortly before Ireth was taken away.

They were quiet for a long moment. Sandis watched the candlelight dance across the wall behind it.

"Do you know what remedial gold is?"

Sandis straightened. "No. Why? What is it?"

Rone set his jaw. Was this what was bothering him? "I visited Kurtz."

Shivers ran down Sandis's legs. "You can't, Rone. He told us not to."

Rone rolled his eyes. "I asked him about the man who tried to nab you."

"The stranger." It was as suitable a nickname as any.

"The stranger. Sure." He rubbed the scruff lining his jaw. "Supposedly remedial gold is taken from vessels' brands and sold on the dark market. Some believe it has mystical health benefits and other garbage. Sound familiar?"

Sandis felt the blood leach from her skin.

They'd never found Alys.

No. Kazen took such good care of his vessels. Alys hadn't been severely injured. Her arm easily could have healed. And Kazen had possessed the amarinth! It would have been easy to . . . to . . .

"Sandis?"

Her thoughts turned to smoke. "N-No. I haven't heard of it."

She reached back until her fingers brushed the first brand in her extensive script. Silence layered itself like sand around them, suffocating, until Rone broke it with a sigh and said, "I also found Dar."

Whipping her hand from her back, Sandis turned to him, the hollowness in her bones evaporating into moths that fluttered under her skin. "Really? Where?" And why had Rone come back alone?

She peered toward the window, as if her fellow vessel might be standing on the other side of the pane. She wasn't particularly close to Dar—of all the vessels, he'd been the most distant. He was always so silent, so stoic, so *unfeeling*. He'd often made Sandis uncomfortable with his mere presence.

But that didn't matter now. He was free, and Rone had *found* him.

She asked again, "Where is he?"

"Working construction in District Three, close to the smoke ring," he answered. Not one smidgeon of her excitement was mirrored in his words or countenance. "He's broken his script, Sandis."

Sandis deflated like pressed bellows. "Oh." Of course . . . Dar had always hated being a vessel, and he didn't know Drang the way Sandis knew Ireth. Of course he'd break his script.

"Friendly fellow," Rone quipped.

Sandis lowered herself back to the sofa. "It's okay. We'll find the others. We can still—"

"The others have probably cut their scripts, too."

She shook her head. "We don't know that."

"Why *wouldn't* they?" he said with a groan. "Even Dar said as much. That they'd be stupid not to."

Her gaze flashed to him, her eyelids hot. "Am *I* stupid, then?"

"God's tower, Sandis. His words, not mine. But he has a point. I get it. Ireth." He gestured to Bastien. "But Ireth is *gone.*"

Because of you, she thought, but held her tongue.

"And keeping your script intact will only encourage Kazen to continue hunting you."

Sandis clamped her fingers tighter until her knuckles whitened. "They might not have broken theirs. Not yet." But Kaili and Rist . . . without Kazen's rules . . . the way they *looked* at each other. A numen had to be summoned into a virginal body. Even if their scripts were unharmed . . .

But there was still Alys. They didn't *know* anything. Couldn't make assumptions. She might be out there somewhere, scared and starving in the city, waiting for Sandis to find her . . .

"I have to try." She released the pressure in her fingers, letting the blood return to their joints.

"Black ashes, you are stubborn." Rone stood and ran a hand back through his hair, then growled when a finger snagged on a knot. "Finding Dar was pure *luck.* How on earth are you going to find the others? They don't have a summoner; you can't just stroll around the city, waiting to sense a numen."

"No, but I—" She paused. Considered. *Grinned.*

Jumping up from the sofa, she nearly embraced Rone, then stopped herself and awkwardly backed away. Rone gave her that childlike look again . . . mixed with confusion.

"*They* can sense a numen, Rone," she explained, bouncing on her toes.

Rone stared at her for a few seconds before his countenance slackened. "No, Sandis. Please no."

But she nodded and smiled. "I can stroll around the city and find them. Or better yet, they'll find *me*."

She need only wait until Bastien woke up. Ireth would never do for the plan—he was too large, too bright. They needed a smaller numen, and Sandis knew just the one. But she'd need Bastien to help her.

She couldn't summon a new numen into him—once a vessel was bound, the bound numen was the only creature that could inhabit the person's body. But Bastien had done all the summoner meditations alongside her, and possibly with his old master, too. He could summon the numen into *her*.

Kneeling beside Bastien, Sandis listened to the sounds of his slumber, hoping its rhythm would change and he'd wake up. It didn't, but Sandis held on to hope.

"Give me one day, Sandis."

Confused, Sandis turned to him. "For what?"

Rone allowed himself a deep breath before answering, "I have one more person I can ask. One more . . . means of getting information. Just give me tomorrow."

She slowly rose to her feet. "How?" A cold feeling creeped into her chest, like someone pressed a ramrod between her breasts.

"Jurris Hadmar," he said. "A contact of mine. I'll go just before dawn. I doubt he's still in the same place, but I can figure out where he went. He might know where Kazen snuck off to."

"You don't sound sure."

He straightened then, like he recognized the slump of his shoulders and hunch to his back and meant to hide them away. "I am sure. I just . . ."

Sandis frowned. "You're not telling me something."

"Doesn't matter." He stood, stretched. "But I'm going alone. Not just to protect you, and him"—he nodded toward Bastien—"but because if I go anywhere near Hadmar with a vessel, he'll kill me without question."

That ramrod began to pierce her skin, despite its metaphorically blunt end. She took a step toward him. "Rone, don't. I can find the vessels, and we'll—"

"You'll what?" he interrupted. "Sit here until Kazen finds you? Until the stranger does?" He moved toward her and placed his too-warm hands on her shoulders. Shivers of heat and ice zapped through her skin at the contact. Leveling his face with hers, Rone murmured, "I'm going to fix this, Sandis. One way or another, I'm going to fix this."

And as she felt a hot, unearthly claw stroke the back of her neck, Sandis found herself desperately hoping he could.

Rone stifled a cough as he plowed his way through the listless crowds in the smoke ring. Between the haze overhead and the shadows draping the buildings surrounding him, the streets looked gray and dreary. He passed a manhole, and the ripe smells of waste fingered his nostrils. He bumped into a man in order to avoid knocking over two kids with dirt-streaked faces. His unfelt apology was muffled against his sleeve as he fruitlessly tried to filter the dirty air entering his lungs.

His destination was ahead. He couldn't see it from the main road, so he took a tight path between two factories and slipped behind a third, getting yelled at by a security guard with a half-finished jug of ale in his hand. It had been some time since Rone passed by this way, and it hadn't been in daylight.

If this was a dead end, so be it. They'd move on with Sandis's plan. But Rone hated not knowing. He hated being useless.

The warehouse he sought looked like a squished sandwich left out in the gutter for a couple of days. Its concrete walls were a sickly sort of gray, and its rows of windows were all boarded up, some broken. It was an out-of-the-way place, one that could be difficult to sneak into.

Rone rounded his way to the back door and pulled out his lock-picks. It took a few tries to get the pins where he wanted them. The door opened about an inch before hitting a bar. Taking the knife from his boot, Rone stuck the blade under the bar and, grabbing the hilt with both hands, managed to lift the thing.

He tried to slip in quickly enough to grab the bar before it hit the ground, but didn't make it. He winced as the sound echoed up the interior stairwell. Sheathing his knife, Rone continued on carefully, slipping one hand into his jacket pocket so he could cradle the amarinth.

It gave him little comfort. His pulse pounded in his neck.

He tried to move as nonthreateningly as he could. He reached another door, picked it, and opened it carefully. Released his amarinth, regrettably, so he could hold out both empty hands to indicate he was harmless. The place seemed abandoned, but he needed to be sure.

He found a third door, unlocked. Beyond that was the body of the warehouse, with metal shelves stacked up to the ceiling. The lighting was spotty and gray where it peeked around the boards on the windows. Rone combed his memory for details of his first job with Hadmar—his second hadn't involved him coming here. It looked different now, didn't it? It had seemed more comfortable before.

He passed the first set of shelves. Peered down a dusty aisle. Cursed. They had moved on—

Footsteps behind him. Rone spun just in time for a club to hit the side of his head.

Pain radiated across his skull and down his neck as he fell to the hard, filthy floor, catching himself on an elbow. A sticky trickle ran down the side of his ear. Despite his disorientation, he could feel his assailant moving for another blow—

"Hadmar," he rasped, holding up an arm to block even as the room spun. "I'm looking for Hadmar."

Another blow didn't come, thank the heavens, but his attacker grabbed the front of his shirt and hauled him upward. Kolin man, similar in size and build to Rone. "Hadmar moved," he spat, his breath smelling like onion. A second set of footsteps announced another man. Rone wanted to say, *Then why are you guarding this place?* But he sensed it would be best not to challenge him.

"I need an exchange of information," Rone said, meeting the man's eyes, forcing his body to remain limp, weak. He didn't think he had anything Hadmar needed or wanted to know, but he had to try. "Hadmar's hired me before."

"But he didn't hire you this time," snapped Onion.

The man behind Rone said, "What should we do with him?"

"Take me to Hadmar. He'll want to see me," Rone tried. "He knows me. Engel Verlad. Our business has been good."

Onion snarled. Scowled at his companion. Something unspoken passed between them. Onion released his collar at the same moment the unseen lackey tugged fabric around Rone's eyes, blinding him. He followed it up with a belt cinched too tight. The pressure made Rone's headache skyrocket, but on the plus side, maybe it would staunch the bleeding.

The unseen man helped him up.

Onion made sure to land a solid punch to Rone's gut before they walked him away.

Rone knew he was in a basement before they took off the blindfold. A very deep basement. He'd tripped over dozens of stairs, and not one of them had led up.

His captors shoved him into a chair that creaked with his weight, then bound his wrists behind him with rope. Tied his ankles. Searched his person. Rone went rigid when he felt them pull the amarinth out of his pocket, but they snickered to each other and shoved it back in.

"How's a girl supposta wear dat, mm?" asked a new voice. "Dis, onda other hand," and he removed the knife from Rone's boot, letting it kiss his chin before hiding it away.

This had been a bad idea. Rone focused on his breathing. On remaining relaxed. He had no qualms with Hadmar. His men had no reason to harm him.

When they finally unbound his eyes, Rone winced, both at the bright kerosene lights and at the blood rushing to his crown. The world around him was blurry for a full minute as Rone tried to blink himself to clarity.

A man in an off-white suit stood before him, well fed with an unfashionable mustache. His salt-and-pepper hair was cut close and thoroughly oiled.

Hadmar.

"Well! It *is* you," the man said, the faintest trace of a southern accent on his tongue. Rone knew the man had been in Dresberg a long time, but perhaps he kept the lilt for nostalgia's sake. Hadmar stepped closer until he was almost in kicking distance, were Rone's feet not restrained. "Engel Verlad. I haven't seen you in a good while." His eyes narrowed. "I have reasons for that."

"I've never crossed you," Rone said, meeting his eyes.

He offered a cheeky smile and shook his head. "No, you're a good dog. But I work around my own schedule, not yours. I don't like snoops."

"In my defense, the warehouse was abandoned."

"Obviously it was not." Hadmar winked. He waved a hand, and Onion brought him a chair. He sat. "I don't like beggars, boy."

"I'm not here to earn money. I need information. Your network is good, Hadmar." Might as well throw a compliment in there. "I knew you'd have accurate accounts."

Hadmar tilted his head to one side. "You've upset me, Verlad. Interrupted my work. But I always was weak to my own curiosity. Exactly what is it you've so stupidly come here for?"

Dragged here, Rone amended, but the words didn't reach his lips. "I need to know the location of a man named Kazen."

Hadmar straightened. Grinned. "A grafter?" So he'd heard of him. "What does a mercenary like yourself want with a grafter? I don't know how well he'll pay you."

Rone didn't mention he'd already been paid. A lot of money that didn't begin to meet the price he'd paid. "It's not business. Not mutual business, at least."

Hadmar studied Rone for a long moment. Long enough for his underarms and spine to sweat.

"You know me, Verlad." Hadmar leaned back in his chair, propping one arm on it. "Grafters, they're like whiny children. Messy and unfocused. I don't call on them. But if a grafter would go anywhere, it would be the dark market."

Rone tried to adjust, to relieve the strain on his bound shoulders, but found he couldn't. "It's my understanding the dark market is more a state of mind." A crook here and a scumbag there, if you know where to look.

Hadmar laughed. "A state of mind. That is good." He waved away someone behind Rone, which made Rone wonder what the lackey was about to do. "You are right, it's sprinkled throughout this wonderful place. But some things aren't easily stowed away in drawers and behind curtains. There's a nice carve out from the Noscon ruins beneath us.

District One, not far from the southeast canal. I can tell you how to get there, but not for free."

Rone took the bits of information and pinned them on the map of the city conjured in his head. Not enough for him to get a clear picture. And if he passed on the haggling, Hadmar wouldn't be happy. He had to play along. It was too late to do otherwise.

"What's your price?" he asked.

"I'm expanding my portfolio, young man." Hadmar shrugged, casual, which put Rone on edge. It was dramatics, a ploy to minimize something big. "That dirty little hovel has some merchandise I can use, and I'd rather not make the expense, see?"

So he wanted Rone to steal something. Fine. "What?"

"Remedial gold. You know what it is?"

His spine stiffened, making the binds on his wrists dig into his hands. He nodded.

"Bring me some. If not, I'll find you and wear your skin for a coat, hm?" Hadmar grinned. "You know I'm good for it."

"Of course." His voice, thankfully, came out smooth.

Hadmar's gaze went to someone else. "I'll give you a drop-off location. Don't keep me waiting." He nodded, and one of his men moved out of the light. "I expect you'll move quickly? You always were efficient."

Rone nodded. A moment later, the binds on his hands were cut, letting the blood run back into his fingers. A man handed him his boot knife hilt first. Rone accepted it and cut the binds on his feet. Checked for his amarinth. It was safe.

Onion approached with a paper with a vague map on it, but Rone knew the place.

Remedial gold. Rone knew nothing about this dark market cave. What if he couldn't steal it? What if Kazen drew him away before he could even find it?

And if Sandis knew . . . that wouldn't go over well.

Better she not know this part.

Rone crumpled the instruction in his hand. "Much obliged."

Hadmar folded his arms, smug. "As you should be. Take him out."

This time, instead of a blindfold, it was a bag.

But the punch still landed in the same sore place.

Sandis worked beside Bastien on the floor in Rone's mother's bedroom, struggling to tamp down her unease and calm her mind. Her meditation would be fruitless, otherwise. She had summoned Ireth, yes, but Ireth was different from other numina. Different with her, at least. Bastien had even remarked that he'd felt a distinct *pull* toward her during the summoning. Like the ethereal beast had been eager to join her.

That had made Sandis remarkably happy.

But if she were to summon other numina into other vessels, she needed to attune herself the way Kazen had. He'd often kept his lair quiet for the purposes of meditation; Sandis had seen his calm, eerie fury unleashed on men who spoke too loudly when he wanted to concentrate.

That was why the grafters used brain dust instead of alcohol. Alcohol makes a person unrestrained and boisterous. Brain dust just makes them foggy. Silent.

Focus. She had to accomplish this. It was her duty.

Red flames began to rim the darkness in her mind.

Sandis jolted, eyelids flitting open. The evening light looked so bright. It took her a moment to recognize her surroundings. Her breath moved too quickly in and out of her throat, drying it out. Bastien remained calm, a living statue.

Rubbing gooseflesh from her arms, Sandis hunched over and evened her breathing. How was she supposed to do this when nightmares kept creeping into her meditation? But she'd stopped it this time. Maybe these exercises of Bastien's would make her stronger against Kolosos, too.

Her gaze shifted back to the Godobian. How she wished she could feel Ireth's warm assurances right now. But she only had her own.

It can't hurt you. Kolosos isn't bound to you. Kolosos doesn't have a body. Kolosos doesn't exist in this realm.

Suppressing a shudder, Sandis straightened back into her meditating pose. *Inhale, exhale,* she scolded herself, closing her eyes again. She worked through the sequences Bastien had taught her, though her body felt stiffer this time. Slow, deep breaths, until her shoulders lightened. Then she broke the inhale into three pieces, the exhale into two.

Rone hadn't returned yet.

In, in, in, out, out. He's fine. In, in, in, out, out.

She didn't understand his plan, but he'd seemed so sure it'd take less than a day. Perhaps he'd needed to use the sewers, and they were slowing him down. But he'd only use the sewers if he were in danger . . .

In, in, in, out, out.

Maybe the stranger had found him. Maybe he was floating in the filthy water, facedown.

Stop it. Rone was fine. He was *fine.* He had the amarinth.

In, in, in, out, out. Concentrate.

Maybe he'd finally decided to leave. Maybe she'd driven him to it.

The next inhale turned ragged. She inhaled deeper, trying to smooth it out. So what if he had? He had no allegiance to Sandis, and she had none to him. Maybe the sewers could carry him right under the Fortitude Mountains, and he could reunite with his mother and live a peaceful life in Godobia, far away from her and her problems. That's all he'd ever wanted, wasn't it? Not Kolosos. Not Kazen.

Not Sandis.

"I came back for you."

Inhale, exhale. *Stop. Thinking. About. It.*

Celestial knew she wanted to trust him. She wanted to forget. To go back to the way things were before. They had been on the run, but by the end . . . she had been so happy. Sitting across from him at that restaurant, laying her head on his shoulder at night . . .

Squeezing her eyes hard until a headache bloomed behind them, she moved on to the third pattern of breathing. Listened to Bastien. He breathed like he was sleeping; she was breathing like she'd just climbed a flight of stairs.

Gritting her teeth, Sandis sucked in air, slow and long, and pushed it out quickly, in two parts. She absorbed the silence around her like a sponge, and for a moment there was only her breathing and Bastien's. She slowed her lungs to match his rhythm. Her head lightened, and she floated away to a strange plane between wakefulness and dreaming. A place where she could—

The front door opened and slammed shut.

Sandis snapped from her reverie and leapt to her feet, pushing through a wave of dizziness as she hurried from the bedroom to the hallway. Rone leaned against the front door, his clothes damp, rubbing the heels of his hands into his eyes.

Thank the Celestial, he was alive.

"Rone?" Sandis came closer, but paused as the rank smell of bad water assaulted her. He'd taken the sewers.

He pulled his hands away, looking tired yet frazzled. Lines etched his forehead, and weights tugged down his mouth. "I didn't want to be followed." He muttered a curse and shrugged out of his jacket, then yanked off his foul-smelling shirt, chucking both into the corner of the kitchen. He stomped to the sink and began working the pump there. Sandis stared, emotions warring for precedence. Relief that he was alive. Fear for what could have followed him, and why. Curiosity for what had taken him so long. And, stupidly, her body warmed at the sight of him, despite the smell. She and Rone had been through so many ordeals together, but they'd rarely resulted in him being half-naked, especially

161

in good lighting. No, *she* was usually the one who managed to burn off all her clothes.

It shouldn't have mattered. It wasn't like she'd never seen a shirtless man before. She'd seen all the vessels that way. Bastien had been completely nude on the floor just yesterday. But Rone had an effect on her she couldn't shake, and while it made her too warm, it also made her chest hurt like it was caving in on itself.

He filled his hands with water and scrubbed his face, his hair, then filled his mouth and spat. As for Sandis, curiosity finally won her internal war.

"What happened?"

Rone grabbed a towel from a drawer and wiped his face, then soaked it in water that had to be freezing, judging by the gooseflesh on his arms. He wiped off his neck and chest before turning to her, his eyes so dark they looked black. "I have a lead on Kazen."

Sandis straightened. "What?" Her heart raced in her chest.

He tossed the towel onto the counter. "There's a physical location for the dark market in District One. I know how to find the entrance. It's as good a place as any for him to hide, and if he's not there, someone down there might have information."

A chill coursed through her limbs before settling behind her navel.

"That sounds . . . dangerous," Bastien said as he came up the hall, twisting his braid in his hands.

Rone raised an eyebrow at the obvious comment.

Swallowing, rejuvenating her voice, Sandis said, "You can't go alone. It's too dangerous."

"I won't." He shoved his hands in his trouser pockets, then seemed to find something unsavory and whipped them out again. He gritted his teeth. "You two need to come with me. I don't know what to expect down there, but an amarinth alone won't cut it. I'll need backup. A threat."

Sandis nodded, though her neck felt rusted. She had the lead she needed, and she would take it, but it was hard to ignore the part of her screaming not to. "If it's a market, maybe they won't be looking for a fight. Just for buyers."

Bastien leaned against the wall, his brows drawn tightly together.

"Bastien?" asked Sandis.

He licked his lips. Hesitated. "I think . . . maybe I've been there."

"Kazen took you?" Rone straightened.

Bastien closed his eyes, forehead crinkled. "I remember a dark place. It was . . . cavernous. I was a slave first, until Oz branded me. I think that's where I was . . . bought."

Sandis put a hand on his shoulder.

"It happened." He shrugged. "But I could be bought again."

Rone nodded. "We'll go in with the pretense of selling a vessel. It'll give us an excuse to ask after Kazen. We just need some handcuffs."

Wincing, Bastien countered, "I don't like being tied up. I . . . don't like tight spaces."

"We'll leave the cuffs loose," Sandis assured him. "And if the worst happens, Ireth can break them."

His blue eyes met hers.

"He's . . . done it before for me." Memories of being inside that armored wagon, scarlets hauling her off to Gerech for being a vessel, surfaced in her mind. She'd summoned Ireth, destroyed the thing. Nearly drowned in the canal, like her brother had. Rone had pulled her from the water.

Rone seemed lost in thought. Was he remembering the same thing?

He came to himself quickly. "Let's do this. Tonight. I have a deadline."

"For what?" Sandis asked.

"I'd rather we have a living line," Bastien said.

Rone shook his head. "Don't worry about it." He sniffed his arm and cringed. "I'm going to wash up. Then we leave."

Biting her lip, Sandis turned toward Bastien.

He sighed. "I'll get the knife. Just in case."

Sandis wore one of Rone's mother's shirts. It was pale, blousy, and had a wide neckline, one that could be pushed back to show where her script started. She hated exposing it this way, showing these terrible people what she was, but she had to be believable as a summoner, just as Bastien had to be believable as a vessel. He wore the open-backed shirt Kazen had given him, even as he followed Sandis with his wrists cuffed in front of him, the chain she held clanking.

Please, Celestial, help me do this. Keep Kolosos away until we can get out.

If she started at the demon's touch down here . . . she feared what it could lead to.

Rone hadn't done much to alter himself, but he'd mussed his hair and, using some of his mother's makeup, purpled his eyes a little. Made it look like he smoked brain dust. He kept one hand in his pocket, where the amarinth rested.

The trio walked through a cold, dank tunnel, one too round to have been carved naturally. The stone took on some color up ahead, and when Rone's lantern light touched the walls, Sandis recognized Noscon art—paints in blue and faded red, studded with some sort of ceramic tile. This had been made by them. She stood in part of their great abandoned city, which her own ancestors had built over. She descended into their heartland.

She wondered if those ancient people had abandoned their homes because of the evil burned into Sandis's and Bastien's backs. Maybe demons had haunted them, too.

She hoped they'd found relief, wherever they'd disappeared to.

Bastien's breathing quickened. Fortunately, light ahead signaled the end of the tunnel. Sandis was so focused on it that she tripped over something—someone. A beggar man, drearily gazing up, his teeth rotted in a way that whispered, *Brain dust.* Gripping the chain harder, Sandis urged Bastien forward.

She could do this. They could do this. They had to.

The tunnel opened up into a larger one with kerosene lamps intermittently spread across rough black walls. A few more beggars lingered here, as well as two men dressed well, one smoking a cigar, the other smoking a pipe. Sandis stared at them until Rone's elbow caught her in the arm. Drug dealers weren't what they'd come for. They had to keep moving.

The two men watched them as they passed, though the beggars didn't seem to notice. The way turned once, then again, snaking deeper and deeper underground. Sandis stepped in a puddle. Something dripped onto her hair. She straightened her back, trying to match Rone's confident stride. Was he really so brave, or was he good at pretending?

Good at pretending. Sandis knew firsthand.

The winding path opened up into an immense cavern with an uneven roof—two stories in some places, as much as four in others. All of it was made of that rough, dark rock. *This* was a naturally made space. Sandis could hear the slightest trickle of moving water far to her left. Another droplet hit her shoulder. She tried not to react to the scent of body odor.

There were several vendors here, though not as many as Sandis had expected. Most were ragtag, set up on blankets or creaking tables. A few had wares displayed, but most had only themselves. Perhaps those who frequented this place knew what their services were, but Sandis didn't. Whom should they question first?

She side-eyed Rone. His stride didn't slow, but his gaze shifted from person to person, weighing them. She noted that he lingered at a stone table selling falsified emigration papers. A new spike of fear stabbed her middle. He wouldn't betray them now, for those, would he? Again?

No, he won't. What Rone had done was done, and though Sandis couldn't trust him, his remorse felt genuine. Guilt was his motivator. He didn't *have* to help her.

Still, sweat moistened her palms and feet. She turned away from the stone table and held her breath.

Then Sandis saw them.

They weren't the same slavers who'd kidnaped her off the street, but something about their clothes, their stance, told her they *were* slavers. They lounged near the natural stream, dressed in Kolin garb, though their faces were obviously Ysbeno. Their pale-gray eyes glinted in the lamplight when they turned toward them. Or, specifically, Bastien.

"You are new?"

Rone paused, and Sandis did, too. The speaker was a plump, pale man behind an elaborate setup of wares. His table had everything from Noscon-looking jewelry to various elixirs strewn about it. A few weapons. Some other things Sandis couldn't identify.

The man's face was a friendly one, though the lines around his eyes were the type that came from scowling. Another pretender.

Rone approached the table, and Sandis followed with as much confidence as she could muster, given the four burly men surrounding it. They had swords and guns on their persons.

"Finding reliable sources in the city is tiring. I heard I could get a better deal here," Rone said, gesturing with a tilt of his head toward Bastien. They'd agreed earlier that Rone would play the part of a broker. Was this how her great-uncle worked, too? But Talbur would never dirty his hands in a place like this. Even he wouldn't stoop so low.

The merchant nodded to one of the armed men. Sandis stiffened when he stepped behind them. He checked their scripts, then returned to the man's side and nodded.

"Two vessels, one obedient?" the man grinned.

Rone snorted in offense. "One vessel. Don't insult my client. She's merely his handler."

The man raised his hands in mock surrender. "My apologies. Names?"

Rone said nothing, merely narrowed his eyes.

"I am Siegen," the merchant said, offering his own in trade. "I can help take him off your hands."

"So could they." Rone motioned toward the Ysbeno slavers.

"I am much more trustworthy."

Rone and Siegen stared at each other a long moment before both started laughing. It startled Sandis. How did he know to follow such cues? He'd been the same with the false Grim Rig.

Because he's a criminal, too, Sandis thought. Guilt stung her.

When the laughter died, Rone said, "You're no summoner."

Siegen shrugged. "I have other means for unwanted vessels." He picked up a slender glass vial from his table and shook it. "And I, too, can broker deals with clients too shy to turn up here."

Rone replied, but the words garbled in Sandis's ears. She stared intently at the contents of the vial. There were flecks of gold and brown in it, hints of rust. All floating in some sort of clear liquid.

Her throat constricted. "Is that remedial gold?" she asked.

She'd interrupted something. Rone rolled his lips together. Siegen raised his brow.

"Why, yes, of course."

Sandis's fingers went cold.

"Which reminds me," Rone went on, "I'm looking for someone. Someone perhaps I could use your *brokering* services for. Kazen. I hear he pays well."

Siegen set the vial down. "Yes, he does, but I haven't seen him in, oh, a week or so. Heard things aren't too great for him. But he might be interested." Lowering his voice, Siegen said, "I happen to know he's recently come into a nice chunk of change."

"Oh?" Rone asked.

He picked up the vial again. "Where do you think I got this from, hm?"

Siegen's lighthearted banter echoed in Sandis's ears.

Remedial gold. It came from Kazen.

Rist, Dar, Kaili—all accounted for. But not Alys.

Not Alys.

"I haven't seen her in . . . four days . . ."

No one had. The memories popped into Sandis's head like gunshots. Alys, bleeding on the floor. The other vessels, unsure of what had become of her. Kazen running from his lair, alone.

Heat of her own making burned under Sandis's skin.

Alys wasn't lost. She was sitting in glass tubes on this table.

Kazen had sold her. Killed her.

And now this man held pieces of her in his fat hands.

"Sandis?" Her name was a hard whisper. Rone grabbed her shoulder. "What's wrong?"

Her skin was so hot the tears running down her cheeks felt cool.

"That's Alys." She didn't recognize her own voice, if she could call it that. It was more a growl.

Rone blanched. "What?"

Bastien's chains bit into her hands. She couldn't speak. He'd . . . He'd *killed her and sold her body*. Taken her to this dark, horrible place. And this man, *this man was peddling her*.

Her body was fire. Pure fire.

Rone stepped in front of her, blocking her from the table.

"No!" she screamed, reeling back from him. "They *killed her!*"

All thought banished from her mind. She didn't think when she tugged Bastien forward. When she grabbed his head, the fresh cut on her arm stinging with her motion. She didn't hear the Noscon words fall from her lips.

She was right. The cuffs melted when Ireth took form.

His fire swallowed the cavern whole.

Chapter 17

Rone dropped Bastien's body, covered only by a sheet stolen from a clothesline, onto his mother's bed. Then he turned around, stepped into the hallway, and slammed the door behind him.

"We are lucky to be alive." His tone was low and dark, but he couldn't lift it. Not now. Not when his bad shoulder was throbbing from carrying Bastien across the city. Not when his pockets were light from bribing the hired carriage. Not when his head pounded from blinding light and smoke inhalation. Thank his damnable god that Sandis had possessed enough sanity to aim *away* from her allies.

She stood at the end of the hallway, hugging herself, trembling.

Rone took three long steps toward her. "You've put a target on our backs for anyone who survived. We better damn well hope none of them have a backbone. Any lead we had is lost. Kazen is lost, and who the hell knows when he'll strike next. Or who."

Slowly, Sandis sank to her knees. A sob escaped her.

Rone closed his eyes and took a deep breath. Then turned and threw a fist into the wall. The sting cleared his head. And dented the molding.

"Not to mention what you did to Bastien," he murmured.

"I know," she whispered. A few tears hit the flat carpet. "I know. He'll hate me."

Rone leaned against the wall and lowered himself to the floor, propping his forearms on his knees. "He won't hate you."

"I . . . treated him . . . l-like a slave."

Those words dug deep. Rone set his jaw against them.

They were silent for a long minute, save for Sandis's stifled sobs as she cried quietly beside him. Rone cracked his knuckles. Picked his nails. Lowered his head. "I'm sorry about Alys."

A new sob broke from Sandis's throat.

And then she screamed.

Rone leapt to his feet. Turned. "What? What?"

Sandis leapt backward, still on the floor, crab-crawling away from him. No, not him. Something in the hallway. Something he couldn't see.

"Leave me alone!" she cried, pinwheeling an arm to fight off some invisible demon.

"Sandis!" He chased after her. Grabbed her shoulders, but she clocked him across the face, panicked. Hyperventilating. So Rone scooped her up in his arms and threw her onto the sofa.

"Sandis! You're here, you're safe!" He shook her. "Sandis, come back to me!"

Awareness flashed through her dark, wet eyes. She stared at him for several seconds before crumpling in on herself, bawling like a newborn. Rone scooped her into his arms. He knew something was wrong when she didn't push him away.

"I-I c-can't d-do this a-anymore," she sobbed. "I-It won't l-leave me a-alone . . ."

Rone squeezed her, letting her tears soak his shirt. He pressed his mouth to her hair.

It. Kolosos.

"I know." What else could he say? He couldn't understand, so he simply held her, protecting her from the world even if just for a moment. The two vials of remedial gold in his pocket felt like bricks, and he prayed Sandis didn't feel them. He'd swiped them off the table as Ireth turned everything to fire.

"We'll go with your plan," he whispered once the fear had died down. "We'll find the others. We'll find them, and we'll find Kazen, and we'll end this."

She mumbled something.

Rone pulled back to hear her better, but the action broke the spell between them. Sandis shifted away, like Rone's arms were the last place she wanted to be.

He ignored the tenderness in his throat.

"Not like Bastien," she repeated, red eyed and weary. "I-I won't treat them . . . N-Never again. Not like that."

He nodded. "Not like that."

She rubbed her palms into her eyes.

"He'll forgive you, Sandis."

But she didn't seem to hear him.

Sandis kept vigil at Bastien's side through the rest of the night and into the day. She was ready with food, water, and apologies when he woke. She knelt at his feet and begged his forgiveness. He gave it to her.

Watching them, Rone wondered, not for the first time, if he belonged in Dresberg.

He still had four days. If he left in the next twenty-four hours, he could make it in time. He might be able to delay two days if he traveled relentlessly through the nights.

It didn't feel like enough time.

Rone waited on the roof that night as Bastien and Sandis prepared to enact her plan. Dead of night or not, he didn't think running around Dresberg with a slagging *numen* in tow was a good idea, but they had so few options at this point, and Sandis . . . Sandis needed this. Rone wasn't sure it would work, but he'd do it. It was as good a time as any to slip by Hadmar's drop-off point, too.

Still, Rone didn't want to be in the room when Bastien summoned into Sandis, assuming he even could. He couldn't hear her scream again. Just thinking about last night made his skin pebble. He ran a hand down his face. *What is she seeing that's so terrifying?*

He felt helpless to stop it. His amarinth had been returned, and yet Rone felt more powerless than ever.

Rubbing a headache from his forehead, Rone sighed, trying to banish memories of another time, when her screams had been his doing.

He whipped his hand from his face. *God's tower, I* came back *for her.*

Did she have to hate him so much? Was everything he did so fruitless?

Footsteps sounded on the iron stairs that wrapped up the side of the building, ending on the roof. A pair belonging to a man, and another set that sounded like . . . a dog?

Rone turned as Bastien's head popped above the roof. The Godobian climbed up, and at his heels crept a giant *rodent*. A weird, bug-eyed squirrel thing with heavy skin flaps between its front and back legs. And feathers. Because that made sense.

It probably weighed two hundred pounds and was about as long as Rone was tall.

It was also strangely adorable.

"I see you were successful." He eyed the numen, who heeled at Bastien's side like a good mongrel. It shook its head, spraying lingering droplets of the purified water Sandis had boiled earlier—a necessity for summoning into an unbound vessel, as was the roach Rone had caught for them. Unbound summoning required a sacrifice, but this thing—this "Hapshi"—was so mild, a bug apparently did the job. There would be a bandage on Bastien's arm under his sleeve from yet another exchange of blood with Sandis—an exchange that would allow him to command the numen at his side absolutely.

Sandis. That was *Sandis*.

No, Sandis wasn't here. This was a mutated form of her body.

Rone chewed the inside of his lip. *She'll do anything to stop Kazen.*

Even obliterate every person and thing in an underground cave. They were lowlifes and criminals, yes, but surely their deaths didn't settle well with her. She was taking on too much for a single person to bear.

How often did Kolosos haunt her? Rone recalled the corpses at Kazen's thwarted summoning of the numen—one a man, one an ox. Compare that to a roach . . .

Bile stung the base of his throat.

They couldn't fail, could they?

"We can walk or fly," Bastien said, peering out over the city. The haze blurred the buildings in the distance, even those with lights on them. The stars were nonexistent.

Wait, what?

"Fly?" Rone repeated.

Bastien crouched and scratched Hapshi's head; Rone tried not to bristle at the pet like affection. Sandis, supposedly, wouldn't remember any of this.

"Hapshi is a level-one numen," the Godobian replied. "Not good for anything but flying, so Sandis said. It should be able to carry both of us, but not far. We can . . . hap to it."

Rone grumbled. "I'm not mounting that thing. I'll take the stairs."

And so he did. By the time he reached the road, Bastien and Sandis—*Hapshi*, not Sandis—already stood hidden in the shadows.

Rone shoved his hands into his pockets, letting the fingers of one hand tangle with the loops of his amarinth and the others slip around the vials of remedial gold. "Let's find some back roads and head toward the lair. We need to stay out of sight." In a city as overstuffed as this one, there was always someone out and about. Rone mapped the path in his mind, including his necessary detour.

More likely than not, the other vessels would be asleep and wouldn't sense the numen, even if it walked right by them. Rone had said so much. Sandis and the redhead hadn't listened.

They would venture close to Kazen's stomping grounds, since that's where the vessels had last been seen. Truthfully, they could be anywhere in the city by now. Bastien let out a long breath, probably nervous to be going back toward the place of his imprisonment. Then again, everything made the younger man nervous. Maybe they'd get lucky and find Kazen back home after all and finally end this nightmare.

"Hapshi can run or fly away if we meet trouble." Bastien's reassurance seemed to be more for himself than for Rone. He gestured to the slim road behind the building, and Hapshi quickly followed him. Rone looked around, listening.

A level one, eh? So if their mercenary friend, the stranger, popped out right now, this numen would be absolutely useless. Except, maybe, as an escape. Given that the ethereal creature didn't have wings, Rone guessed it was more of a glider. Which was useless if they were at ground level.

He stalked after the two vessels anyway.

They walked in silence for nearly an hour, changing routes twice— once to avoid a cluster of beggars and again to circumvent, shockingly, a trio of white-robed Celesian clerics. Why the religious men would be out in the city at this hour, Rone didn't know, but he also didn't care.

They had just passed into District Four, where Kazen's former lair was, when Rone stopped and said, "There are some good hiding spots around here. We'll cover more ground if we split up. Why don't you go north? I'll head around this way," he pointed, "and meet up with you at the canal."

Bastien hesitated. "I . . . I don't think that's a good idea."

Rone shrugged. "If something happens, fly away, right?"

174

Bastien pressed his lips together, but nodded. Rone waited until Bastien ventured up the street with Hapshi before slipping down another alleyway, righting an empty garbage bin as he went. The street narrowed, dipped, and nearly pinched off where two buildings practically made love with one another. Rone squeezed through and slipped down an unlit path clear of debris and people.

A shadow moved nearby.

Rone put up both his hands. "Delivery for your boss."

The shadow shifted—Rone thought it holstered a gun. "Verlad," said a low voice.

Rone nodded and reached into his pocket for the vials. He felt dirty, palming them and offering them to this man, knowing what they were. *Who* they were. Any shred of amiability Sandis felt toward him would be killed if she saw him now.

He'd done it for her. To catch Kazen, even if that hadn't panned out. And as he let the vials roll into the awaiting lackey's hands, Rone offered up a sacrifice of his own.

No more Engel Verlad. He pulled his hand back as though the remedial gold had burned it. *No more thieving, no more jobs for scum like this. I'm done.*

He'd leave it all behind him when he went to Godobia anyway, but there was weight to the promise. Engel Verlad was finished.

The man said nothing, merely pocketed the goods and waited for Rone to leave. Which he did, quickly. He hurried toward the canal, leaving his lies and bent truths behind him.

He got there before the Godobian, but thankfully didn't have to wait long before Bastien and Hapshi came into view. They joined up silently, obviously both empty handed, and took a winding path back through the smoke ring. It didn't smell as bad at night, since about half of the factories set their smokestacks and furnaces to low after sundown. They were careful to avoid the few factories that were still open for nightshifts, driving back the haze with their lights.

"What's the distance on this thing?" Rone finally asked after another hour so he wouldn't think about the pain growing in his feet, his final transaction as a thief for hire, or the puddle of Celestial knows what he'd just stepped in.

Bastien's braid fell off his shoulder. "What?"

Rone gestured to Hapshi. "How close do we have to be for the other vessels to sense us?"

Bastien considered for a moment. "I'm not sure. Not terribly far. A mile or less, I'd say. I haven't experienced that . . . sense . . . as often as I imagine Sandis has. My master was more frugal with his vessels."

Rone studied the oversized rodent bird, waiting for a flinch or gesture of some sort to show it was listening, but there was nothing. Not even a hint that it recognized its host's name.

No wonder the Celesians hated these things. They were utterly inhuman.

"I'm guessing"—Rone pointed down an alleyway with a garbage bin at the end of it, something they could use to get over the fence behind it—"that if we have no luck tonight, she'll want to do this again tomorrow."

Bastien rolled his lips together. "I think so. It would be healthier for her to take a day in between."

Rone sighed. "She won't."

"She said she met you in a tavern."

"Yeah, I'm not in the mood for sharing backstories right now, kid."

Bastien frowned. "I'm not a child. I'm nineteen."

"And I've got six years on you." He grabbed the lip of the garbage bin and heaved himself atop it, then jumped over the fence, falling about nine feet to the ground. Bastien eyed the height—Rone guessed athleticism wasn't in his repertoire. Instead, he climbed on Hapshi's back, and the numen leapt gracefully and silently onto the garbage bin and over the fence, gliding gently down to the road on the other side.

Bastien fell off regardless. Rone walked ahead to hide the grin pressing against his lips.

He paused as he turned the corner. They could go three directions, but all of them led toward lit buildings. Best bet was to the right, where a shop had only a single lantern hanging on its door. Then they could circle back to his mother's flat and start a new route tomorrow.

Shoving his hands into his pockets, Rone tilted his head toward the shop. "This way. Let's—"

"Bastien?"

All three of them, including the numen, turned around at the baritone voice. It came from the left, from a shadow that moved carefully, slowly down the narrow road sandwiched between two tall brick buildings.

Bastien took a step toward it. "R-Rist?"

The figure strode toward them until it stepped into the muted moonlight. He lowered a pistol. Rone vaguely recognized him. He was about Rone's height and probably a few years younger. His straight dark-brown hair was overgrown and hung over one of his eyes. He was broad-shouldered but looked like he could use a meal. Or five.

Sandis's plan had worked.

Rist eyed Rone. "You were the one following her all over the city." He paused, his eyes dropping to Hapshi. Rone had first seen Rist on the back of Kazen's horse, chasing after them with the rest of the summoner's men. Then his numen form had sheltered the bastard when Sandis first summoned Ireth into herself.

Rist hesitated before shifting his attention to Bastien and the numen.

"Sandis." Bastien twisted his braid as the oversized rodent sniffed the cobblestone. "I . . . summoned into her."

Rist didn't show any surprise, just rubbed the back of his neck. "When I sensed you . . . I didn't know who you were. I thought Oz, maybe."

"Oz?" Rone asked. He'd heard the name before.

Bastien licked his lips. "My master, before Kazen."

Great. More grafters. Rone shoved his hands into his pockets. "So you thought you'd get caught again? Work for someone else?"

Rist shot him a glare. "I thought I could make a deal."

"A deal? For what?" Bastien moved closer.

Rist's shoulders slackened. "Kaili. She's . . . sick. I haven't been able to find a job. Can't afford a doctor. Managed to pocket something for her, but it didn't help."

So they'd stuck together—Sandis would be relieved they'd found two for the price of one. She deserved a victory.

He wondered what Kaili needed a doctor for.

"We can help," he said. "Take us to her."

Rist lit a candle and took it over to a pallet on the ground. They'd slipped through a grating into an underground delivery tunnel that connected a warehouse and what had once been a cotton factory. When Rone asked, Rist had muttered something about the factory going bankrupt and someone repurposing it for clockworks. The warehouse, no longer needed, had been divided into storage rooms and offices that were rented out to whoever could make the monthly payments. The tunnel was more or less forgotten, except by the handful of homeless who had claimed different nooks and offshoots of it.

Rist led them to one of the nooks—a short hall that branched off from the main tunnel and split into two rooms, one of which looked like an old closet. They followed him into the larger room, and Bastien shut the door behind them.

Even in the poor lighting, Rone could see the reason for Kaili's sickness, even before Rist knelt beside her and gingerly removed the makeshift bandages across her back.

The woman's golden script shimmered in the candlelight, marred between her shoulder blades by a dark split in the skin that pussed at the edges. Tendrils of red snaked between the Noscon symbols.

"We split up." Rist's tone was suddenly softer, almost reverent. "Lost each other in the confusion. I didn't know where she went, so I helped Jak get home—"

"Jak?" Rone asked.

Rist frowned. "One of the new kids Kazen took to brand. His parents were still around. But Kaili got scared and took a knife to her script, not wanting to be arrested. She thought maybe she could plead her innocence if it was obvious she didn't *want* to be a vessel." He shook his head. "I've cleaned it out, used salve. Washed the bandages. I just don't have the right supplies."

The pain in his voice was clear. Kaili stirred but didn't wake.

Rist added, "She's been sleeping more and more."

"I've got money. We'll get the supplies," Rone said, and for the first time, Rist looked at him with benevolence. "I have a flat we can take her to—"

"Too risky," Rist cut in.

Rone gritted his teeth. "Do you want her to sleep on the dirty floor or a bed? It's not far. She can take San—I lapshi."

Rist eyed the rodent. Rone wondered exactly how long they had before it just poofed back into a naked woman. Did numina poof?

Bastien said, "Please, Rist. Sandis . . . she's the reason we found you. She wants us together again. To fight Kazen."

Rist reeled back. "Are you crazy?"

"The way I see it," Rone butted in, "is you come with us, get your girlfriend the medicine she needs, and listen to what Sandis has to say when she comes to, *or* you can fester here and watch Kaili die."

Rist shot up to his feet. "You piece of—"

"Kolosos."

The name was weak, the feminine voice groggy. Rone watched the fight leak out of Rist like water from a sponge. In less than a second, he was at Kaili's side again, smoothing hair from her face. Hair, Rone noted, that was cut in the same style as Sandis's.

Kaili pressed her hand against the floor as if to get up, but her elbow buckled. Bastien moved the candle closer to her pale face.

"He killed your brother," she whispered. Rist tensed. "We should . . . listen."

Rone wiped a hand down his face. It wouldn't matter—even if they got Kaili well, her script was ruined. Just like he'd thought it would be. Sandis's plan had already failed. However . . . Rist had sensed Hapshi's closeness *and* said he'd planned on making a deal with whatever summoner roamed the streets. Which meant . . .

"Rist."

The younger man glanced at him.

"Your script?" he asked.

Rist frowned. "I haven't broken it yet. I didn't want . . . to end up like her."

Rone took a deep breath and let it all out at once. "Get her on the rat. We'll argue about it in the morning."

Chapter 18

Once, Kazen had been convinced the heavy smoke pumping from the factories made him sick. He'd thought he needed fresher air. A new way of thinking. A divine purpose. So he'd sought it out. In the end, it had nearly destroyed him.

The time had long since passed for him to return the favor.

He considered this as he approached an oversized factory, one that pressed into the street, ruining its symmetry. Valves and pipes wound up one side, and a single smokestack belched from its secondary building. The security guard outside the door sized up Kazen. He expected no less; his coat fit too well for a menial factory worker, the material too expensive. His hands lacked the calluses, though he admitted the largeness of his knuckles made him appear to be one who stressed his fingers in labor. Not so, but it wouldn't matter regardless. The clothing was enough.

In a city like Dresberg, the wealthy always had the upper hand.

The sounds of clinking metal pressed against the walls of the small foyer he stepped into, a space that offered no comforts—no chairs, rugs, or refreshments. The right and left walls had large glass windows that revealed rooms filled with working employees, all paid barely enough to live on. Kazen ignored them.

Instead, he stood in front of one of the windows and pressed his silver-capped cane into the floor before him, resting both hands on it.

He stood erect, though the joints of his lower back protested, trying to make him feel his age. His posture remained stiff.

It took a few minutes before someone noticed him and ran off, and a few more before a short yet burly man stepped through the door. He looked to be in his forties, pale with a round face. He ate well. Yes, he was a superior.

Excellent.

"I'm here to review your employee roster," Kazen said, reaching into his well-tailored coat to retrieve a badge he'd purchased for an overly handsome sum in the dark market. It was a bronze medallion the length of his palm and about two-thirds its width, the front engraved with a sailless boat. Words in all capitals surrounded it, but no one paid attention to those. Most of the laboring class couldn't even read. It was the shape of the badge and that boat that mattered. Made him look like a city officer.

The man frowned, but he gestured Kazen back through the door he'd exited. "What's this about?"

The sounds of clanking metal increased threefold as Kazen stepped out of the foyer. Men broke up sheet metal to his right; to his left, children broke down boxes and pallets. The air carried the scents of oil, sweat, and chloride lime. It was oddly humid.

"That is information I cannot share, my good man. Your name, for the record?" Kazen didn't care who the fool was so long as he proved useful, but a police officer would have asked, and Kazen did not make mistakes.

The man muttered an answer Kazen barely heard. They wound around men and machines until they reached a cramped closet space filled with boxes and filing cabinets. The man took an aggravating amount of time sifting through them to find what Kazen had requested.

Disorder. Filth. Incompetence. All things Kazen loathed. He'd loathed Galt for similar reasons. But he waited with practiced patience, the only sign of his frustration the tapping of his index finger on his cane.

"Here we are," the factory worker said. "What years are you looking for?"

"Last ten."

He pulled out a thick book, then another, and set them atop a stack of boxes. "Don't take them, just look. Sir." He checked a clock on the wall. "I need to check on a line."

Kazen merely nodded, and the thick man pushed past him to the door, which Kazen closed with his heel. He brushed off his sleeve where the man had touched him and opened the book.

Its records ended last year. He flipped back pages, scanning inked passages. Flipped, scanned. Careful, slow. He did not enjoy doing things twice. Precision was the key to success.

By the time he found the name he sought, his unwanted partner had returned. "Well?"

Kazen pressed the tip of his finger to the name. The man leaned in and looked it over.

"Oh, I remember him." He sounded surprised, as though the functioning of his own brain was a shock. "Good one. Left a few years back. Lily Tower, so I heard."

Kazen pressed his lips together and let out a small hum of confirmation. The Lily Tower, was it? How interesting.

Leaving the book open, Kazen turned and stalked out of the room.

"Hey, do you need . . ." the man called after him, but Kazen was already gone.

Chapter 19

Sandis's eyes shot open, and her lungs gasped for air. For a moment she didn't know where she was. Didn't recognize the uneven paint strokes on the ceiling above her or the drawn curtains over the window to her left. The bed—this wasn't her cot. Nor was it the wide, soft bed she'd been given in her great-uncle's home.

Rone's mother's bed. Rone's mother's flat.

She sat up and cradled her head, her blanket slipping down to her hips. Her pulse throbbed under her skull, but the awakening was different this time. The numen she'd hosted was not the creature that had once been part of her very soul. She blinked, eyelids sticking to her dry eyes. She noticed a pitcher of water and a cup on the small table next the bed and blessed Bastien—Rone—whoever had left it there.

Ignoring the cup, Sandis gulped straight from the pitcher, dribbling cool, stale water down her naked chest. It hit her stomach like ball bearings, but she downed nearly half the contents before setting it aside and wiping her mouth. No nightmares this time. Just blissful emptiness. Praise the Celestial.

Then she remembered.

Gooseflesh rose on her skin as her memory relived those last moments.

Bastien's shaking hand sliding over her forehead. The splitting, tearing, *ripping* sensation of being possessed. And then utter darkness. She remembered nothing of the night's journey. But she remembered before.

The cavern, the dark market, the screams as fire engulfed everything. How many people had she killed? But they were slavers, criminals, killers. Celesia condemned them.

Just like it condemned her.

Her headache spiked, and she winced. It felt like another lifetime, a different story set beside hers on a bookshelf. *Oh, Ireth, forgive me.* She wiped grit from her eyes. *I used you, too.*

She glanced at the light edging the curtains. What time was it? Afternoon?

Then she heard voices.

Slipping from the mattress, she listened. Rone's voice, smooth and mellow. She couldn't hear what he said, but the sound of him reminded her of the pain medicine Kazen had given her after a summoning. She'd had too much once, and its sweet relief had faded into a feeling worse than the headache.

She closed her eyes, but that made her focus on the pounding in her head.

Another voice. A man's. Too low to be Bastien . . .

Sandis snapped to attention. Rist? Had they found Rist?

Hope sparked in her like lit gunpowder. Sandis ran to the dresser with two broken drawers, where she had placed her dress before last night's summoning. She pulled it on, nearly popping a button, and ran out of the bedroom, headache forgotten.

She ogled them in amazement. They sat at the dining table—Rone on the left, Bastien at the right, and at the head was *Rist*, who met her gaze as she barreled in. He looked a little ashen, a little tired, but he was *here*.

Her plan had worked.

"You came," she whispered, stumbling toward the table. Rone stood to help her, but she gripped the table edge and held herself upright. "We found you, and you came."

"Hi, Sandis."

She spun at the woman's voice. The sight of Kaili stretched across the couch, propped up on pillows, brought moisture to her eyes. She looked *awful*—too pale, with dark rings around her eyes—but she smiled, and that sad but sweet expression reminded Sandis of her first week in Kazen's lair. Kaili had crept to Sandis's cot in the dark and whispered that everything was going to be okay.

Sandis rushed to Kaili's side, burning her knees on the carpet in her haste to get closer. "Are you sick? Are you okay?"

"Just an infection." She offered another weak smile. "Feels like I got my brands all over again."

It was then that Sandis noticed the bandages sticking above her collar. The shirt wasn't the open-backed sort they'd worn as vessels, but it was too big for her. An alarm like the gong of a bell tower sang in Sandis's head, and for a moment she thought someone had skinned her friend, taken her gold . . .

But Kaili wouldn't be alive if someone had done that.

The second option dawned on her. Sandis's shoulders drooped.

"You cut your script."

Kaili nodded. "I didn't have a reason to keep it. I did it wrong. But your friend here got me medicine, and it doesn't hurt as much today."

Rone met her eyes briefly before looking away.

"Thank you," Sandis said. And if the medicine somehow failed to stop the infection, they had the amarinth as backup.

Rone shrugged. "You still can't use her to summon."

"But she's going to be okay." Her gaze shifted to Rist. "Right?"

Rist didn't answer. He looked like worry personified. Kaili answered for him, "I'll be fine. And Rist is still good."

That tenacious hope sparked inside Sandis again. "Your script is still intact?" And she assumed, he and Kaili hadn't . . . With her infection, they probably couldn't have . . . done anything else to hurt their summoning ability.

Rist scowled. "I escaped that place so I wouldn't have to be some demon's puppet anymore."

Rone snorted.

Glowering, Rist asked, "What?"

"I think you mean *we freed you* from that place so you wouldn't have to be a demon's puppet anymore."

"Rone," Sandis warned.

Bastien looked between the two before muttering, "But we did it . . . no strings attached."

Rist wheeled on him. "Do you think *now* is a good time for your stupid jokes?"

"Rist, please," Kaili said, then coughed, and Rist deflated like a struck dog. He mumbled something that sounded like an apology, but wouldn't meet anyone's eyes.

Kaili's too-warm hand reached over and took Sandis's. "I'm glad you came back for us. And that you didn't go the way Heath and the others did."

The others were the kidnapped children from the newspaper. At least one of them had survived. Sandis paused, then glanced to Bastien and Rone, stiff. "You told her? About the summoning?"

"*Just* the summoning," Rone said, a subtle promise that her nightmares weren't common knowledge. He sounded tired, reserved. He looked . . . sad, but why? She couldn't tell. He had become harder and harder to read ever since—

"I had my suspicions," Rist said, studying the tabletop. "I'd seen notes. I . . ." He set his jaw.

"But you couldn't read them," Sandis filled in for him.

Rist looked at her, but his gaze was annoyed. "I can read. So could Heath. Kazen knew it, too. Why else would he have thrown me in solitary for snooping?"

This was news to Sandis. "He knew?" she asked, at the same time Bastien said, "You can?"

They both looked to Kaili.

She shook her head. "I can't. Neither can Alys."

The vessel's name pierced Sandis like an icicle. Her breath caught, drawing the others' attention to her.

Averting her eyes, Sandis bit the inside of her cheek to stay present. "What's wrong?" Kaili asked.

A moment passed before Bastien answered, "Alys . . . *couldn't* read."

"That's what I said."

Sandis glanced back in time to see Rist rise from his chair. "Couldn't," he repeated.

Bastien nodded.

Rone was straightforward, as always. "Alys is dead. We found her remains in the dark market. Kazen sold her for remedial gold."

Rist blanched. Kaili gasped and covered her mouth with one hand.

Hearing him say it transported Sandis back to that dark, dank place. She saw the smug look on the merchant's face, followed by fear as Ireth reared up beside her.

Silence fell over them like sludge. Kaili was the first to break it.

"What's . . . remedial gold?"

Sandis stared hard at the floor while Rone explained. Then the silence settled again, suffocating and cold. But they couldn't dwell on it. They couldn't mull in the shock, the hurt, of Alys's unjust passing. They had too much to do. *And the best way to avenge her is to destroy Kazen.*

Composing herself, Sandis searched for something, anything, to put them back on track. To shield the news of Alys.

Her focus fell on Rist. "Y-You and Heath went to school?"

Relief highlighted Rist's features, as though he was just as glad to move away from Alys's death as she. "We had private tutors." He slowly returned to sitting. "Our parents owned the Fricada shipping yard."

Sandis's mouth formed a long O. Rist and Heath had been . . . wealthy? She'd assumed the vessels had all come from backgrounds similar to hers.

Rist closed his eyes. "We were picked up by slavers. Me first, then Heath."

Sandis stood, forcing strength into her legs. "But then your family . . . they're still—"

"They're dead. The slavers killed my parents in front of Heath and burned down our house. Thanks for bringing it up, though."

"Rist," Kaili pleaded.

"Kaili," he said, matching her tone. After a second, he added, "I saw the Noscon glyphs when I snuck into Kazen's office. I can recognize a lot, but not those particular characters. Koh-Lo-Sos. He had diagrams. My brother's name was scrawled at the top of one."

The failed possession had turned Heath inside out in a fountain of blood and innards. It was a stubborn memory that took effort to push away. The colors of it stayed in the front of her mind, making her stomach churn.

Celestial, I can still smell it.

Had Rist already overcome his brother's death? Or did it eat him up inside, the way Anon's drowning still did to her? But she couldn't ask. Not with Alys's demise so fresh.

Sandis asked, "Have you seen Kazen since leaving his lair?"

"No. Thank goodness." Kaili shifted on her pillows, winced, then settled. Rist stood from his chair and moved to the counter, where a pile of ointments and packets lay. The medicine. At least Rone's betrayal money was good for that.

She noticed Rone staring at her, but when she met his eyes, he looked away. Perhaps the same thought had occurred to him.

Sandis took a seat at the table as Rist brought a cup of water mixed with pain powder to Kaili. "I know most of his men are gone, but he doesn't need them to summon Kolosos." She tensed, as though saying its name would bring the numen's attention upon her. "He just needs to find the right host. If only . . ." She glanced at Bastien. *If only Ireth were still with me, I could figure out what he was trying so hard to tell me.*

Rist shook his head. "Kolosos isn't our business. You freed us, yes, but you're sucking us right back into this mess."

"Last I checked," Rone growled, "you walked here on your own two legs."

Rist turned a hard look on Rone. "What do you know? Let me see *your* brands, then maybe I'll listen to your slag."

Sandis stood up, knocking her chair to the floor. "Kaili and I would both be dead without Rone, and you would still be in that *cage*, Rist! So just . . . shut up so we can think, okay?"

To Sandis's surprise, Rist smiled. "That's probably the meanest thing I've ever heard you say, Sandis."

Rone's lips twitched with a smile of his own. Somehow, that twitch deflated the pressure building in her chest, leaving her with just the subtle, distant hurt she'd been nursing for the last month.

Sighing, Sandis added, "Rone and I spoke with a priestess at the Lily Tower. She said Kolosos is the name of the antithesis of the Celestial. That it is chaos, and hell is in its heart. Kolosos will affect all of us."

She thought she smelled sulfur and turned, but saw nothing. Rone stood, but Sandis shook her head, and he settled again.

"I don't . . . I never fully understood what Ireth was trying to say to me, and Bastien has been unable to communicate with him," she continued. "But this is important. If nothing else, why shouldn't we band together?"

"It might not hurt," Kaili spoke more to Rist than anyone else, "if we pooled our resources and took care of one another."

Hope pulsed in Sandis's core, warm and agonizing all at once. Hadn't she thought the same thing? But the sentiment had come too late to save Alys.

She couldn't bring herself to reveal the truth about her. Maybe Rone and Bastien already had.

Sandis rubbed her eyes, masking the unease worming beneath her skin. "We'll figure this out, one way or another."

Silence fell over the table for several seconds.

"What about . . . the stranger?" Bastien asked.

"What stranger?" Rist asked at the same time Rone rubbed his forehead.

"Kazen isn't working alone." Sandis's voice was soft, but it carried in the silence settling over the table. "He's hired out. There was a man who attacked us and tried to abduct both Bastien and me—"

"What?" Rist asked, shooting to his feet. "So you pulled us into *more danger?*"

Sandis put up her hands. "We don't know that he's coming back!" *Please don't go. Please don't go. Ireth, help me explain—*

Oh.

Kaili said, "I don't know if we were ever out of it."

Scrambling for a solution, Sandis said, "Maybe my great-uncle could help."

Bastien asked, "Great-uncle?" at the same time Rone said, "Absolutely not."

Sandis's fingers curled into fists. "We haven't even tried. He might know where Kazen is."

"Not anymore, he doesn't," Rone snapped. "Kazen's deal with him was a one-time thing."

"But he might have—"

"*Sandis.*" Rone stood, hands planted on the table. "Your great-uncle is *exactly* like those crooks in the dark market!"

Sandis stepped back as though Rone had taken his hand to her. Little cracks in her heart seemed to spread outward, like pressure applied to splintered glass. Talbur had obvious shortcomings, yes, but he was still family. He had taken her in when she had nowhere to go.

She hardened, darkened, clutched her chest as though she could stop the cracks from spreading. In a voice soft and cold as winter snow, she said, "Remind me how you're any different."

Regret chilled her at the look on his face. The way Rone paled like he'd been shot in the gut, the way his arms and mouth slackened. Only for a moment, but long enough for Sandis to see.

Then he hardened, too. Slammed his chair against the table as he pushed it in with too much force. Nearly knocked Bastien over as he stormed toward the door.

"Where are you going?" Bastien asked.

Rone wrenched the door open. "I'll find Kazen myself."

Sandis hurried toward him, remembering his guttural scream when the stranger snapped his leg. "You can't. We've tried. And what about the stranger?"

He whirled on her, and Sandis stopped for the heat of the gaze. "I'm not asking your permission."

His hands slipped into his pocket—checking for the amarinth, no doubt—and he stepped out on the walkway, slamming the door behind him.

Chapter 20

Rone hadn't taken his bag with him when he left, but that was for the better. He'd be past the southern wall by now if he'd remembered it.

He'd walked for a long time with no destination in mind. Busy streets, empty streets, sometimes retracing his steps or taking too many right turns. Urgent steps filled with false purpose, until the sun began to sink and his muscles strained.

So he found a railing outside a canal and sat on it, staring into the current below.

He still had time. If he left tonight, he could make it to the border before the papers expired. Be with his mom by the end of the week, even. Slough off this life like old skin and start anew. Surely the hurt and the worry and the guilt would abate after enough time passed. In years, maybe, but he'd learn to forget it.

All he had to do was go back and grab the pack by the couch. They were always on the go, so he always kept it ready. He could do it in less than ten seconds. Then disappear for good.

And yet, he couldn't.

Sandis could hate him, hit him, berate him. But he couldn't leave her. Not like this. She could reject him over and over, but he couldn't run in her hour of desperation. God knew he'd tried, and that had been the biggest mistake of his life. One he continued to atone for.

He should write to his mother, but his paper and pens were in that pack. Besides, maybe he'd find another way out. A smuggler, maybe. A few well-placed bribes.

But he wasn't Engel Verlad anymore, and Kazen's money was quickly running out. He'd have to take a job as a sewer boy again, or maybe work his way up to factory management. But even factory managers didn't have the kind of money that swayed border guards.

Cradling his head in his hands, Rone let out a stale breath. How had his life gotten tangled into so many knots? Was there truly nothing he could do to win her back?

In the long run, it didn't matter if he did or not. Kazen was a real threat, and not just to Sandis and the vessels. If nothing else, he could attempt to be noble and fight for the good of the city he so deeply despised.

Rone leapt off the canal guard and rolled his shoulders. Night was descending. He should head back. Figure out what to do next. Hopefully someone in that flat had an idea.

They were sitting ducks if no one did.

Sandis wrung her hands together as Rist attempted to cook something on the narrow stove. Kaili took up most of the couch, so she sat on the side of it, facing the door, curled up in the corner where it met the wall. She glanced at that door every now and then, waiting for the handle to turn, the hinges to creak. Hours had passed, and nothing. But Rone would come back. He'd left his pack. He had to come back.

Right?

She should apologize to him. Regardless of what had happened in the past, he'd done a lot to help her and the others. She was indebted to him for that, even if her sore heart thudded in reminder of his betrayal.

She'd never been one to cave to anger. Why was she doing so now? Lack of sleep, maybe. The stress. The waiting.

A shiver coursed up her script. She rubbed the base of her neck, where Ireth's broken name tattooed her skin. Just a shiver, nothing more. Perhaps she should let Bastien summon Hapshi into her again soon, if doing so kept worse monsters at bay.

Cupboards opened and closed as Rist scuttled about the kitchen. "Has he ever heard of a strainer?"

"Just use a plate," Kaili said. Her voice was stronger. The infection was healing. Good.

Bastien rose from the table to help Rist look.

The door opened.

Rone stepped in, and Sandis leapt to her feet. Everyone turned to look at him. Stiff silence permeated the room. The anger had faded from Rone's features, but Sandis couldn't read the blankness that had taken its place.

He shut the door. "Smells good."

"Rone." She sidestepped to get a better look at him. "I didn't mean what I said. I wasn't thinking, and—"

She barely registered the loud crash as the front door ripped from its jamb and smashed into the wall behind it, revealing a tall, pale man clad in black.

The stranger.

Quick as a firing pin, Sandis knew.

Rone had been followed.

The stranger's dark eyes landed on Sandis at the same time a vile word spewed from Rone. The man only made it one and a half steps before Rone leapt at him.

The stranger moved like water, blocking a well-aimed punch with his forearm before delivering one of his own.

"Move!" Sandis shouted, stumbling backward and grabbing Kaili's arm. She pulled her off the couch; her friend stumbled, but remained upright. "Out the bedroom window!"

Rist rushed to Kaili's side and scooped her into his arms before bolting for the bedroom, no questions asked.

A sleeved arm came down around Sandis's neck and hauled her backward, cutting off her air and lifting her feet off the floor. The smell of cigars filled her senses.

Sandis struggled against the stranger's grip as he flew through toward the hallway so quickly the colors of the flat blurred into dark shades of gray.

Rone flashed before her, a bleeding bruise on his forehead. His knuckles sailed for her face—no, the stranger's.

The stranger released her, and Sandis fell hard onto the floor, desperately sucking in air.

Rist barreled in to help, aiming for the stranger, but the tall, lean mercenary shoved Rone out of the way and backhanded the vessel, sending him crashing into the dining table. The momentum lifted Rist's shirt up a few inches, enough to show the golden script burned into his skin.

Sandis leapt for the stranger's legs and coiled herself around them, forcing him to fall. The stranger flipped over, his strength greatly exceeding Sandis's, and bucked like a fish, throwing her off his legs. In another seamless movement, he aimed a kick up and over his head, blocking a blow from Rone. Rone teetered to the side, and the stranger rolled backward and onto his feet.

Within half a second, they were fighting again. Rone spun under a thrown elbow and managed to land a kick to the stranger's side, only for the stranger to grab a fistful of his hair and slam a fist into his nose. Blood trickled down Rone's lips. He hadn't had time to spin the amarinth.

Sandis turned, only to see Kaili helping Rist to his feet. *No, run! You were supposed to run!*

She didn't have much time. If the stranger landed the right blow—

Bolting for the bedroom, she found Bastien near the open window, pale and quivering and unsure.

"Now. We have to do it *now!*" She should still have some of his blood in her from the night before. She prayed she did. But she would *not* do this without his permission. Not again.

Bastien nodded, and Sandis placed her hand on his head.

"Vre en nestu a car-car—" She cursed herself for the slip and bumbled over the words. *"Vre en nestu a carnath. Ii mem entre I amar. Vre en—"*

Kaili screamed.

"—nestuacarnathIrethepsigradenid!"

Bastien exploded in a burst of blinding light. Heat singed her nostrils and burned away tears. The very power of the summoning disheveled her hair and forced her back several steps.

Her beautiful fire horse loomed over her, dark and menacing and *powerful.*

Sensing her wishes through the blood bond, Ireth charged past her. He was wider than the hallway; the walls buckled, splintered, and burned as he galloped through them.

Rone was on the ground. Rist bled from his mouth.

At the sight of the numen, the stranger dropped Kaili's hair and stared, wide-eyed, before sprinting for the door.

Ireth reared and spat an arrow of fire after the man. The blaze was too brilliant, too bright, for Sandis to watch.

Seconds later, the stranger was gone, and the flat was on fire.

Chapter 21

Rone's gums were bleeding.

Holding his side, he spat onto the carpet. His left eye was swelling shut, but he was alive. And he could walk. His nose was broken, again, but he didn't think anything else was . . . *Please let that be a bruise,* he thought as agony flared in the ribs under his fingers. The stranger had been favoring his left arm—the one Sandis had grazed with a bullet. It was likely the only reason those ribs weren't swimming in his belly.

He looked up at Sandis as smoke swirled around them and flames climbed the walls. The mere presence of the horned fire beast pushed back her skirt and hair like wind. She embraced its dark muzzle lovingly, murmuring something to it. Ireth whinnied and then winked out of existence.

Bastien, naked as the day he was born, fell to the floor, embers and ash snowflaking around him.

Grunting against the pain in his side, Rone pulled out his amarinth and spun it. He felt his nose painlessly shift over, his ribcage straighten, his bruises lighten. It could be a risk, using up the amarinth's power like this when he didn't know what the next twenty-four hours had in store, but he did know one thing: he wouldn't have been able to carry Bastien otherwise.

Coughing, he tossed the amarinth to Sandis and slung Bastien over his shoulder. God's tower, Kazen had fed this boy too much. Rist, hacking up a lung, came out of the hallway with Kaili. They both fell over. Sandis rushed to Kaili's side and forced her pinky to curl around one of the amarinth's loops. Kaili's eyes widened—either because she was shocked to see the ancient artifact or because she, too, felt its healing power stitch her script back together. Wounds that old would leave a mark, so Rone doubted she'd be able to host a numen.

Flames surged onto the ceiling.

"Out!" he barked at Kaili and Rist. "Sandis, my bag! It's next to the couch!"

Sandis startled and spun around, as though noticing the flames for the first time. She darted to the couch and grabbed Rone's bag, then reached under the couch for her rifle.

Rone pushed her toward the door with his free hand, nearly dropping the nude weight on his shoulder. A tug on his pocket told him Sandis had returned the amarinth. People above him screamed. The iron stairs rattled with the neighbors' hasty departure.

Sandis paused. "We have to help them—"

"There are two fire exits in this place!" Rone shouted. "We need to *go* before the scarlets show up!"

Her eyes widened, but urgency took its hold, and she sailed down those stairs, nearly tripping over the other vessels.

Thank goodness night had fallen, providing cover for Bastien's exposed script.

As they ran into the shadows, Sandis pulled one of his shirts out of his bag and threw it over Bastien. Black ashes, these people ruined *all of his clothes*.

Police whistles pierced the night air.

Rone glanced back toward the burning building.

He'd failed again. That stranger would have killed him had Sandis and her numen not shown up. He would have taken all of the vessels, and it would have been Rone's fault for not realizing he'd been followed.

Worse, the man in black was still alive.

Sandis grabbed his elbow and pulled him down the road. Kaili and Rist were already at the end of it, Kaili waving frantically for them to follow. Her pale face shone like the moon. Hopefully she hadn't reopened her wound.

Running. Right.

Picking up his feet, Rone peered one more time at the fire behind him.

Watching his mother's old flat go up in flames only served to remind him of how much he was going to miss her.

"Set him over here." Kaili placed a tattered blanket on the cement floor in the hallway of the makeshift living space Rone and the others had retrieved her from roughly twenty-four hours earlier. The light was darker than dim, thanks to the shortage of lamps burning in the underground tunnel, but it was out of the way and, for now, safe.

Rone tried to set the unconscious Godobian down as gently as he could, but his shoulder pulled as he did, and Bastien sort of flopped onto the blanket. Rone kicked up a corner to cover the vessel's manhood.

Wincing, Rone rubbed his shoulder—the same one that had been crushed in that sewer collapse three years ago. The one Sandis had fixed. Apparently carrying dead weight halfway through the city was bad for it. Rolling his neck, Rone stepped back and examined the rest of their new hideout.

The other misfits who occupied the underground tunnel were spread out, quiet, and kept to themselves, from what Rone could tell. Rist and Kaili's offshoot of the tunnel was sizable, if dark, comprised of a wide but short hallway, an old storage room, and a large closet. The fact that the others hadn't crept in during Rist and Kaili's time away meant Rist had probably done a good job marking his territory earlier. Some of the walls still had hooks and nails in them, perhaps to hang orders or damaged goods returned from the warehouse. An abandoned wheeled cart acted as a sort of door.

"Get some rest, wherever you can," Kaili murmured. She rolled her shoulder, as if unable to believe her back had healed. "We don't have much, but—"

"It's fine. This is plenty," Rone said.

Kaili offered Rone a small smile before slinking off into the larger room, where Rist brooded like a thundercloud. Rone felt much the same way.

Twice. Twice now, Rone had fallen to this stranger. And he hadn't just lost by a few points—he'd gotten *pummeled.* If Ireth hadn't come galloping in . . .

It occurred to him that the stranger hadn't seemed surprised to see Rone uninjured, his leg completely healed. How long had the guy been watching him?

Grumbling, Rone pushed his hand back through his hair. His shoulder tightened in protest. Kneading his fingers into the muscles at the base of his neck, Rone ventured toward the smaller room, moving past the Godobian in the hallway.

Sandis sat on the floor, her eyes heavy, her knees pulled to her chest. She'd lit one of the candles from his pack and placed it on a shelf jutting from the wall. Her skirt had crinkled around her hips, exposing most of her legs. Smooth, flawless legs. The candlelight flickered across them and danced in her tired eyes. She simply stared at it, as though lost in thought.

Pulling his hand from his neck, Rone lingered in the doorway. "You okay?"

Without looking at him, she nodded. A few heartbeats later, she said, "Thank you for carrying him."

Rone glanced behind him to where Bastien slumbered. He tried to wake the guy, but he was out cold. Would be until morning, maybe afternoon.

He sighed. "Thanks for saving *me.* I'm sure you wouldn't have minded if that guy had taken me out."

She turned to him, her brows drawn together, giving him the sort of look that punched him in the gut.

Black ashes, she could knock him out faster than the stranger.

"How could you say that?" she asked.

Rone straightened. "How could I not?" When the *look* didn't relent, he added, "God's tower, Sandis. I *sold* you. I abandoned you. You lost Ireth . . . It's a wonder you talk to me."

She hugged her knees closer to herself. "Your mother . . . You had to save her, Rone. I understand that."

"Then why do you treat me like . . . like some kind of executioner?" His voice was a little too loud for the quiet place. He took another step into the room, his heart beating too fast. "Like I'm only here out of necessity? God's tower, Sandis. I'm *trying*—"

His voice hitched on that last word, and his mouth snapped shut to swallow the sound of weakness, the sound that threatened to reveal the hurt that clung to his insides like leprosy. He rubbed his eyes, reasserting control. When he dropped his hand, Sandis was looking at the candle again, only her eyes glistened with tears and her fingers gripped the folds of her skirt, knuckles threatening to pop. The sight bruised him too deeply to be borne. Black ashes, when had he become so soft?

"I tried to apologize," she whispered.

"I'm not talking about that."

She didn't respond.

Crouching at his bag, he grabbed his last set of clothes and stepped back into the hallway. "Get some sleep."

"But where will you—"

Rone shut the door behind him, pulled the shirt over his head, and lay down on the cement floor across from Bastien.

He didn't sleep well.

Bastien was still out when Rone finally got up for a meager breakfast in the morning. He dug his fingers into the stiff muscles around his bad shoulder, trying to loosen them up, but immediately stopped when Sandis stepped into the small space between the two rooms, combing her fingers through her tresses. She was pale, droopy eyed. Unrested. *Nightmares.* Rone knew it instantly. At least they hadn't been horrid enough to make her scream again.

Kaili, full of color and energy thanks to the amarinth, scrounged up a few apples—if Bastien didn't wake up soon, maybe Rone would eat his.

He had just taken his second bite of the first fruit when he noticed their numbers. He asked, "Where's Rist?"

Kaili swallowed her own mouthful. "He left about an hour ago."

Rone paused before taking his third bite, a spike of panic lancing him. "What? Where?"

Kaili blinked. "To look for a job. He had a lead with a smelting company before—"

"Are you kidding me?" Rone dropped the apple and crouched down, forcing his voice to lower. "We. Are. In. *Hiding.* He can't *go* to work! What if he's followed? Black ashes and hellfire." A headache sparked behind his eyes. "We don't know what happened to the stranger. We don't know if he lingered, ran, or actually got hurt. There are too many unknowns in this situation. Rist leaving is a huge risk. Did he at least take back routes?"

Kaili turned to Sandis, as if expecting her to save them from Rist's idiocy. Sandis looked just as alarmed as Rone felt. "I don't know. He was hoping to . . . pick up more medicine for me, too." Her voice drifted.

Rone cursed again. "How far away is he?"

Kaili considered. "The smelting factory is about a forty-five-minute walk."

He cursed a third time.

Apparently three was the charming number, because Kaili bristled. "What? Kazen doesn't know where we are, and that *man* is dead—"

"He's not dead."

Kaili gaped.

Rone rubbed his eyes with his middle finger and thumb. "I don't know how injured he is, but looked to me like he cleared the window. Our best bet is that he's too crispy to be looking for us today."

Sandis put a hand on Kaili's knee.

Rone rolled his lips together. Thought for two seconds. "We should leave anyway. There are too many witnesses down here. I know a few places that rent on cash alone, no papers. Places easy to abandon. Maybe the warehouse next door has space until we find something better."

Kaili hugged herself. "We don't have money to—"

"I'll cover your expenses, okay? But Rist has to forfeit the job."

"We can only hope," Sandis said, much softer than he'd been speaking, "that you and Rist aren't targets. Kazen wants you, yes, but Bastien and I can host larger numina. If Kazen's attention, and this stranger's, is focused on us, Rist will be okay."

Kaili paled, then reached back as if to feel her script. "Kuracean is only a level lower than Ireth."

Sucking in a deep breath, Sandis said, "One level matters, where Kolosos is concerned."

She tensed then. Squeezed her eyes shut.

Rone tensed, too.

"Sandis?" Kaili asked.

To Rone's relief, Sandis relaxed a second later. "Nothing. Just a headache."

She was getting good at lying.

"I-I don't know when he'll get home." Kaili dropped her hand. "If he gets hired, maybe not until after dark. We can't leave before then; he won't know where to find us. I can look into the warehouse—"

Rone shook his head. "No, we'll stay here. Hole up." He sighed. "I don't think our cover is blown yet. If Kazen's lackey had followed us a second time, he would have already carried Sandis off with him."

Kaili asked, "Why Sandis?"

"She's the lightest. Easiest to carry away."

Sandis averted her eyes. His guilt grew thorns. He couldn't stay here idle all day. He just couldn't. Maybe . . .

Rone nodded, paused. "But there's something I can do while we're waiting."

Both women looked at him.

"The Riggers might have information about the stranger."

Kaili frowned. "You just said we should lie low."

"I also would like to know more about our enemy and, Celestial willing, find us a new hideout where a hundred or so mobsters can stand between him and us." Rone tried to keep the annoyance from his voice, but judging by the way Kaili's eyebrows tensed, he hadn't done a very good job.

"There's always the cathedral," Sandis suggested, mouselike. "If we're careful, we can take a day there."

He rubbed his eyes. "When will Bastien wake up?"

"Soon." Sandis's voice was quiet, her eyes focused on the Godobian. "Your ammo?"

Her gaze switched to him. "I have plenty. But Rone—"

"You'll be fine, then. Only one entrance to guard." He stood. They would be fine. As for Rist, Rone could only hope. When he got back, they'd all be in danger, but Rone had until nightfall, if Kaili was right.

Rone desperately wanted to feel useful. If nothing else, he could buy medicine and clothes. At least he had confidence in his bank account.

The dawn had only just begun to break up the dark blues of the sky when he emerged on the street, using the same grating in the alley Rist had used to get them down there. He made sure he wasn't seen before venturing to the main road, noting that he still smelled, faintly, of smoke. Better than sewage.

The sun had risen by the time he reached the three-story boardinghouse on the corner in the heart of the smoke ring. People already milled out in the streets, some dragging screaming children, others pushing their way through the masses to get to work. A young girl set up her newspaper stand, getting ready to hawk the day's stories, and a carriage pushed through the masses, the driver cursing out those who crossed in front of him as he pulled back on his horses' reins.

It struck him how normal the boardinghouse looked. A little run-down, but most buildings around here were. Sludge dropped by years of rainfall stained the sides of the place, and nearly every room with a window was unlit.

The bit that ruined the illusion was the darkly dressed man loitering near the narrow set of concrete stairs off the back of the property. The guy looked like he spent all his time doing pushups and eating steak.

The man noticed him approach and folded his arms, accentuating a large chest beneath a shirt that barely fit him. If this guy got angry, he'd likely lose a button. Yet when Rone got within a few paces, the guy's stance relaxed.

"I need to speak with your boss." Rone kept his voice low, his eyes trained on the guard. He had to be all confidence and determination with these people.

To his relief, the man nodded. "Jase Kipf has been greened," he said, whatever that meant. "Go down the stairs. Rufus will help you from there."

Rone slipped by the guard and took the stairs down. He opened the door at their base, only to meet two more men just as large as the first. The one with the darker complexion said, "I know you."

"I hope so. Your friend said Rufus would take me to Sherig."

The lighter-haired brute grinned. He was missing two teeth, and one of his canines was gold. "This way, then. I trust you don't have any weapons?"

Rone checked his pockets. He was fairly certain the amarinth didn't count as a weapon, and it was spent anyway, so he merely nodded. It would seem the Riggers were still grateful for the loot they'd raked in, because they didn't check for themselves.

Rufus opened a side door and led Rone into the maze. It felt as though they were taking more left turns than before, and indeed, the door Rufus eventually opened didn't reveal the "throne room," but a small lounging area where Sherig reclined on a threadbare sofa. A cigar was tucked between her lips, and she was reading a book Rone recognized—the same romance novel he'd purchased for his mother for their journey to the border.

Huh.

A trio of red-eyed mobsters sat around a small round table, playing cards. Another snoozed in the corner, a half-empty, unlabeled bottle nestled in the crook of his arm.

Sherig glanced up from her book and grinned. "Well, well, well, look what the cat coughed up. Better make it quick; this story just got interesting."

Rone folded his arms as Rufus retreated back into the hallway, closing the door behind him. "Duke taking his shirt off?"

Sherig snorted and sat up, patting the cushion next to her. "You look like you got into a tussle. You got another tip for me, boy?"

"Unfortunately, no." Rone came closer, suddenly self-conscious about the bruising around his nose. He chose to stand rather than get too comfortable with the woman who could order her underground army to draw and quarter him at any moment. "I'm hoping you have information for me."

Sherig frowned. "I see how it is. And what do I get in return?"

Rone grumbled. He had some cash on him, but not a lot. "How about the fact that I didn't take any of Kazen's loot?"

The woman shrugged. "What do you want to know? I'm in the middle of a real good scene here, Jase."

"I'm trying to find the name and location of a fighter-for-hire type. I'm guessing he's around thirty-five years old, tall and thin. Really pale, with black hair. Knows seugrat impossibly well."

Sherig opened her mouth to reply, then closed it, pondering. A few seconds passed before she said, "He doesn't use the old style, does he?"

The question surprised him. "I'm . . . I'm not sure."

"Pat. *Pat!*" Sherig shouted at one of the card players. "Go get Snuffs."

The youngest man at the table laid down his cards. "Aw, come on, I'm about to win."

"No, you ain't," chimed in the man to his left. "I can see yer cards."

Pat growled and threw his hand on the table. "He's sleeping anyway," he muttered as he slipped out into the hallway.

Sherig wasn't one for small talk—she returned immediately to her novel, as if Rone weren't there. He didn't mind. He took the opportunity to study the room—a shelf of cigar boxes, a few board games of all things, some dried fruit. There was a metal loop in the floor near the gaming table that looked like a hidden door of sorts—

"Don't get comfortable with the place," Sherig said without looking up from her book.

Rone frowned. "I take it you're not up for playing hostess, should Sandis and I need it." He didn't mention the others. It would be easier to earn Sherig's hospitality with two than with five, and if Rone got it, he'd figure out some way to weasel Bastien, Rist, and Kaili into the deal. He stupidly felt responsible for them, too.

Without looking up from her page, Sherig said, "I'll have no grafters among my men."

"I can make it worth—"

She interrupted the lie. "That was the law long before I ever took over, Rone." She met his eyes. "There is a thick line that divides us from them, and mob law is the one law I will not break. Don't ask me again, or I'll break your fingers."

Rone swallowed his irritation. "All of them?"

She didn't respond, so Rone turned his eyes to the ongoing card game until Pat came back with a balding man whose tanned skin whispered of southern heritage.

"Snuffs"—Sherig set her book down again—"didn't you once talk about some mercenary fellow who knows old-style seugrat? Maybe two years ago?"

The man paused for a moment, confused, then snapped his fingers. "Oh yeah, Verger. That the one?"

"Hell if I know." She turned back to her book.

Rone offered his description of the stranger, and when Snuffs started nodding, a spark of hope ignited in Rone's gut.

"Sounds like the guy. Creepy fellow, real stoic?" Snuffs shuddered.

Rone nodded. "That's him."

"Name's Verger. Scary guy. Wouldn't want nothing to do with him myself, but Bens hired him out a couple times for touchy stuff." The Rigger said the name Bens like Rone was supposed to know who he was. Another Rigger, he assumed.

"Competent guy, though. Doesn't feel pain, I swear it. Doesn't feel *anything*—the few times I saw him get injured, he reacted like a statue, but the guy moved like the wind."

Doesn't feel anything? Could this Verger have an amarinth? But no . . . Sandis had shot him, and the wound hadn't healed—he'd still favored his bad arm back at Rone's mother's flat. Whatever it was that made the guy so unfeeling, it wasn't Noscon magic.

"Always tried to stay on his right side, I did," Snuffs went on.

Rone blinked. "His right side?"

Snuffs tugged on his ear. "Pretty sure he's deaf in that one."

Rone chewed the inside of his lip, mulling. The man—Verger—did have a habit of tilting his head when he threw a punch. He turned a lot, too, like they were in a boxing ring. Was that due to this older style of seugrat or because it was the only way he could listen to what might be behind him?

This could be useful. Not a solid tip—Rone wouldn't rely on it if he and Verger crossed paths again—but the information could prove handy. "How do I find him?"

Snuffs shrugged, and that spark of hope fizzled out. "No idea. I didn't handle him, just Bens, and he's dead. Sherig?"

"Never heard of him." Sherig turned a page. "That's all I got, Jase. Sorry."

Rone sighed. "Sorry won't cut it this time." But he had a name and a potential weakness. He should be thankful for that. He touched his bruised ribs.

"There's your freebie." Sherig closed the book and set it aside, then stood, reminding Rone just how imposing her large frame was. "Next time, it's a trade or your ass is on the street, hear me?"

Rone gave her a mock salute. "Loud and clear."

Snuffs escorted him back out; a new guard stood by the stairs, but he was no less beefy than his predecessor. Rone pushed past him, apologized with a nod, and headed back into the city. There was a market not far from here, and he still wanted to pick up a few amenities, although he'd have to take a complicated way back to make sure he wasn't being followed—

He paused as he crossed the street, earning a hard word from a middle-aged man he'd cut off.

Sorry doesn't cut it.

Sorry.

He felt like his bones had turned to ice water. His heart shrunk in on itself.

Sorry. God's tower . . . he'd never actually apologized to Sandis, had he? All the things he'd done—coming back to rescue her, teaching her how to defend herself, following her when she worked to make sure she'd be safe, buying the rifle—it had all been as penitence. To *show* her he was sorry. That he cared. That he—

But he'd never actually said the words, had he?

He sifted through his memories as the crowd finally pushed him toward the gutter. Their fight after escaping Kazen's lair. His time following her on Talbur's jobs. The nights they'd spent hiding. The attack on Kazen's lair. All of it . . . He couldn't remember saying it once. There had been awkward silences and defenses and arguments . . . but no apology. Not for that.

He felt like wet laundry being wrung dry. Was it too late to tell her? Too late to atone for misleading her, betraying her? Or was it all simply not enough, just as his actions to date had never broken through the wall she'd built around her? The wall made of bricks *he* had supplied?

He had to try. It was all or nothing at this point. And if it were the latter, then it was finally time for Rone to stop hoping and move on.

As if the option of moving on were that easy.

Chapter 22

Kazen's age gave him the upper hand in this place. Everyone who might have recognized him was dead.

The gray pilgrimage band cinched around his upper arm like a tourniquet, but he suffered it patiently. Suffered it, the other moon-eyed pilgrims, the wayward priests and priestesses, even the hypocritical droning of the Angelic himself. How easy it would be to . . . but no, it would be no different than before. *Patience,* he crooned to himself. That was the key to their destruction. Patience.

He choked down a meal quietly, exchanging pleasantries with a single mother and her teenaged daughter as he did so. It took an amazing amount of concentration not to reach up for his hat. He'd left it behind, exposing every angle of his face and thinning hair. *Patience.*

Kazen didn't ask to see the pilgrimage records from years past; he knew where they were. He slipped between marble columns and moved silently across plush carpets to the small records room. Went straight to the drawer he needed, as he knew how they were organized. He thumbed through them until he found the desired ledger. Opening it, he scanned name after name, slow and precise. His reward came easily.

"There you are," he murmured, tearing the page from the center of the ledger. But . . . oh, it wasn't merely a pilgrimage, was it? How interesting.

Kazen tucked that tidbit of knowledge into the back of his mind and slipped from the room. A little more sleuthing and he'd have the information he needed. Winding deeper into the tower, he ventured toward where the acolyte records were kept.

If memory served him right, he knew exactly where to find them.

Chapter 23

Sandis put her blanket on Bastien's lap as he sipped cold tea, which was little more than water with some herbs floating in it. Kaili didn't have the means of heating up the water without borrowing the fire from the beggars who lived down the corridor. They only lit that on occasion, and only at night. Sandis couldn't see the sky from their underground hideaway, but it was certainly evening by now. Rone had been gone a long time.

She focused her attention on Bastien to evade her worry—and to distract herself from the things that liked to lurk in her thoughts when she was idle. Bastien's recovery was slow, perhaps because their food was so sparse. Kaili, at least, had medicine left over from her battle with infection, and that seemed to help Bastien's summoning pain. He didn't say much after Sandis explained their situation to him, however, and Sandis hadn't felt a need to break the silence. Perhaps she should have, to counter the loudness of her anxiety.

The Riggers' headquarters weren't terribly far, were they? What if Rone had been wrong and the stranger had waited for him to emerge so he could kill him? But then the mercenary would have come for Sandis, Bastien, and Kaili by now, right? Could Rone have run into other trouble?

Had the Riggers simply been an excuse to leave?

Needing time alone, Sandis retreated to her little room and attempted to meditate. She closed the door and sat in the light of the nearly spent candle, crossing her legs in front of her. Focused on her breathing.

She couldn't get past the first pattern.

When Rist got back, would they leave without Rone? Should they look for him? What if his body was floating in a canal somewhere or stuffed into a garbage bin?

What if he didn't *want* her to look for him?

The idea pierced her core with needles, and she cringed. If he left . . . but she had Bastien now. And Rist and Kaili. They would be fine. They would . . .

Celestial save me, I don't know what I'll do if he leaves again.

She hated this constant war inside her, this battle between fear and want and anger. The raw hunger at her center. It was the same broken part of herself she'd tried to give Talbur. The one Anon had left gaping. The one Rone had begun to fill before stripping her bare.

Was it so wrong to be wanted by just *one person*? To love and be loved in return? To just . . . *mean* something to someone?

Rubbing a knot in her shoulder, Sandis looked at Rone's pack. He hadn't buttoned it up all the way after retrieving his shirt last night. It sat there, staring at her.

He'll come back, she told herself. Yet an insidious whisper insisted she couldn't trust anything about Rone, no matter how badly she wanted to.

Her stomach tightened and rumbled. Giving in, she crawled to Rone's bag. Surely he had something to eat in there.

She pulled the buttons apart, finding a torn pair of slacks on top. She removed them, his soiled shirt, then his underclothes. A mess of bandages clumped under those, intermixed with candles, matches, a pocket knife, and other knickknacks and essentials.

An apple.

She snatched it but hesitated. This was Rone's food. Not hers.

Why couldn't she stop depending on him?

She put the apple and the other things back, then pushed the pack away. Something crinkled beneath her hand.

Pausing, she noticed a pocket on the side of the pack. She opened it and found an envelope full of cash. She shrunk the moment she pulled it free, worthlessness spiraling around her like a serpent. It was the money Kazen had given Rone to betray her. He mustn't have spent much of it.

She fingered through the bills. There were so many . . . her lips parted when she read the numbers on their centers.

This was a lot more than a thousand kol, the amount Kazen had told her he'd paid for her. A *lot* more. Kazen had lied about this, too.

As Sandis put the envelope back, her fingers brushed something else. Papers. She grabbed them and pulled them free. Loose papers, four of them, folded together. She opened them and tilted the pages toward the light.

Her hands went cold.

She stared at the first paper. Read it, reread it. Turned to the second page and read, then the third, then back to the first.

This was a set of emigration papers. But how? She knew a set of papers had been part of the deal, but Rone's mother had used them to leave the country. Travel to Godobia. She would have needed them for every checkpoint.

So how were these here?

It hit her like a gun hammer fired. Kazen had given Rone two sets of emigration papers. *Two* sets. Rone hadn't just meant to leave her, but the country. Alongside his mother. So why was he still here?

She moved closer to the candle and set the papers right beside it. Her eyes hadn't fooled her. Legal papers, notarized and everything. Why was he still here? Why?

A single tear traced the shape of her cheek. *Me?*

She struggled to believe it, but what else could it be? He hadn't taken a real job since they'd run from Kazen's lair. Even after getting his amarinth back. He hadn't done anything but stay with *her*.

She wiped the tear away. Saw the numbers in the upper left-hand corner of the page. An expiration date.

It was two days from today.

She stared at the numbers for a long moment, numb, until her thoughts stirred enough to do the math.

Didn't it take *four* days to reach the Fortitude Mountains and the pass out of Kolingrad?

The door opened. Sandis blinked, sending more tears cascading down her cheeks. She turned to see Rone standing in the doorway.

His eyes went straight to her, then to the papers in her hands. He stepped inside and closed the door.

Her fingers shook, making the expiration date dance in the candle-light. "You'll never make it in time," she whispered.

Rone stood there a moment, then stepped over to his bag. Was he angry she'd gone through his things? But this, how could he not have told her about—

"I'm sorry."

His voice was low and soft, like feathers. She clutched the papers in her hands. "Why are you—"

"I'm sorry, Sandis." He took another step toward her, then another. "I did it for my mother, yes, but I should have told you. We could have figured out a way to thwart them and still save her . . . maybe. I don't know. But, Sandis." He reached forward and clasped her shoulders. "I'm so, *so* sorry."

His voice hitched again, just like it had this morning. She stared at him, his dark eyes endless as the night sky, a soft glisten to them.

Her heart daggered in her chest.

His hands slid down her arms. He dropped to his knees in front of her. "R-Rone," she croaked, but her throat swelled shut. More tears slipped from her eyes.

"I'm sorry," he whispered. "God, Sandis, if I could do it again . . ." He pressed his forehead to her stomach. "I'm sorry. I'm sorry. I'm sorry."

Something broke inside her. Cracked, split, crumbled.

He wasn't the same. *This* was not the same Rone who had lured her into an alleyway. Who had broken his promises. Who had broken her heart.

She dropped the papers and pressed a hand over her mouth as a sob escaped her. She fell into him, wrapping her arms around his neck, his soft curls brushing the bridge of her nose. She wept into his hair, and his arms encircled her, crushing her against him.

Sandis wanted to whisper her own apologies, but she couldn't speak. So she held him tighter, wetting his neck with her tears. He didn't complain, didn't adjust, didn't move. His breath swept across her collar in uneven spurts, and when she pulled back, there was moisture on his lower eyelashes.

A weird pressure came up her throat, something halfway between a laugh and a sob. She carefully ran the pad of her thumb under one of his eyes. "I-I'm sorry," she whispered. "I'm sorry for not listening. For always thinking—"

"God's tower, Sandis." Rone shook his head and stood, pulling her against his chest. He spoke into her hair. "Don't apologize. Please don't."

His shirt absorbed another tear. The fabric smelled of smoke and rain and *Rone*.

He kissed the top of her head. Lightning coursed down her limbs from the soft pressure of his lips. "When this is all done, we'll start over," he murmured, and the candlelight flickered in the corner of Sandis's eye. "You won't be running from anything, and I won't be an ass."

A hoarse laugh trapped itself between Sandis's mouth and Rone's chest.

"We'll go off somewhere, and it'll be just you and me. No city, no scarlets, no vessels, no Kazen. No deals or jobs or psychotic uncles." He held her tighter and bowed down, brushed his cheek against her temple. "I'll follow you anywhere, Sandis. To the Arctic Ribbon or the heart of hell. Anywhere you want. I promise."

Sandis knew those two words—*I promise*—were the truest words she'd ever heard. They enveloped her in an unfamiliar but blissful warmth. She pulled away from him, just enough to see the beautiful sincerity in his eyes.

He was so close, she didn't even have to stand on her toes to kiss him.

There was no hesitation in Rone's response. He gave in to her with an eagerness that made her heart fly to the stars and back. She clutched fistfuls of his shirt, and they stumbled back, clumsy with their balance, but Rone's arm snaked around her waist and steadied her. His free hand grabbed the shelf, jolting the candle. The kiss didn't break, but Rone turned his head and claimed her lips with a new and undeniable wanting.

The shock of it burned through her mouth and across her jaw, down her neck . . . waking parts of her she hadn't known she had. Filling her with fire and light. Rone's hand released the shelf and knit into her hair, pulling her even closer, like he was the desert and she was water.

A small sound escaped her throat, and Rone pulled back, misinterpreting it. He didn't get far. Sandis followed him, releasing his shirt so she could hold both sides of his face and guide him back to her.

His mouth swallowed her lower lip, sucking on it gently. The stubble on his cheeks tickled her fingers. She swam in the masculine scent of him until up was down and she was entirely lost.

She didn't want to be found.

She broke away for air, only for his mouth to crash down on hers again halfway through the breath. But air didn't matter. His mouth danced across hers, his hands knotted in her hair. Sandis parted her lips, and Rone's tongue traced the shape of her mouth, seeking hers. She gave it to him, barely hearing the knock on the door—

The hinges creaked. Rone groaned. Rather than break their connection immediately, he slowed the fervor of the kiss, which only served to build a defiant ache in Sandis's chest. When he did pull away from her, he moved just enough to angle his head toward the light splitting the doorway. Sandis's hands trailed down his shoulders and chest as she followed suit. Her hazy vision barely made out the form of Kaili.

"Rist is back," she said. Her voice carried no indication of embarrassment. If anything, it was anxious. "If we're leaving tonight, we should do it now."

Rone's arms slackened. "Make sure Bastien's ready."

Kaili nodded and closed the door to a crack.

Shifting back to her, Rone leaned his forehead against hers. Closed his eyes.

Sandis carefully kissed his mouth. "I never stopped loving you, Rone."

His dark eyes shot open. "Sandis—"

"Rone?" It was Bastien's voice outside the door. It sounded pathetic and tired. "Do you have more of that pain powder?"

Sandis licked her lips. They were swollen, but she wanted nothing more than to torture them to their limits. To curl up in Rone's arms forever. She kissed him once more, stopping any words he might say. He'd made enough promises to her tonight. She wouldn't expect any more.

Chapter 24

Rone felt strangely rejuvenated when he stepped into the small hallway between the rooms. Energetic to the point of being antsy, but full of frustration at having been interrupted. If he hadn't seen Rist immediately, a pack strapped to his back, he would have accused Kaili of subterfuge.

More than anything, he was . . . happy. Weirdly so. He was sneaking into the night with *four* illegal vessels, hoping to find refuge from an assassin trying to kill the lot of them, while stopping the man's boss from summoning a scriptural monster, and he had to bite the inside of his cheek to keep from grinning like he was hopped up on brain dust. His stomach felt better than it had in weeks. A strange sort of peace filled him, soothing all the cuts and scrapes caused by *not knowing*. It was like . . . Well, Rone had never really felt this way before. Unfortunately, the current situation did not allow him to savor it.

He forced his attention to Rist. For a moment he thought to lecture the man for potentially putting all of them at risk, but Kaili already whispered to him with a worried expression on her face, and Rist looked more broody than usual. The job was probably already done.

Sandis murmured a few things to Bastien before looking at Rone almost sheepishly. God's tower, she was beautiful. He wasn't sure he deserved her, but he wasn't going to complain, either.

Focus.

"We should head out now, while we have cover. Just in case," Rone said to the others. He slipped back into the room they'd just left and grabbed his packed bag. Rone picked up the emigration papers and checked that they were all there before cramming them into a pocket in his pack. It was unlikely, but maybe Rone could doctor them enough to make them passable. And somehow make a copy for Sandis. Then again, maybe the code stamped on the bottom of each page prevented counterfeiting. He wasn't sure, but now wasn't the time to worry about it.

He returned to the hall and watched the others prepare. Sandis rebraided Bastien's thick mane. Kaili pulled on a tattered coat that looked like it'd come out of a low-end charity bin. She looked over the nook with a note of sadness. It wouldn't be long before another drifter found the space and claimed it.

Rist said nothing, just took the lamp—it had a hook hanging off of it, so it was probably stolen—from Kaili and started down the length of the tunnel toward the grating they'd used to exit and enter.

"Rist," Sandis said as they neared, "snuff the light."

Rist grumbled, but did so.

For a moment, impenetrable darkness colored their path. Rist moved the grate, the sound of metal sliding over concrete too loud to Rone's ears. His eyes slowly adjusted. He stepped out last, right after Bastien. This was a darker corner of the city, but it would only take a block or two to reach light.

Sandis was right—for now, the cathedral was the safest place for them, until Rone could scout out something better. It'd buy them an extra day. Hell, maybe if their options became too few, they'd do the pilgrimage all over again.

But they couldn't hide for long. Each day they spent cowering was another day Kazen had to find a way to summon his monster. And if the macabre nature of his near summoning with Sandis was any indication . . . that man would do anything to win.

"Be quiet, but keep your head up," Rone whispered after dropping the grating back in place. "We don't want to draw attention, but if we do, we don't want to look guilty."

"You should be a scholar," Rist quipped, leading the troupe out of the alley and down a narrow street clustered with empty garbage bins.

Rone held back a retort and increased his pace. Sandis paused at the corner. For a moment Rone thought she was waiting for him, but as he neared, letting Bastien get ahead of him, he noticed the tightness of her shoulders. She'd folded her arms, hugging herself, her fingernails digging into the skin above her elbows. Her eyes were cinched closed.

Rone touched her. She felt feverish. Gripping her upper arms tightly, he said, "Sandis, you're here. Stay with me."

She shivered. He moved one hand to cradle her face, feeling the tautness of her jaw.

"Sandis."

She relaxed. Opened her eyes. This time they brimmed with conviction, not fear. "I'm all right," she whispered. "It's gone."

Rone kissed her crown. "You're safe. Just stay close."

She nodded.

They turned onto a larger street, this one dimly lit by a few shops that had brightened their doorways to discourage burglars, as well as a small tavern at the end of the row that bustled with conversation. Wasn't that the same one where Rone had met Sandis?

Their small group pulled away from the tavern—the cathedral was in the opposite direction—but Rone looked long enough to catch movement near the gutters across the street. Light from the tavern windows highlighted a man's dark jacket and . . . scarlet pants.

The policeman looked directly at them, even stepped farther into the street for a better vantage point.

Rone stiffened but kept moving. *Act natural. We're just out for a good time—*

The policeman turned around and ran the other way.

Rone slowed, watching him go. He *ran*, not walked. Rone and the others were the suspicious ones, dressed in ill-fitting clothing and traveling the dark streets with an unlit lamp. Rone's picture had been circulated by Kazen, too. So why did this scarlet run the other way? For backup?

Why didn't he have a partner?

What exactly had he been waiting for?

Rone's stomach sank. "He's been paid off."

"What?" Sandis asked.

Rone spat a curse like old tobacco and grabbed Sandis's hand, hurrying her toward the rest of the vessels, who had kept walking while he dallied. Reaching them, he said, "Go faster. *Move.*"

"What's wrong?" Kaili asked.

He might have been wrong, but erring on the side of caution had saved his life almost as many times as the amarinth had. "A scarlet ran off at the sight of us. The stranger, Verger, might have a network of them." Kazen sure as hell did. "We need to get to the cathedral *now.*"

Could he hire a cab to fit all five of them? But he'd have poor luck finding one this late at night, especially in the smoke ring. No one who could afford a carriage spent their time or money here.

And even if Rone was wrong about the scarlet, literally every single one of them was a criminal in one way or another. Best to leave the police to themselves.

Rone took the lead. He pulled the group down a few side streets, doubling back only once to cover their tracks. Couldn't do it too much, or they'd never get to their destination. The Central Cathedral of the Celestial wasn't exactly next door.

They ran for a bit. Sandis did the best at keeping up, thanks to all the running for their lives they'd done recently. Kaili, despite her long legs, was slow, but Rist took her hand and pulled her along. Bastien puffed like he couldn't get enough air. He didn't protest, however, even when he tripped on the leg of a sleeping beggar and nearly broke his nose on filthy cobblestones.

Roofs. They should have gone for the roofs. But with this group, maybe it would have slowed them down.

They switched to a fast walk when they reached a main road, trying to catch their breaths. They crossed a bridge over a branch of the canal. All the while, Rone looked back and forth, but he didn't see any other scarlets or lurking shadows. The sight of the cathedral spire up ahead encouraged him to pick up his pace a little, and the others followed suit. They rounded a corner. A merry glow met their eyes. The cathedral windows were always lit for wayward pilgrims or those seeking forgiveness or whatever other nonsense the Celesians preached. Odd that Rone couldn't remember anymore. Once upon a time, he could have recited every service provided by the cathedral in alphabetical order.

He didn't feel bad, forgetting.

"Okay," he said between breaths, still jogging, "we're from Unstacht, swung south to pick up our Godobian convert. We're so sorry for being late, got it? If you can't act the part, then don't talk—"

Horse hooves. Barreling closer. *Too close.* Why hadn't he heard them before?

Rone turned around to see a black gelding galloping down the lane, an equally dark rider astride it.

Verger. Aimed right for them.

"*Go!*" Rone shouted. His grip on Sandis's hand tightened, and he hauled her toward the cathedral. Toward sanctuary. Kaili yipped and nearly tumbled over herself. Bastien huffed, too slow, *too slow.*

Metal horseshoes struck cobblestones. Right behind them. Sandis was the easy target.

Rone yanked her into his chest and dropped, rolling over the hard street while protecting her with his arms. His head hit on one of the rotations, and the stone battered his wrists, but the horse passed.

They stopped rolling, and Sandis sat up, gaping at him.

Kaili screamed.

Verger had a handful of her dark hair in one hand, and the other grabbed her collar and yanked her onto the horse with him. Rist bellowed after them. One moment Kaili was struggling, and the next she fell limp across the saddle. Verger galloped at alarming speed down the street.

"No!" Rist sprinted after him, but even if he hadn't just run four miles trying to get to the cathedral, the horse was too fast. Verger disappeared at the next intersection, the thundering of hooves fading to memory.

Still, Rist ran.

Sandis pushed Rone off and ran after him, her rifle bouncing against her back. "Rist! Stop!" She charged after him. Bastien fell to his knees right in the middle of the road, heaving hard enough to puke.

Rone ran after Sandis.

Rist's body tired, and he stumbled, not even halfway to the intersection. Sandis ran around him and grabbed his shoulders.

"We can follow him!" She wheezed. "Rist, let me summon Hapshi into you. He can fly."

Rist stared at the empty road ahead of them. Panted. Shook his head. "I'm still bound to Kuracean."

Sandis fumbled over the pocket of her dress before turning to Rone. "Knife?"

Rone plucked one from his boot and handed it to her.

"I'm going to cut it," she told Rist. "Just enough to break the bond. Okay?"

"Do it!" Rist snapped.

Pulling away, Rone scoured the street for the other preparation they would need for the summoning. There, a loose cobblestone. Rone pulled it up and found a worm wriggling beneath it—just enough to summon a level-one numen, if Rone understood his occult. He grabbed it and ran back over.

Rist didn't even flinch as Sandis pulled his collar back and dug the knife into the very edge of the tattoo marking the skin above his script, the brown-inked Noscon symbols reading, "Kur-A-Cean." She handed the blade back to Rone, and he exchanged it for the worm, which she tore in half and dropped at Rist's feet. In a fluid series of movements, Sandis grabbed a vial of purified water from her pocket, uncorked it with her teeth, and dumped the liquid over Rist before pushing her hand into his hair.

Rone thought he saw her lips move to the words of a prayer before she began the Noscon incantation that somehow pierced the ethereal plane. Rone stiffened—if this didn't work, Kaili was lost—

A flash of light burned his eyes. Through the residual spots of color it left in his vision, he saw the oversized hamster appear on the street, right in view of any who thought to look out their windows.

"Sandis—"

"We're going to follow them." She motioned Rone forward before mounting the beast, but when Rone saddled up behind her, the numen could barely even walk. Bastien had been wrong about its ability to support two riders.

Sandis turned around, terror written in her features.

Sandis was lighter. Hapshi would go faster with only her.

"Go," Rone said, hopping off. "Get some altitude first. The longer we wait, the harder he'll be to track."

The terror in her eyes morphed into determination. She nodded, dismounted, and grabbed the loose skin over Hapshi's neck. She led the creature over the gutters and down another street. She nearly knocked over a man, who yelled after her to watch her dog. Rone followed, but when Sandis raced up the exterior stairs of a theological library, he stayed on the ground so as not to be an obstacle. She climbed up to the second story before remounting the rodent.

This wasn't going to work. The little monster didn't have real *wings*—

The numen leapt off the stairs and splayed out its limbs, the flaps of skin on its sides extending. Defying physics, it soared straight, gaining height slowly, and flew in the direction Verger had gone, never so much as flapping its arms.

Rone stared after Sandis as she vanished. His mouth was dry. He'd never get used to the occult. Never. *Please don't do anything stupid. Please come back to me.*

Bastien limped up beside him, strands of loose strawberry-blond hair sticking to his face. "W-What do we do now?"

Rone sighed. "We wait."

Sandis's fingers dug into a row of rough feathers and gripped the loose skin beneath. She pressed her knees into Hapshi's sides until her thighs hurt. Her skin tightened and pebbled with the cold wind, and she could barely keep her eyes open for all the stinging smoke that amplified the darkness.

In another world, this would have been bliss. Flying over the city, free from its chains . . . but this was a chase. This was Kaili's life.

It scared her.

The height, the flight, the lack of things to hold on to. Her unfamiliarity with Hapshi, so different from Ireth. She had none of Rist's blood beneath her skin, so she could only guide him with the tug of her hands and lean of her body. Smoke stung her nostrils and amplified the darkness; it took all of Sandis's concentration to keep her eye on the stranger—Verger—without letting him sense her presence. She and the others had managed to thwart him twice, but one-on-one, Verger could overwhelm her easily.

She heard the occasional shout down below, but whether someone had spotted her or had nearly been run down by Verger's mount, she couldn't be sure.

Hapshi seemed to like her company, or at least the opportunity to stretch its legs. When Sandis tugged its skin to the right, it turned right. When she coaxed it higher or lower, it obeyed. And if only for its own preservation, it naturally avoided spires and smokestacks that Sandis might have run them both into.

The galloping horse helped her pursuit. When she passed through puffs of smoke or poorly lit chunks of buildings, she followed the hammering horseshoes barely audible over the wind singing in her ears. She didn't dare release her grip on Hapshi long enough to use her rifle. Her fear of falling aside, it was too dark, and the distance—she was about eighty feet off the ground. She could hit Kaili, and she'd never practiced firing while *moving*. And if she missed altogether, it would spook Verger and ruin her chances of hunting down his hideaway. So the rifle stayed at her back, and her eyes and ears remained trained on Verger.

Maybe now, at least, she would know where Kazen was hiding.

After nearly half an hour of pursuit, the galloping slowed. Sandis panicked, for in that moment she could neither see nor hear Verger. Pushing down into Hapshi's shoulder blades, she coaxed the numen lower, her eyes watering as she held back a cough. She blinked and saw shadow move against shadow. Heard the faintest nicker of a horse.

They were still in the smoke ring, outside a brick wall. From the street, Sandis would have thought the wall another factory, but from the air, she could see it masked a short building within.

Licking her lips, she pulled up on Hapshi's skin folds, her knuckles aching with the strain. "Come on, friend. We need to get back to the cathedral. I need you to fly as fast as you can."

Hapshi didn't understand her, of course. Not without the blood bond. But the numen didn't complain when she directed it back the way they'd come. She tried massaging her knees into its sides to increase its speed. When that didn't work, she dared to release one sore hand and scratch the beast behind its ear.

Hapshi let out a soft sound, something between a purr and a giggle, and zoomed through the sky.

When Hapshi landed on the street a short ways from the cathedral, Sandis clung to its feathered fur and coughed smoke from her lungs until her stomach nearly emptied itself onto the poor creature's head. She pried her hands from its neck, her fingers stiffened into crooks. Sliding off the numen's side and onto her knees, she winced at her sore muscles and the tendons running up and down her legs.

Hapshi began to pull away from her, its attention caught by something else. Sandis clung to the creature. "No, stay. *Please.*"

Hurried footsteps sent a spike of alarm up the back of her neck, but the two men running toward her were Rone and Bastien. A small sigh of relief escaped her. Small, because Kaili was still in danger.

Bastien went straight for Hapshi, grabbing the numen's ears and forcing it to stay where it was. Rone knelt on the cobbles in front of Sandis, who nursed flexibility back into her hands.

"What happened?" he asked.

"I found her." She coughed again. "He went west, I think into District Two. Some . . . short building, square, surrounded by a wall. It's dark."

Rone ran his hands down her arms, his touch almost too warm against the chill in her skin. "Could you find it again?"

She hesitated, drawing out the flight in her mind. "I think so. Yes. But Hapshi can't carry us all."

Rone and Bastien exchanged a look.

"Okay," Rone said. "You fly, we'll follow." He put up his hands. "Don't get mad, but I'm going to steal a horse."

"A horse?" Sandis repeated, then glanced to the cathedral behind him. "From the *pilgrims?*"

Bastien, wringing his braid in his hands, looked down the street with trepidation. "W-We can't argue about this. Kaili."

Biting her lip, Sandis nodded. She dug into Rone's pack until she found a few smashed crackers. The food commanded Hapshi's attention, and she led the numen back to the building with the stairs as Rone and Bastien hurried back toward the cathedral. Once Sandis had fed Hapshi its treat and mounted, she again heard the sound of horseshoes against cobbles.

She scratched Hapshi behind the ears. "Let's fly."

Sandis landed atop a brick building—no, that was the wall she'd spoken of. Rone scanned it as he pulled back on the reins of the mare he'd commandeered. While Bastien didn't know how to ride a horse—Rone himself barely did—he knew how to saddle one, which had helped immensely. Rone didn't think he could have ridden the horse bareback.

He'd stopped the horse some distance from the wall, not wanting the sound of its approach to alert anyone. The mare heaved in protest from having carried two grown men on her back in the middle of the night, but she'd gotten her revenge, as Rone discovered when he awkwardly dismounted. Groaning, he resisted the urge to rub his crotch. That was going to hurt in the morning.

"H-How do we get in?" Bastien sounded like he might pass out if given an answer. He'd pull his braid right from his scalp if he didn't stop tugging on it.

Rone shook his head as he led the horse to a sign hook above the door of a nearby building. He looped the reins around the hook and then carefully approached the wall, keeping one eye on Sandis. "I don't know,"

The thing wasn't scalable in the least. Could the numen carry each one of them up? But it couldn't take off from the ground, right?

"How long until Rist . . . reverts?" Rone asked.

Bastien considered. "Without being dismissed? Uh . . . whenever his body gets too tired to hold its p-possession. Hapshi is easy . . . so he'll stick around awhile, I think."

Creepy. He paused, squinting at Sandis. She waved her arm toward the south. "Come on." He crossed the street, Bastien behind him.

Scanned the narrow road that passed the east wall. Silent. Not even a beggar trespassed.

Rone ran his hand along the south wall, the darkness bloating the farther along it he got. What meager light came off the smog-choked moon was blocked by another building looming not far from this place. His hand found a gate. A latch. Locked.

"Rone." His name was soft as a spring breeze. He looked up, barely making out Sandis's shape above him. She lowered her rifle over the wall, then dropped it.

Rone caught it and, grimacing, smashed the firearm's butt against the lock twice before it gave way. The noise felt like a beacon. The narrow gate creaked when he opened it, so he pulled it only wide enough for him and Bastien to slip through. He waited to be ambushed, but the narrow courtyard ahead of him remained silent.

Hapshi landed on the ground a few feet in front of him, startling him. He bit down on a curse. Rubbing her hand, Sandis dismounted, then took a cord from Rone's pack to tie Hapshi to a piece of exposed rebar. "Here. Somewhere."

Rone handed her the rifle—she was far more proficient with it than he was—and slipped his left hand around the amarinth stowed in his pocket. He needed every advantage against Verger he could get.

I can't lose again. If I lose this, I lose everything.

Because Sandis was here, too.

Sandis took Bastien's hand as they approached the flat, single-story building. It wasn't especially large, and its squat shape was an anomaly in Dresberg. Maybe the wall had been erected so no one would notice the available space. Or, simply, to keep people *out*.

They reached another door, also locked. Rone knelt in front of it, squinting to see as best he could in the dim moonlight. He knew this kind of lock. Fumbling through his bag, he found something to pick it with. It took a stupidly long amount of time to hear the telltale *click* of success.

The darkness was thick as concrete, forcing Rone to dip into his bag to retrieve a half-spent candle.

He braced himself as he lit it, but the space was empty. All of it.

Sandis stepped through first, her rifle at the ready. Rone followed behind her, holding the candle high. It was a single room without windows, a few pieces of junk lying around. Dust covered everything. Some of the walls were peeling.

"Sandis," Bastien whispered. "Are you sure?"

She nodded.

Rone held the light lower, scanning the floor—

There. Tracks in the dust. He followed them around a bend in the wall, to a narrow staircase without a rail.

He looked at Sandis, whose eyes seemed to shiver. Pressing her lips together, she nodded once.

Rone handed the light to Bastien. There couldn't have been more than twenty stairs leading down, yet Rone felt as if it led to the center of the earth itself. He told himself the quiver in his legs was from the horse, not fear.

You have the amarinth. It would only last for a minute, but it was a minute Verger wouldn't have. Rone clutched one of its loops. He wouldn't miss the opportunity to use it this time.

This door wasn't locked. Rone pushed it open with his toe, its bottom scraping gently along the concrete floor. Light burned his eyes, though it wasn't bright. A hallway greeted them. He stepped through it, rounded the corner.

A familiar voice said. "Really? I hadn't thought so."

But it wasn't Kazen's voice.

It was Talbur Gwenwig's.

Chapter 25

Sandis's grip on the rifle slackened. Her heart skipped a beat, making her blood thicken. She pushed past Rone, into the light coming from several hot-burning lamps in a small room scattered with tables, odds, and ends. Two people occupied the space—the stranger, Verger, a shadow leaning up against the wall and across from him, on the other side of one of the tables, was Talbur Gwenwig, her great-uncle.

A new part of her heart shattered at the sight of him. Not Kazen. Talbur. *Talbur.* Her family. The only blood relation she had left.

It had been him all along. He hadn't simply let Sandis go; he'd sent Verger to hunt her like some prized quarry. This wasn't about Kazen wanting her body for Kolosos, it was Talbur wanting her for . . . what?

The vials on the table. The smile on the merchant's face.

Alys.

She struggled to breathe. Her movements seemed so slow, like they fought a heavy current. Like time had grown lethargic. In the half second it took for Talbur and Verger's eyes to find her, one thought solidified in her head.

Their bond of blood had never meant anything to him.

When had he decided she was worthless? Had he planned this from the beginning, or only once she'd started defying him?

Neither man hid his surprise well, but Verger leapt to action, swift as a swallow, ready to earn another paycheck.

Rone nearly knocked her over in his rush to intercept.

Rone ducked under Verger's hook and yanked his amarinth from his pocket. As he brought it down to spin it, however, Verger intercepted, his long, pale fingers seizing Rone's wrist. For a fraction of a heartbeat, Verger stared at the artifact, confused.

So Rone shot the heel of his hand into the man's face.

He'd aimed for the nose, but fighting Verger was like fighting smoke, and a last-minute dodge ensured he missed his nose and hit his cheekbone instead. Still a painful blow, which sent Verger reeling, but not an incapacitating one. Rone immediately spun the amarinth and slid it across the floor to some sort of metal contraption in the corner, where its floating lodged it out of sight.

One minute.

Rone launched at Verger, leaning toward his left—Verger's right. The man in black saw him coming and spun around, sending a long leg out for his head. Rone blocked it with both forearms. His shoes slid on the smooth floor. He dropped his guard, and Verger's knuckles collided with his stomach in a well-placed uppercut.

Didn't hurt. Sucker.

Rone grabbed Verger's arm and twisted with the intent to throw Verger over his shoulder, but the man somehow used the motion to his advantage and spun away, landing a hard blow on Rone's kidneys as he went. That one would have sent Rone to his knees, had Noscon magic not spurred him forward.

Rone feinted, then sidestepped again to Verger's supposed deaf side, noticing the awkward way the man turned his head to better hear him. He punched; Verger blocked and swung. Rone ducked and kicked out a leg to knock the other man to the ground, but Verger leapt and executed a very similar move, only higher. The top of his foot clapped loudly against Rone's ear and knocked him over. Rone rolled out of the way barely in time to avoid the man's next attack.

This doesn't matter, he thought, and he jumped to his feet, only to take a foot to his belly. He slammed back into the wall. *It doesn't matter if he's completely deaf. I'm not sneaking up on him. He sees me.*

Rone pushed off the wall and skirted a table, trying to put more space between himself and Verger, barely glimpsing Sandis and Bastien running through a door on the far end of the room. Good; better that they avoid the brawl.

He focused his energy on Verger.

His seconds ticked away.

Talbur didn't speak, didn't give her a speech, didn't smile or frown. He just ran.

Sandis hadn't noticed the door tucked into the far back corner of the space until Talbur rushed for it. She hesitated only a moment— Could Rone defeat Verger on his own?—but Talbur had Kaili.

She made the choice quick as a firing pin. Trust Rone. Save Kaili.

"Bastien!" She rushed for her great-uncle, and her friend followed. Talbur pushed through the door five paces before Sandis did. Lowering her rifle, she slammed her shoulder into it. The door whipped into the concrete wall behind it.

She nearly fell down the handful of stairs leading to another open area, this one about twice the size of the first room, lit again with overly bright lamps. All of it was concrete and metal and . . . the *smell*. For a moment Sandis was back in Kazen's lair, peeking through the door as he turned Heath inside out. The room where he'd chained her to the floor while human and ox blood pooled at her feet.

It smelled like death and chloride lime.

Three men in smocks jumped from their work and scattered like roaches to the walls of the room. The only exit was behind Sandis and Bastien, guarded by Rone and Verger's ongoing fight.

Sandis rushed toward her great-uncle, then stopped when she saw the table the smocked men had jumped from like flies from feces.

The blood. The body. The hair. She lay prone on the table, her back cut open like a pig's, her spine glistening.

Bile burned Sandis's throat. Her heart crumbled like the end of a lit cigar, and the ache of it radiated like a star.

They'd already harvested her.

Kaili was dead.

Rone hit the wall again, but this time he tasted blood in his mouth. Time was up.

He barely managed to duck a fist soaring for his eye. It was a bit of luck that he landed a knee to Verger's hip, slowing him down for half a second so he could get some space. Some air. Anything.

This old style of seugrat . . . Rone couldn't predict it. Yet Verger seemed to know every move Rone tried the moment he thought it

They spun, danced, feet, legs, arms, hands flying. Rone took another blow to his still-sore ribs and nearly crumpled from the pain that shot through his abdomen.

He was going to lose.

Sandis couldn't look away.

The sight of Kaili slaughtered on the table, her golden script ripped from her flesh, made her sick. Cold. Distant. But she couldn't look away. Even when Bastien's hand found her shoulder. Even when the smock-clothed murderers tried to push their way to freedom.

Not until her great-uncle's voice grated her ears did she find the strength to pull her hot eyes from the massacre.

"Dear Sandis," he crooned. "What a surprise."

She gritted her teeth until her jaw flared with pain. Pinned him under her stare. He was so calm, so nonchalant.

She hated him.

He opened his hands, palms upward. "There is a saying on the northern coast that goes—"

"*Shut up!*" The butt of her rifle bit into her shoulder when she fired. She didn't remember raising the gun.

Talbur's eyes widened as crimson squirted from his thigh just above his knee. He collapsed, a hard gasp ripping from his throat.

"*My* turn to talk," she spat, taking a step toward him, then another. Talbur stared at her, his wrinkled face pale, his expression . . .

The slack lips. The wide eyes. The cowering stance. He was scared.

"How could you?" She hated the way her voice trembled, just like the rest of her. "You were my *family*." Her vision blurred, forcing her to blink. "I would have given you everything, didn't you know that? But you had to take it. You took it all. And when I left, you *stole* it." She pointed a finger back toward Kaili, and heavy tears coursed down her cheeks. "You *stole* the closest thing to *real* family I had!"

The revelation tore into her like Isepia's claws. Fire had taken her father. Sorrow, her mother. Drowning, her brother. But she'd formed a new family. It was a delicate one, built on feathers and threads, but she'd built it all the same.

And she'd left them. And now Kaili . . . *Alys* . . .

Talbur tried to right himself, but he wheezed and fell hard onto his injured leg.

Sandis took another step toward him. "I have no family, Great-Uncle." Her voice sounded too low, and it scraped the floor as she walked. "That means you have no family, either. Will anyone miss you when you're gone? Take the money away, and would anyone care if you lived?"

Talbur swallowed. "S-Sandis—"

She pushed the gun's muzzle into his neck. Her hand wasn't on the trigger, but he trembled anyway. A roach with its foot stuck in honey as the predator approached.

That's when she noticed it. His dark eyes, so like hers. Never leaving hers. Never glancing to the firearm in her hands. Not once.

He wasn't afraid of the gun. He was afraid of *her*.

Summoner, vessel, weapon. She was all of them.

Did it have to be a bad thing?

She blinked, her jaw relaxing. "I'm stronger than you," she whispered, and the knowledge burned bright in her belly. "I'm stronger than you. I always have been." *Stronger than Kazen, too.*

She pushed the muzzle harder into his neck, right above his larynx. "What was the plan, Talbur? To turn me into money, too, or to eliminate your greatest threat?"

Rone knew he was long due for a haircut when Verger grabbed his locks and hurled him backward into his knee.

Rone's back *popped*, and for a terrifying minute, he thought it had broken. But when Verger tugged on his scalp to turn him around for another blow to the face, Rone managed to push himself up onto two still-working legs, dig his fingernails between the bones in Verger's hand, and slam his palm up into Verger's elbow, forcing the man to release him while twisting his arm and sending him toward the floor.

But Verger recovered swift as a blink. He hit the other side of his elbow, forcing his arm to bend. Rone knew this part—he'd try to turn their hands to gain control; then he'd wrench Rone's shoulder from his socket and send *him* tumbling to the floor. Knowing Verger, he'd keep turning and turning until Rone's arm popped off like the leg of a crustacean.

A realization hit him like knuckles to the face.

Even as Rone tightened his fingers into a fist to keep Verger from grabbing his hand, even as he swept out for Verger's legs, knowing the other man would try to block and be forced to release his hold, Rone's brain spun. It wasn't that he couldn't predict what Verger would do. It wasn't an old style versus a new style—new styles were created to *better* the old ones, not to weaken them. No, this was about *intent*.

Rone never fought to kill. Both his father and his master had preached against murder. Rone had taken their words in stride; he didn't want to kill, either.

But Verger did. He had no moral restraints holding him back. Rone fought to incapacitate; Verger fought for death. And one was obviously more powerful than the other.

Rone spun out of Verger's grip, feeling blood drip down his face. If he wanted to win this—if he wanted to protect *her*—he had to change his mindset. He had to be willing to kill.

Pulling his knife from his boot, Rone said, "Let's end this, Verger."

"You should meet him. Ireth." Tears continued to run down Sandis's face, but her hands remained firm on her rifle, so the tears dripped freely from her chin. "You deserve his fire. You killed her. You *killed* her." She whispered, "Bastien, please—"

His hand grasped her elbow. Sandis backed away from Talbur—ensuring he couldn't grab her rifle—before turning to summon into her friend.

But Bastien's face was severe, his brow tight, his jaw set. "This isn't the way, Sandis."

She gaped at him. Pointed toward the corpse on the table. "Look what he *did*, Bastien!"

He shook his head. "I'm not saying he doesn't deserve to die. But not like this. Do you really want to use Ireth to kill? Use him the same way Kazen did?"

The brightness at her core snuffed into ash, enveloping her in coldness.

Ireth. Her Ireth.

Didn't he hate the killing as much as she did?

Death. His or Verger's. There was no other option. The amarinth was spent.

Verger lunged. Rone didn't dodge but rushed into it, landing a blow to Verger's neck even as the man's knee connected to his stomach. Rone doubled over, but his knuckles had pinched the artery running up to Verger's brain. The other man stumbled. Rone pushed the pain away and launched himself at him, returning the nausea-inducing blow. A sound escaped Verger's lips when his fist connected—the first sound he'd ever heard from the man.

He had a sudden image of this man carrying Sandis out of his mother's apartment. Had he been an instant later, Verger would have brought *her* here.

If he failed, if he let this man live, Sandis would never be safe.

Rone grabbed Verger's face and shoved him back, sending another uppercut into his stomach. Then another.

I won't leave her alone again.

He twisted under a weak block and rammed his elbow into the man's jaw, feeling the joint rip apart from the impact.

Never again.

Verger started to fall, but Rone grabbed him. Pulled him closer.

Never. Again.

He brought his foot down on Verger's leg just as Verger had the first time they'd fought. Rone had thought he would die right there in his flat. He would have, had Sandis not sent a bullet into Verger's arm.

Rone's heel dug into Verger's kneecap until it bent the other way, shattering the man's leg into two pieces.

Verger mewled and fell to the floor. But he was too strong. Too powerful. Rone couldn't let him come back. *Wouldn't* let him.

He spun around, gaining momentum, and slammed his heel into Verger's temple, right above the man's broken ear. Verger crumpled to the floor and didn't rise again.

Something *thumped* behind them.

Sandis whirled around, eyes flashing to the door. *Rone.*

She couldn't lose him, too.

"Watch him," Sandis said to Bastien as her great-uncle's blood steadily dripped onto the floor. Readying her rifle, Sandis ran back up the stairs, following the retreat of the cowardly men who had ripped Kaili apart, ready to send a bullet through Verger's head—

The men in smocks were gone. The tables had been shoved into walls and tipped over, debris littering the floor. Rone stood in the midst of the mess, one of his eyes and half of his lips swelling. A streak of drying blood marred the side of his face.

But he was alive.

Something between a sob and a laugh caught in Sandis's throat. She ran to him, dropping the gun, and threw her arms around him. She felt him wince, but one of his arms came around her waist. He teetered, then caught himself.

"Kaili?" he asked.

She pulled back as though he'd sent a knife through her chest. She shook her head, unable to speak, the relief she'd just felt mutating into something spiny and cold.

Rone closed his eyes for a minute, a sharp breath leaving him. "I'm sorry, Sandis."

He followed her to the other door, a slight limp to his step, and pocketed the amarinth. Talbur was right where she'd left him, supporting himself with trembling arms as blood soaked his pant leg.

She knew the moment Rone noticed Kaili's body on the table. The shock that both whitened and greened his face, the snap of his neck when he looked away too quickly.

Oh, Rist, Sandis thought. *What will we tell him?*

"Wh-What should we do?" Bastien asked, his tired eyes on Talbur. He seemed defeated. Sandis laid a hand on his shoulder blade, and the Godobian sighed.

"His crimes number more than what lies within these walls," Rone said, almost like he was reading from scripture. "We can lead the scarlets here. Even if he pleads innocent to Kaili's death, his involvement in the occult will send him straight to Gerech."

Talbur stiffened at the suggestion. "No. Please." He grunted, trying to sit up, but he gripped his leg and moaned, falling down onto an elbow. "I can pay you . . . We can barter, Verlad. Isn't that what we've always done?" His smile made Sandis sick. "Barter . . . whatever you want."

Sandis lifted her rifle. Hesitated. Rone took it from her hand and clubbed Talbur with the butt before handing it back. "That will keep him quiet, at least."

Sandis gripped the weapon. Nodded. Gerech was suitable punishment for this man. Turning from him, but not daring to look again at Kaili, she said, "How will we carry her?"

Rone's shoulders slumped. "Oh, Sandis. I . . . I don't think we can."

She swallowed against a tight throat. Turned again. "Bastien?"

Bastien pressed his lips together and shook his head.

"She's dead weight." Rone winced when he realized the dual meaning of the phrase. "We have nowhere to bury her, and she's . . . evidence."

Tears blurred Sandis's vision.

"It isn't just her," Bastien said, almost a whisper. "Th-The script from her back is . . . there." He pointed, but Sandis didn't look. "This place is some sort of facility for harvesting remedial gold. There's evidence enough."

Rone frowned. "We only have Hapshi and the horse. Dawn will be here any minute."

Sandis wiped at her eyes, but it did little good. New tears replaced the old ones instantly. "They'll throw her in a pauper's grave."

They stood together a moment, surrounded by silence.

"The walls are stone."

Rone's shoulders hunched, making him look shorter. Meeting her gaze, he said, "The walls are stone. If we take her to the corner, if Ireth can burn hot enough—"

Her heart twisted inside her. It wasn't what she wanted for Kaili, but it would be quick and dignified. "Bastien?"

He was already nodding. "Just tuck me away somewhere the scarlets won't find me, eh?" He pulled off his shirt. Sandis pushed her palm to his strawberry hair . . .

"Kind of him," Rone said. They stood on a rooftop, watching the first tendrils of sun creep over the city wall, turning the smoggy sky a sick shade of pink. They watched a dozen men in scarlet uniforms push through the gate on the south side of the harvesting facility. Within moments they would find Verger dead and Talbur alive. They'd likely give him medical treatment before taking him to Gerech. The wound Sandis had inflicted on him wouldn't be lethal if treated within the next hour or so, but the man would likely have a limp the rest of his life. Granted, Gerech didn't tend to give its prisoners long to live.

Sandis nodded. Hapshi lingered nearby, still carrying a dressed but unconscious Bastien on its back. They'd go as far as the unbound numen would take them before its host's energy ran out. Hopefully all the way to Rone's flat. He would rather not have to carry both men, especially in the growing daylight.

"He's always been kind." Sandis brushed some of Bastien's unbound tresses from his face. Her other arm curled around a glass container they'd taken from the facility. Within it was a mound of gray dust—Kaili's ashes. Sandis wanted to let Rist decide what to do with them, once he woke up. Rone had a feeling the man wasn't going to take Kaili's death well.

Sandis turned from the facility and the scarlets, walking toward the other edge of the roof, Hapshi following her. It was only a four-foot jump to the next roof, and the next.

"Sandis."

She paused and looked at him, fatigue dripping from her features, sorrow lining her eyes.

"What can I do?"

She offered him the smallest smile he'd ever seen—barely an upturn of one corner of her lips. "Just . . . stay."

Rone nodded. Put a hand on her shoulder, then moved it to the nape of her neck. Leaning down, he kissed the top of her head. "I promise," he whispered.

It was a long way back.

Chapter 26

The sun burned too bright overhead, making even the dust on the road reflect its brilliance. This far from Dresberg, there was no smoke to mute the sky or burn Kazen's lungs. Everything here, a day's journey from the northern coast, was fresh and open. He had to admit to enjoying it, though his time in Kolingrad's farmland would be short. He had too many plans. Maybe, after he fixed the world, he would retire here. He chortled at the thought of retirement, though his knees, sore from travel, would have appreciated time to relax.

Soon, he thought, planting his cane in the road as he approached a barn. Farmhands often slept out with the animals and not in the house, which was a good half acre from the barn and walled in by rows and rows of nearly ripe corn. Kazen had left his horse and small covered cart not far away. Close enough for him to do what needed to be done. The Lily Tower was precise with its information; he had no doubt that it was accurate. This was the place.

One of the two barn doors was ajar, and Kazen resisted the urge to cover his nose when the scent of pigs wafted over him. He stepped over a pile of droppings and into the large structure with its gabled roof and long, hay-stuffed loft. The sound of scraping at the other end of the barn drew his attention. Kazen lifted his cane and walked quietly on unaided feet.

There were two horse stalls here, both unoccupied, and a young man—barely more than a boy—raked out the farthest one, sweeping soiled straw onto the barn floor. He was thin, tan, and had short dark hair. His farm clothes hung loosely from his body.

Kazen leaned on his cane.

The boy turned, then started at the sight of him. "Farmhouse is that way, sir," he said, pointing.

Kazen smiled at the lad, seeing everything he needed to see. He had been right. The boy was perfect.

"I've been looking for you," he crooned, stepping close enough to crush straw under his shoe. "We'll accomplish great things together, you and I."

Gripping the silver top of his cane in both hands, Kazen swung for the boy's head.

Chapter 27

"No." The rawness in Rist's voice burrowed into Sandis's ears like twisting razors, and she shook as she forced herself not to turn away. The walls of Rone's flat amplified the sound. Now that Verger was no longer a threat, they'd seen no reason not to return there.

Bastien found his voice first. "I-I'm so sorry, Rist."

Rist shook his head, dark hair skirting his forehead. The skin around his eyes tightened, and fresh embers burned in his gaze. "She's not. She's *not*." His volume raised with every word, and he turned fiery eyes on Sandis. "I let you summon into me! We chased after him! She's not . . . she's not . . ."

The fire snuffed, and the rawness returned. Sandis's healing heart grew a new crack, and she grasped at her breast as though she could physically hold it together.

At least he hadn't had to see it. At least that macabre image of Kaili, torn open, spine gleaming like bloodied pearls, wouldn't be embedded in his memory forever. Right beside the image of his brother, mutated into a bleeding heap on the floor.

"I-I'm so sorry," she whispered, choking on the empty apology. What could she possibly say to him? "We went as fast as we could."

If only she hadn't gone back for Bastien and Rone. Could she have forced herself into the facility before those men cut into Kaili's back?

Could she have shot Verger before he could hurt her, shot Talbur, shot every last one of them and gotten Kaili away?

Rone had told her again and again, as they waited for Bastien and Rist to wake, that it wasn't her fault. But part of her didn't believe it. Rist's pain twisted her insides into tight, chafing, *guilty* knots.

Rist flew to his feet, his energy hitting her like a shock wave. Rone stood, too, ready for confrontation. But Rist didn't strike her with his fists. They went instead to his ears, pulling as if he would rip them from his head. Then to his eyes, the heels of his hands pressing, pressing—

"*You* did this," he growled.

Rone shook his head. "We did all we could—"

"*You* did this!" Rist's shout echoed off the walls of Rone's flat. He ripped his hands from his red eyes, tears glistening over brown irises. "You"—he turned to Sandis—"and your stupid scheme to fix what isn't broken. You drew us in. You led him to her!"

Sandis stood on shaky feet. "I didn't mean for any of this to happen." Her throat tightened around the plea. "I loved Kaili, too."

"No." Rist pointed an accusing finger at her, and Rone took a step closer as if to intercept him. "Don't you dare say that to me. None of you loved her. *None* of you did."

Bastien raised his hands, palms up. "R-Rist, let us tell you what—"

Rist turned and shoved Bastien hard enough to send him backside-first to the floor. He stormed past him to the couch where he'd woken up. Looked at one side of it, then the other, until he found the bag that held his meager belongings.

Sandis felt eyes watching her. She jumped, turned, but the monster wasn't there. Only Rist, hurting and broken. Packing his bag to leave.

"Verger is dead," Rone said, but that statement did nothing to slow Rist's movements as he checked to assure all he needed was there. "He's dead, and Talbur is in Gerech. Her killers have been punished." Minus the rats who'd fled at the first sign of trouble.

Rist shouldered his pack and spun around, dark as a shadow. "You should have died." His eyes shifted to Sandis. "*You*. They were after *you*."

Rone seized Rist by his shirt collar.

"Rone, please!" Sandis grabbed his elbow and tugged it toward her.

Rist moved his hands as if he were going to hug Rone. "We should have sold this and escaped," he spat, pulling his fingers from Rone's pocket, holding the amarinth between them. "Still could."

Rone released Rist and snatched the artifact from his fingers. "If you think money will fix that hole inside you, you're wrong."

Rist reeled back as if Rone had stabbed him. Then he gritted his teeth, sneered, and said, "I hope you rot in hell." A tear ran down his cheek, and he slapped it away. "All of you."

He turned his back on them and strode to the door, yanked it open on its bent hinges, and slammed it shut behind him.

Rone startled awake, his eyes searching the darkness that surrounded him. A narrow window in his bedroom let in a smidgeon of orange light from a lamp across the street. He cocked his head, listening, but the air was still, as were the shadows. The quiet was a relief, after a day filled with tears and mourning, both for Kaili and Rist. He was a light sleeper—Sandis must have shifted. Rone wasn't used to sharing a bed; he'd had a few women briefly in his life, but he'd never stayed the night. It had felt too vulnerable.

Closing his eyes, he felt Sandis's ribs slowly expand and contract under his hand. Her forehead pressed against his shoulder, his half-numb arm holding her close. He shifted to rest his chin on her soft hair. The world outside this flat was slowly going to hell, but here, it was easy to ignore it. To count his blessings. To have *her*, finally.

Her breath hitched.

"You awake?" he whispered, but Sandis didn't respond. He listened for a moment, until her breath hitched again. Her chest was moving a little faster now.

Thinking of her nightmares, Rone sat up and pulled his arm free. "Sandis," he said, and squeezed her side. "Sandis—"

Her eyes fluttered open. In the dim light he could make out confusion in them—and then it melted away. She blinked a few times. Rubbed her eyes.

"Thank you," she muttered.

Rone lay down beside her, propped his head up on his arm. "Nightmare?"

She nodded. "It was strange. I knew Kolosos was there, but I couldn't see it. I was running for a long time . . . running on the stars."

"The stars?"

Sandis rolled onto her back. "I can't even remember it now. The harder I try, the more it slips away . . ." She thought for a moment, and Rone let her have the time to do so. After a minute passed, she turned to him and smiled. Kissed him, her mouth featherlight against his. It lit his body like a torch.

He studied her face when she pulled away. "What was that for?"

"Keeping the monsters away."

He trailed a hand up her leg. "I know better ways to keep the monsters away."

She gave him a pointed look. But she couldn't blame him for trying, no?

She settled back against him. Rone held her to his chest, breathing in the scent of her. It took him a long while before he felt back asleep.

Something felt off, but he couldn't put his finger on what.

Rone had only been awake for two minutes when he figured it out, and his heart sank clear to the arches of his feet.

Sandis looked up from where she lay sprawled on the mattress. "What's wrong?"

Rone's hands checked his pockets again, then his pants. He moved to the bed and ripped the blanket off her.

Sandis sat up. Her voice took a serious tone. "Rone, what's wrong?"

He stepped back, his brain taking too long to connect to his mouth. "I can't find it." He took off his jacket and shook it out. Checked all his pockets again, even the ones he never carried the amarinth in.

Sandis leapt off the bed, instantly knowing what he searched for. She lifted the pillow, checked the cracks around the mattress, then pulled the entire mattress off the bed.

No glint of gold. Nothing.

Rone cursed, then cursed again, and a third time. He dropped to the floor, looking under the bed frame. Sandis rushed to his bag, but he already knew it wasn't there. He always slept with it on his person. If it hadn't fallen out while he slept . . .

He froze, remembering starting in the middle of the night. Sandis had slept so soundly beside him. He'd assumed she was the one who'd woken him up—either by shifting or making some sound—but what if it was someone *else*?

Sandis must have followed his train of thought, for she ran to the front room and called, "Bastien? Have you seen the amarinth?"

A crisp memory rose to the front of Rone's mind. Of Rist holding the trinket, chittering about selling it.

Rone stormed out of his bedroom. Sandis and the Godobian stood in the kitchen, the latter making breakfast. "Have you seen Rist?" he pressed, his tone hard.

Bastien looked pale, his blue eyes flicking between Rone and Sandis. "H-He came back. Last night. I . . . I thought he'd changed his mind. I saw him . . . and I went back to sleep."

Rone cursed and ran out the door and down the stairs until he reached ground level. His pulse felt like a thousand hammers under his skin, beating his bones and muscles to pulp. He bolted out into the street, earning a hard word from a carriage driver. He spun, bumping into one man, then another. Found his bearings and *ran*.

He ran until his lungs burned and his legs ached, then moved at a brisk walk until he could force himself to run again. He'd left without any cash to hire a cab. So he continued to run, past the point of hurting, until his ribs were fingers of pain and his feet were numb. Until he coughed for the smoke in the air.

He lowered himself through a familiar grating in a familiar alley, limping his way toward the underground connection where the five of them had holed up before heading to the cathedral. As he turned to the two rooms Kaili and Rist had first occupied, however, he found only two men, one sleeping with a bottle of ale beside him, the other crocheting with black yarn. The latter looked up at him, questioning.

Rist hadn't come back here. Where, then? To a jeweler? To a goldsmith? To a dark market merchant? Would Rist sell it above ground or below? Kazen was missing, ready to summon the monster that had *killed Rist's brother*, and Rone didn't have the amarinth to use against him.

He had a sinking feeling that no matter how hard he looked, he wouldn't find Rist or the precious amarinth.

But God knew he had to try.

Chapter 28

Kazen bolted the lock on the solitary room deep in his lair—the underground home he'd half carved out himself, only for it to be raided by low-life mobsters, his goods stolen and his means upturned. He'd paid a beggar to scout the place out for him—seemed no one cared to continue searching for him. No matter. The beggar was dead, Kazen's prize secure, and his timetable down to hours. He didn't plan on staying long. The final steps simply required some careful planning. Careful tending to his new acquirement. If he wasn't enough . . .

But Kazen refused to acknowledge the possibility of defeat.

He paused en route to his office. Soft steps sounded in the next hallway. He listened, muscles coiling. So the fool boy hadn't been thorough. A man's footsteps, judging from the weight of them, slow but not inhibited. A Rigger? What would a pathetic mobster want with this place?

His hand moved for one of the pistols on his belt. Stepping into the hallway, Kazen drew it.

Then stopped. Tamped down the surprise bubbling beneath his skin. He forced his shoulders to relax and let his head tip lazily to one side.

"Rist," he said. "How unexpected."

The tall, lean man paused in the hallway, his left eye twitching, his jaw set. His eyes were bloodshot. Why had the vessel returned after his taste of freedom? Had the streets been too much for him?

He had a pistol in his hand, leveled with Kazen's gut. But surely the lad hadn't come back for *revenge*. How quaint, if he had.

Kazen pressed his tongue against the roof of his mouth to prevent a smile from contorting his lips.

Rist squared his shoulders. It was a strange stance on him. He had always been so quiet, so restrained. Almost as meek as his brother, save for that time Kazen had found him snooping in his office. He was the last of the vessels Kazen expected to surprise him, and yet . . .

No amount of feigned nonchalance could keep his eyes from widening and his breath from catching as Rist pulled the *amarinth* from his pocket. Kazen knew it immediately for the real thing, not the golden decoy Rone Comf had carelessly tossed in the summoning room the night he'd damaged Alys. Nothing could mimic that diamond-esque core that shined with a faint internal light. Nothing could mimic *immortality*.

Questions surged through his mind. How had the boy obtained it? Where had he been? But Kazen smoothed both face and thoughts. Brought his cane in front of him and rested both hands atop it.

"You've come to barter." His heartbeat quickened in his chest.

Rist palmed the amarinth. "I want papers like the ones Comf has. Emigration papers. And money for the journey."

Kazen allowed himself a grin. "You want to leave? Run away?"

Rist growled. His grip on the pistol tightened, but Kazen held his ground. If the boy shot him, he wouldn't get what he wanted, now would he? "I want the cash and the papers, and you can have your precious trinket. I don't need it." Red bloomed around his eyes and up his neck. Anger? No, something else. The boy had recently experienced something unsavory.

Kazen nodded. "A fair deal. And fortunately for you, I have the papers in my office." He shook his head as he crossed the hall and pushed open the door to his personal space, still in shambles from the raid. The lock was broken, too. Savages. They'd be sorry.

Ignoring his own desk, Kazen strode to Galt's. It was a worthless piece of furniture—had been even when his assistant was alive—but it was deeper inside the office than his own. When setting a trap, one had to ensure the bait was large enough to catch the intended prey. True, it would be easiest to just turn around and shoot the man with his hidden pistol, but why kill for the amarinth when he could have it *and* Kuracean? Rist was one of his strongest vessels, and he'd finally come home. If he'd damaged his script, on the other hand . . . well, Kazen had means of recycling that as well.

Kazen opened drawers until he found a sheath of paper half-stained with some kind of food. He pulled the papers free, shielding them with one arm, and set his cane down so he could leaf through them.

"If you change your mind, returning isn't nearly as bureaucratic," he commented.

"I won't come back." Rist's voice was low and gravelly. The pistol trained on Kazen's left kidney. But Kazen knew Rist. He wasn't trained in firearms. Not like Kazen was.

Kazen took a few papers from the middle of the stack and folded them in thirds. Then he opened his coat pocket and began counting bills. "One thousand."

"Two."

Kazen raised an eyebrow. "You push your limits."

Rist held up the amarinth again. "We both know this is worth ten times what I'm asking."

Kazen paused, acting like he was considering, then nodded. Pulled all the cash from his coat and pretended to count it. He set it on top of the papers, gripped them, and extended his hand.

Just like a weasel to a snare, the vessel came forward to accept his prize. The moment Rist's fingers touched the paper, Kazen shot out his own, striking the boy's wrist. The pistol clattered to the floor, and Kazen's other hand jabbed him just below the jaw, on the artery that supplied blood to the head.

Rist staggered, then dropped, the amarinth falling from his fingers.

Kazen opened the cupboard in the corner of the room to find a tube connected to a needle and some restraints.

Yes, this was coming together quite nicely.

Chapter 29

Rone was utterly and completely exhausted.

He'd barely slept in the last four days. He'd spent money all over Dresberg, hiring carriages and horses to take him from one side of the city to the other. He'd visited every goldsmith and jeweler inside the walls, and even harassed merchants outside the walls. He was a hair's breadth away from filing a Celestial-damned police report.

Sandis met him on the street outside the tall, narrow building that housed his flat, taking his arm as if her slender body could support his. God's tower, she could strip down to pure skin and throw herself at him, and he'd be too tired to do anything about it.

Probably. Maybe.

"It's gone," he mumbled, leaning into her as she guided him to the stairs. "It's just . . . gone."

"But you're not." Her words were featherlight and smooth. She and Bastien had upturned the entire flat, just in case, but they all knew Rist had taken it. Rone appreciated their efforts, nonetheless.

He groaned.

"You beat Verger without it." She kept her voice down as they climbed to their floor. "You can beat Kazen without it, too."

Rone shook his head. "Try this again in the morning. I'm too pissed off for your reassurances to work right now."

She stopped halfway up the stairs.

Sighing, he said, "I'm sorry. I didn't mean—"

"No, not that. There's someone here for you. He showed up around noon and refused to leave until he spoke with you."

Rone managed to pull some of his weight onto his own legs. "Who?"

"His name is Liddell." She searched his eyes while she spoke. "*Cleric* Liddell."

"She's one of them, isn't she?" His father spoke in his memory.

Rone's stomach tensed. "You and Bastien, does he know—"

"I don't think so. He wants *you*, not us."

Rone rolled his lips together. A priest, at his flat? Wants him for *what*? Curiosity renewed a fraction of his energy. He and Sandis closed the rest of the distance between themselves and the flat. The abused hinges protested loudly when Rone opened the door.

Bastien sat on the floor, his legs crossed as though he wanted to meditate, his eyes glued to the man on the couch. Cleric Liddell was not much older than Rone. He had hair as black as Verger's, bound back into a small tail at the nape of his neck. His nose was too large for his face, straight and pointed, forming a near-perfect triangle. He had a weak chin and close-set eyes. He also wore a white robe with little silver embellishment, save for a small four-petaled lily on the chest. The cloth turned gray at the knees and darkened until it reached a hem filthy enough to impress any pilgrim.

His eyes—hazel instead of common brown—shot directly to Rone when he entered, and he flashed to standing, his entire body stiff and erect like a soldier's. He was about a hand's width shorter than Rone. His eyes gleamed with victory.

"What the hell do you want?" Rone asked. Sandis elbowed him in the side.

"Rone Comf?" the man asked. Like he needed a confirmation. When Rone nodded, Cleric Liddell said something Rone had not expected.

"My brethren and I have been searching for you. Please, come with me to the Lily Tower. The Angelic needs you."

Rone stared. Blinked. Stared.

He mustn't have heard right.

Cleric Liddell stared straight back at him. Bastien stood. Shifted from foot to foot.

After clearing his throat, Rone managed, "Pardon?"

"The Angelic needs you, Mr. Comf. We've been searching for you for nearly two weeks now, per his request. You have been difficult to track down."

Sandis said, "He wouldn't tell us why. He only wanted to speak to you."

Rubbing his eyes, Rone made his way to the sofa and sank into it. His head hurt. His stomach rumbled. Sandis must have noticed, for a few seconds later, she came to him with a bowl of noodles. It smelled . . . Godobian.

Those clerics he'd seen in the city the first night they took Hapshl out . . . could they have been searching for *him*?

"This is of the utmost urgency." Cleric Liddell moved to him. "We must go now, while the sun is high."

Sandis put a hand on his shoulder. Whispered, "This might be what we've been waiting for."

It could be, yes, but Rone had learned long ago not to trust his father. But before he could ask any questions, Cleric Liddell added, "You have a duty to God—"

"Your god can drown in the sewers for all I care." Rone shoveled more food into his mouth.

The cleric actually gasped. Rone chewed to hide a grin.

After swallowing, Rone lifted his head. "What does he need?"

Cleric Liddell frowned. "I am not at liberty to discuss it."

"My father didn't tell you why he needs me, did he?" Rone cocked his head to the side. "You do know he's my father, yes?"

Cleric Liddell didn't answer either way. His shifted from side to side, obviously uncomfortable. After a moment, he dropped to his knees. "Please, Mr. Comf. We've scoured the city, and now we've found you. The Angelic is in great distress."

Rone slurped up another noodle. "Do you get promoted if I say yes?"

He might as well have slapped the man.

"Rone." Sandis sat next to him on the couch, her hand on his shoulder. Leaning close so only he could hear, she said, "Kolosos."

Rone nodded. What else could the Angelic possibly want? Not Sandis—Cleric Liddell had wanted her left behind. Rone had never told her the Angelic suspected her, either. Sandis had enough on her plate to worry over.

Setting his bowl aside, Rone stood. "I'll come." They needed help. Allies. Maybe the Celesians had discovered something new.

"Excellent." Cleric Liddell rose to his feet. "Let us go now, while the light is out. The Godobian can walk the woman home."

Sandis paused. Rone snorted. Bastien scratched the scalp under his braid.

Cleric Liddell's gaze moved over all of them, and his ensuing sigh was nearly a sob. "Celestial, save me, they live in sin." He covered his face dramatically with both hands.

"I wish," Rone muttered, and headed toward the door.

Cleric Liddell insisted their journey was not a parade, and only Rone need come, but Rone brought Sandis anyway. Bastien volunteered to stay at the flat to ease the priest's nerves.

Cleric Liddell hailed them a cab to the east entrance to the city, the one closest to the Lily Tower. Rather than pay the driver, he merely showed him a pendant denoting his Celesian authority. Rone hadn't known the priests held enough political clout to commandeer carriages.

Nerves danced across his skin, but no anger flamed in his belly as they approached the tower this time.

It felt strange to hope, where his father was concerned. But the power of the Lily Tower might make it possible for them to stop Kazen. To stop Kolosos.

Cleric Liddell led them up six flights of stairs. There were no pilgrims that Rone could see; either they were scheduled for a later time, or no one wanted to trek to the tower today. Sandis's fingers squeezed his a little tighter with each step, reminding him that her kind was not welcome here.

He'd kill all of them if they tried to touch her, amarinth or no.

The communion room was empty and spotless. Cleric Liddell's stride didn't slow when they reached it; he walked toward and then through the sheer curtains behind the small stage, making haste for the Angelic's private office. When the cleric knocked, Sandis put her other hand over Rone's, but he simply nodded. He was all right. So far.

A familiar voice on the other side of the door beckoned them inside, and Cleric Liddell turned the knob, immediately bowing as he opened the door.

"My Angelic, I have found Rone Comf, as you insisted."

The Angelic stood from his white desk. The bags under his eyes were larger than the eyes themselves. His eyes paused on Sandis for but a moment before he said, "Mr. Comf, come in. Liddell, thank you. I will note your diligence. I would speak to them alone, but do not go far."

The priest nodded and backed out of the room without ever turning around. He closed the door securely in his wake.

The Angelic waited a few seconds before speaking. "I fear what you spoke of before is true."

Relief and fear speared down Rone's spine. They finally had an ally . . . but if the Angelic's hard disposition had been swayed, then their situation was dire.

Sandis's hand went to her heart. "Kolosos?"

Rone's father winced at the name. "Kolosos opposes the Celestial. I have studied. Prayed. I fear this macabre *thing* has great power, and foolish men seek to bring it into the mortal realm." He shifted his attention to Rone. When Rone said nothing, the Angelic added, "I expected a snide remark from you."

"Told you so," he offered.

The Angelic fell back into his chair. "I am doing what I can. Pulling my sway with the government and the triumvirate, though our power in Kolingrad is not what it once was. I will not start fearmongering by spreading word of this. But you, both of you"—he nodded toward Sandis—"have said you know of one who worships this numen. A summoner who wishes to bring him to our plane."

"Kazen, sir," Sandis said. Rone wished she were a little less respectful, after how little the Angelic had cared for her and her opinions in the past. "His name is Kazen."

The Angelic nodded. "I thought that was the name. I've checked the city records against our own. There was a cleric named Kazen who left the church some forty-five years ago, before my time. He was ousted for blasphemy."

Sandis stiffened. "It . . . couldn't be the same person. Kazen"—she rubbed her arms—"Kazen has never feared God."

Rone said, "We know where his hideaway is, but it's abandoned. He recently had a . . . collision with some mobsters."

His father considered. "Perhaps there is something there that could be of use to us. I will send you with a team, as well as some police officers who are loyal to—"

"I'm not taking your goons around the city with me."

The Angelic frowned. "You would rather go unarmed? Vulnerable?"

The absence of the amarinth suddenly made his jacket too light. "I'd rather be clandestine." That place had been pretty cleaned out— Rone didn't think there'd be much of use. But he supposed they might as well leave no stone unturned. Besides, he knew his father. They'd need to cooperate if this man were to help them.

The Angelic's lips pressed into a thin line, but he nodded. "Then scout. You will take Liddell with you."

"I don't think—"

"Yes," Sandis spoke over him, "he may accompany us."

Rone withheld further complaint.

His father nodded. "Come back here and tell me what you find, and I will do likewise. Kolosos cannot be unleashed."

Rone exchanged a glance with Sandis, remembering her collar and chains, the blood at her feet. With those red images beneath his eyelids, all he could bring himself to say was, "I know."

Chapter 30

Sandis wasn't sure if the silence that clung to the dilapidated buildings like cobwebs made her feel better or worse.

Rone led the way, searching every broken window and intersection. Sandis walked not far behind him, close enough to Bastien that their arms brushed. She wondered if his legs were as leaden as hers. He certainly looked afraid, but that was common for him. Still, despite his anxieties, he somehow took everything in stride. He hadn't hesitated to help her pursue Kazen during the Riggers' attack on his lair. He hadn't hesitated to go after Kaili and Verger. Was it easier to face one's fears when one had so many of them? When there wasn't a choice *not* to confront them? She wanted to ask, but it seemed wrong to break the silence that engulfed them. Even the cleric stepped lightly.

Thoughts of Kaili stirred a sensation not unlike rain pattering down the length of her torso. She started counting windows on a leaning building up ahead, if only to prevent the image of her friend on that table from rising in her thoughts.

When they reached the entrance to the lair, Rone said, "Stay here." Sandis didn't want him going in by himself, not without the amarinth or her rifle, but he slipped in the moment he delivered the order, giving her no opportunity to protest.

When he emerged a few minutes later, relief bloomed in Sandis's chest like a lily. "Still abandoned." His attention went to Sandis and Bastien. "You'll know where to look better than we will."

Shoring herself up, Sandis took the stairs down into the quiet lair, her footsteps resounding like drums as she went through the hall. The others followed her, but she moved as if in her own little world. Her fingers brushed chipping paint on the wall, while her other hand grasped the strap of the rifle pressed against her back. *I am stronger than you,* she reminded herself.

She opened the door to the vessels' room first, noting it was unlocked. The cots were empty and overturned. Two missing. Had the Riggers taken those?

Crossing the hall, she checked solitary, also unlocked. Inside lay a cot and a bowl of water, half-filled. The water made her wonder if someone had been here recently. Shouldn't the water have gone into the air by now? But solitary was a dark and small space . . . She had to be mistaken.

She thought she saw the shadows move across the walls, skeletal wings fluttering in the dark corners. She slammed the door shut and locked it.

Cleric Liddell hovered in the main hallway, taking in the white washed walls, moving with the steps of a babe. "There is evil in this place," he whispered, causing the skin on Sandis's arms to pebble.

Rone approached and set a hand on her shoulder. A very large part of her wanted to sink into him, to close her eyes and pretend she was somewhere else, but instead she offered him a weak smile. "I'll look through his office; do you know where his bedroom is?"

Rone nodded and walked down that way. Bastien followed Sandis into the office.

She approached Kazen's desk first and pulled open drawers. They were sparsely filled, if not empty, but she checked everything, every page in every letter, every spare paper.

"What should I look for?" Bastien asked.

"Anything that might tell us where Kazen could be." She recalled that Bastien couldn't read. "Set aside papers that look important. Any . . . maps. Letters to friends. Anything, really."

Bastien nodded and began to search.

Sandis opened another drawer, empty. Kazen kept a lot of documents in his office. Had the Riggers taken them? But no, she'd searched for her own documents after the raid. She hadn't found them, but she could have sworn these drawers weren't empty.

She checked the door as a shiver passed through her back. She caught a glimpse of Cleric Liddell passing by, gnawing on his thumbnail. Lines around his mouth sank deep into his skin. He did not want to be here. None of them did.

Just there, in that corner, was where Kazen had painted symbols up and down her arms and legs, readying her for Kolosos . . .

Sandis opened drawers with renewed fervor. She found another ledger, but it was blank. She checked all its pages and the insides of its covers anyway, then started thumbing through the disheveled bookshelf behind her, forcing herself to focus on the titles, begging her eyes to read faster, like Rone's did.

Several minutes passed before Bastien said her name.

Sandis pulled one book, then another, from the shelf, dropping them to the floor and searching beneath and behind them, though in the back of her mind, she knew she'd find nothing. Kazen wouldn't hide some secret to unhinge him here. "What, Bastien?"

When he didn't reply, she turned around. He'd left Galt's desk and stood at the narrow cupboard in the far corner of the room—the same cupboard from which Kazen had retrieved the razor he'd used to break the name *Ireth* on her back. Bastien had opened it, and Sandis saw tubes and needles, dark bottles. She shivered.

But Bastien's blue eyes bore into hers like twin suns. Stepping away from the books, Sandis said, "What did you find?"

"You."

Sandis didn't understand.

"I found you. Or you found me." He ran his hand over the cupboard shelves. "I . . . I want to give him back to you, Sandis."

She moved around the desk. "Who?"

"Ireth."

She froze four paces from him.

"I-I've thought about it for a while," he continued, "ever since you first summoned him into me. He wanted you, Sandis. I *felt* it. I've never . . . I've never felt that pull from any numen before. Even Grendoni. And I've been a vessel for seven years."

Dryness clung to her throat and tongue. "You can't just . . . give him to me."

"Why not?" He offered her an unsure smile. "It's all here . . . and you have most of his name still, don't you? I could fix it. I could break my bond and give him to you."

Hesitant, Sandis turned back to Kazen's desk. "The sphere is gone. The Riggers took it."

Bastien tapped on the inside of the cupboard door. Carved into the wood were two circles comprised of ten rows of Noscon script. Diagrams of the astral sphere that hid the names of all numina. "But I don't need it," he added. "I saw your marks, Sandis. Kazen didn't take that much away."

Hope flared in Sandis, but she caged it with shaking hands. "It has to be done with mixed blood, Bastien. Mine and Ireth's."

"Then summon him."

She parted her lips, unwilling to believe Bastien would do this. That he'd let Ireth rip his body apart, *again*, just for the drop of blood they'd need. Would breaking the bond hurt him? Would it fill him with an echoing emptiness like it had Sandis, or would he feel no different?

"You'll be dead," she said, referring to the deep sleep that overcame a vessel after possession. "You won't be able to fix Ireth's name on me."

"I can."

Both Sandis and Bastien turned to see Rone in the doorway. He shrugged, as though the gesture excused his eavesdropping. "I found nothing of use." He glanced to the cupboard. "If you show me how the needle works, I can fix Ireth's name. There's nothing here. This won't slow us down."

She shifted her weight from foot to foot. Whispered, "The cleric."

Rone shook his head. "Might make him faint, but if the Angelic wanted you in prison, you'd be there." Then, perhaps seeing her alarm, he added, "Don't worry about it."

Sandis swallowed. Stared at Rone, then turned back to Bastien, who offered her a smile.

"*This* is what we have," the Godobian insisted. "I-Ireth tried to tell you something before. Maybe he can help us. But first we have to bind him to someone who knows how to listen. Don't say nay, Sandis."

It wasn't until he grinned that Sandis caught the terrible joke. *Neigh*, he meant. Like a horse. A wet laugh, so close to a sob, burst from her throat. Bastien's lightly freckled face blurred in her vision. "Thank you," she whispered, feeling her heart rise up her throat and drop into the words. She threw her arms around his neck and squeezed. "Thank you. Thank you. Thank you."

Ireth. Wait for me. I'm coming.

She barely felt the needle when Rone pushed it into the skin just below her neck, mending the symbol Kazen had broken to prepare her for Kolosos. They'd locked out Cleric Liddell, who'd finally stopped pounding on the door. Bastien now slept, clothed, on the table Kazen had used for tattooing and branding alike. Rone had dressed him, and Sandis had rebraided his hair. She'd placed a kiss on his forehead and gratitude in his ears, hoping the Celestial would bless him with blissful dreams and not timeless darkness.

A part of her—a very small part of her—was sad, knowing that with Ireth bound to her, she would never again be able to behold his magnificence. She'd summoned him right there in the office, careful not to ignite the walls. The fire horse had seemed to understand what she needed, and after allowing her to embrace his warm muzzle, he'd turned his head so she could draw a few drops of blood from his strong neck. It felt wrong to break the dark silver of his skin, but she did, and Ireth's heat had burned back her joyful tears.

She knew the exact second Ireth's name became whole. Not because the needle stopped pricking or because Rone leaned back, unsure, but because an otherworldly warmth wove between her ribs, and a familiar pressure pressed against the inside of her skull. Sandis gasped and stood, knocking over her chair, hugging herself as she had hugged Ireth minutes before. Closing her eyes, she savored the sensations of distant fire, of being too deep underwater, of faint but decided *love* that filled her veins. Then she spun toward Rone, who still held a needle and a small vial of blood.

He smiled in awe. "It worked."

Sandis nodded. "I feel him. I *feel* him, Rone!"

She cried, and Rone set down the supplies so he could enfold her in his arms. "I feel him," she whispered into his neck. "He's here. He's here."

Rone held her for several seconds before loosening his grip. "Can you talk to him, Sandis?"

She chewed her lip. Even before their separation, communication between her and Ireth had been . . . vague. Fleeting sensations and the occasional vision. Even now, the warmth and pressure faded from her body, as if it strained the numen to remain with her so long.

Stepping back from Rone, Sandis let her mind work. The visions . . . She got them when she slept sometimes. Once when she'd stared at the amarinth long enough, but they'd lost that.

"The Noscon writing," she whispered. When Rone raised his eyebrow, she said, "Ireth showed me something when we were with the citizen records. The Noscon ones. Maybe that would spur something again." Even she heard the uncertainty in her voice, but she had to try.

Rone nodded. "I'll calm down the priest and be right back, okay?"

He left, and Sandis turned toward the open cabinet. Approached it and studied the two engravings on its door. She stared at them a long moment, feeling no increase in heat or pressure within herself. So she traced the careful symbols on the astral sphere, most of which meant nothing to her. She found Ireth's name on the fourth row down.

Something pricked her thoughts, and she leaned closer, studying the symbols. Her fingertip sank to the bottom of the higher carving, to three symbols carved together. She recognized the three marks from the Noscon words Kazen had painted on her limbs. Koh-Lo-Sos. *Kolosos.* She chewed on her lip, staring at the writing. Not daring to trace it, as if doing so would bring the red-eyed monster's wrath upon her.

Leaning back, her eyes moved to the top of the sphere, tracing the symbols there. She couldn't help but wonder . . . if Kolosos was at the bottom, what was at the top? She didn't know any of these symbols, even as pieces from the other vessels' tattoos.

"This is for a greater purpose," Kazen crooned in her memory.

"I'll expose their lies."

"We'll finally show the world the truth."

"The only 'god' you need to concern yourself with is the one about to join us."

The only god.

Only god.

God.

The Angelic's voice merged with Kazen's. *"Kolosos opposes the Celestial."* Opposes. Opposite?

Sandis's stomach slammed against her hips. Chills spiraled through her body, and strength left her legs. She returned her finger to the symbols on the bottom row of the first carving of the astral sphere. Kolosos. Then, dragging her finger upward, she pressed it into the symbols on the very first row. Could this, too, be a god?

"Celestial?" she whispered, her mouth dry.

Was this the truth Kazen was so adamant to reveal? Was he indeed the same Kazen the Angelic had told them about, the one who'd left the Lily Tower for blasphemy? A cleric? A man who might have learned that the Celestial . . . was a *numen*?

Was her god a numen? Was he even a god at all?

Sandis sank to her knees, the pressure growing in her head not at all Ireth's doing. She'd been told she was an abomination. A blasphemy. People like her were denounced, arrested, and killed. But if she was right . . . they were hypocrites. All of them.

She was wrong. She had to be wrong. She—

"Show the world the truth." That was what Kazen had said.

Rone came back into the room, then rushed to her side. "Sandis? What happened?"

It took her a moment to come back to herself, to separate her heavy, clustered thoughts from reality. Trembling, Sandis clutched Rone's arm. "I know where Kazen is."

She thought of the missing papers—papers the mobsmen wouldn't want. Considered the bowl of water in the solitary room. Kazen *had* been here. With someone else—someone stronger than Sandis. And he'd already left.

"What?" Rone gripped her shoulders. "How? Where?"

She shook her head and pushed herself to her feet. "We have to go. *Now.*" Bastien would have to stay. They could lock the door, keep the cleric from seeing his brands.

"Sandis—"

The skin between her brands perspired. She pushed Rone toward the door. "We have to go *now*!"

"Where?"

"The Lily Tower!" she cried. "He's going to summon his god where everyone will see it. Where everyone will be forced to admit to the truth!"

She didn't take time to explain. Couldn't. She ran for the lair's exit while Rone yelled at the cleric to care for Bastien. Then his steps thundered behind her.

Sandis couldn't move fast enough.

Sandis knew she was right when the crowds in the streets started running the same direction, away from the east wall. Away from the tower. Knew she was right as she pushed her lungs and legs to carry her close enough to hear screams. Knew it when she saw the broken stone around the gate in the city wall.

She felt Ireth's heat in her muscles, pushing her farther, faster. Her body succumbed, letting her run on numbness instead of pain, on desperation instead of sustenance. The closer she and Rone got to that gate, the more the crowd thinned. Weaving through the panicked people was like trying to fly in a hailstorm. But despite the warnings of several scarlets, Sandis and Rone burst past the wall and toward the white tower that gleamed in the light of the lowering sun.

The first thing she saw was a great shelled beast, its front legs laden with enormous pincers, its head that of a giant turtle, lips sharp as blades. Kuracean. *Rist.* Sandis nearly tripped at the shock of it. But had Kazen recaptured him or called Kuracean into another vessel? Sandis had freed the numen from its binding when Kaili was abducted. Yet somehow, as if Kaili's spirit whispered it, Sandis knew that creature's body belonged to her angry, heartbroken friend.

The numen beat its massive claws against the tower, sending stone and marble flying. Two priests rushed from the front door, and Kuracean slammed both pincers into the ground hard enough to shake the road beneath Sandis's feet. When the dust cleared, only one priest was still running.

Screams echoed from the tower. A priestess leapt from a third-story window, only to crumple when she hit the ground. Thoughts of Priestess Marisa pushed Sandis harder still, running on a strength not her own. Rone's heavy breaths swirled through her hair as he kept pace. The tower grew larger and larger, even as Kuracean beat into it like a knife to clay. Sandis had no vessel to summon into, but she had Ireth, and if need be, she would sacrifice her wakefulness to bring his power into her body. To stop Kuracean. To stop Kazen.

She heard Kazen before she saw him, the voice which he never raised now bellowing into the dust-clogged air, shouting over the screams of fleeing pilgrims and priests. A few lingered nearby, transfixed, listening. *Run, you fools!* But Sandis could not stop for them.

"Today is the day of your recompense! Now is the time for your blindness to be cast away!" Kazen's black clothing contrasted with the white temple behind him. Sandis focused on his face. So close. Rone would have to carry her away when she was done. *Ireth, be merciful and let me wield your fire long enough to stop him. Give me strength!*

She pushed her hand into her crown, the words of summoning hoarse in her burning throat. At the same time, Kazen's hand pushed into the dark hair of a young man kneeling in front of him, a man with bound legs and arms. A glint of gold caught Sandis's eye, and she stumbled in her run.

The amarinth.

And it was spinning in the hand of the vessel.

"No!" Rone shouted. He must have seen it, too. His speed increased, and he barreled toward Kazen even as Kuracean ripped another chunk of the tower free and threw it at him, missing by mere feet.

Focus. Sandis uttered the next lines to summon Ireth, her palm slick with sweat. Pressure built in her bones. The third line, then the last words—

The last words . . .

The amarinth spun, reflecting sunlight, but it was the vessel who seized her attention. The color of his hair. The familiar slant of his eyes, which met hers with a wideness that was not merely fear.

It was recognition.

Sandis tripped over her own feet and fell to the road, skinning knees and palms. She stared, the screams fading from her ears, the pressure vanishing from her limbs. His name formed on her lips more as a wish than a word. It couldn't be. It *couldn't be.*

"Anon?" she whispered, and at the same time, her brother mouthed, *Sandis.*

Then his body exploded in a burst of red light that grew until it consumed the Lily Tower, black and burning and terrible.

Kolosos.

ACKNOWLEDGMENTS

First, I want to thank my readers for continuing down this new path with me! I am so grateful to each person who picks up one of my books. Without you, these books wouldn't happen.

I have so many people to thank for their immense help in getting this story in shape! Cerena, Laura, Caitlyn, Tricia, Leah, Rachel, Rebecca, and Whitney. *Thank you* for reading my many, many words and offering feedback to make them stronger. And Jason, Angela, Marlene, Laura, and the staff at 47North: you have my utmost gratitude.

Thank you to my assistant, Amanda, for giving me the time to write and to my husband, Jordan, for the same. Another thank-you to Jordan for being so good-looking. It really does help the writing process when one's spouse is fiendishly attractive.

Thank you to those who have offered me kind and encouraging words in person, in letters, and on social media. I cherish all of them.

Also, thank you to my cousin Adam, who did the architectural design for my basement remodel for free. I told him I'd repay him by putting his name in this book's acknowledgements.

And once again, thank you to that great Divine Being who continues to be patient with me and helps me put weird ideas into what I hope are good stories.

ABOUT THE AUTHOR

Author photo © 2017

Born in Salt Lake City, Charlie N. Holmberg was raised a Trekkie alongside three sisters who also have boy names. She is a proud BYU alumna, plays the ukulele, owns too many pairs of glasses, and finally adopted a dog. Her *Wall Street Journal* bestselling Paper Magician Series, which includes *The Paper Magician*, *The Glass Magician*, and *The Master Magician*, has been optioned by the Walt Disney Company. Her stand-alone novel, *Followed by Frost*, was nominated for a 2016 RITA Award for Best Young Adult Romance. She currently lives with her family in Utah. Visit her at www.charlieholmberg.com.